not a thing

A CONTEMPORARY ROMANCE

SEDDLEDOWNE SERIES
BOOK TWO

SUSAN HENSHAW

*For my readers whose pasts seem too much to overcome. I hope
this love story shatters the darkness and lets in the flood of light
waiting for you. You deserve love and happiness. Yes,* **you.**

*And for the **four best (adultish) kids on the planet**.*

Will*, who's always been a determined guardian and protector.
And who kept us together when it all fell apart.*

Emma*, who faces the darkness daily and chooses to live. And
who I can always, always count on to sing with me in the car.
Top of our lungs, girl.*

Cole*, who's at the bottom of the world right now. Don't cry for
me Argentina? I cry occasionally and miss his hugs daily. But I
couldn't be more proud of his brave example of sacrifice and love
for the Lord. He is our Ashton. Without the table pounding.
Love you, bud.*

And for my baby (who is now driving, what?!) **Adelaide***, who,
in spite of thinking everything I say or do is a complete
embarrassment, lights up our home with sunshine, sarcasm, and
like Anna, hilarious Gen Z slang. And when she sees this will
surely purse her lips and say, "Bruhh."*

a let

Dear Reader,

There is a **content warning**
don't want to read spoilers, skip di

This is a realistic, contemporary, s
story. **It is not a rom-com**. Hard
Will you laugh? Absolutely! But, i
will also cry, swoon, and hopefully

If you're okay with intense er
and swoony kisses, you're in the ri
glad we found each other.

All to pieces,
Susan

content warning

Your mental health matters. For your information, this book deals with **toxic relationships, bullying, suicide, and a stalker.**

Heat level comparison: If you enjoyed the angst, mild swearing and spice in The Twilight Saga by Stephenie Meyer, you will love this book.

Now that we've gotten that over with, hold on to your cowgirl hats, because hottie Holden is waiting on the next plage. Yeehaw! And let's move 'em out!

playlist

Find the playlist for Holden and Christy's story on Spotify.

- Into the Stars...Benson Boone
- half of my hometown...Kelsea Ballerini feat. Kenny Chesney
- I Knew You Were Trouble...Taylor Swift
- Change...Churchill
- One Man Band...Old Dominion
- Heart Like a Truck...Lainey Wilson
- Flowers...Lauren Spencer Smith
- Be Someone...Benson Boone
- If He Wanted to He Would...Kylie Morgan
- Before You...Benson Boone
- Die From A Broken Heart...Maddie & Tae
- better off without me...Matt Hansen
- Drunk In My Mind...Benson Boone
- To Love Someone...Benson Boone
- Ghost Town...Benson Boone
- If You Love Her...Forrest Blakk and Meghan Trainor

- Break Up In A Small Town...Sam Hunt
- i wish you cheated...Alexander Stewart
- Wine Into Whiskey...Tucker Wetmore
- Till That Day...Emma Nissen
- My Greatest Fear...Benson Boone
- lacy...Olivia Rodrigo
- Cry...Benson Boone
- Beautiful Things...Benson Boone
- Bless the Broken Road...Rascal Flatts
- All Your'n...Tyler Childers
- Worth the Wait...Spencer Crandall

one

I'm not normally a honker. My mom raised me better than that. But sometimes on the DC beltway, when Joe Blow is meandering down the fast lane like he's out for a Sunday drive, you gotta do it.

I pounded my hand into the center of the steering wheel, blaring my custom horn noise. "Moooooooo." Nobody expected to hear an angry cow in the middle of rush hour traffic. Just a nod to my Dupree Ranch roots. Which was fitting, since that's where I was headed.

Slow Poke rewarded me with the middle finger and a hard brake tap. An opening in traffic appeared to the right, and I sped around, putting him squarely in my rearview and out of my mind.

Just then, my car's digital voice, which I'd brilliantly nicknamed Tessie, announced an incoming text in her silky, smooth tone, "Sullen Silverado said, 'Seriously, tool? You didn't think to tell me Christy was the new principal of Seddledowne High?'"

I snorted, annoyed at my brother Silas's text. Because first

1

of all, I'd just been trying to think up a better nickname for him now that, according to our mother, landing his dream girl had turned his disposition perpetually smiley. Pshaw. Apparently, not today. And second, it was irritating that he thought I had some kind of pulse on his ex-fiancée, Christy, and her life plans. And third...just wow.

Christy had accepted a job in Seddledowne?

As a principal?

I mean, yeah, I'd known she interviewed for a job with the Seddledowne School District for an eighth-grade teacher position. I would've told him that if I'd thought there was any point. But I'd assumed that, when everything fell apart between the two of them, she'd headed straight back home to Laramie, Wyoming. Why poke the bear with useless information?

My stomach did a backflip at the realization that she was in my hometown, not two thousand miles away like I'd thought. My heart kicked into a trot.

Snuff it out, loser. She's not for you.

I pressed the button on the steering wheel to reply. "Man, I honestly didn't know. That's crazy. Thought she went home weeks ago." I held my breath as I flipped the blinker and merged onto I-66, headed west.

Christy was moving—no, it was the first day of school— she'd already moved...to my hometown? The question was why. She couldn't actually think she had a chance of getting Silas back, could she? Then again, she didn't know he and Lemon were already married. At least, I hadn't told her. Maybe that's exactly what she thought.

Jealousy growled like a beast in my throat.

Tessie again. I groaned. "Sullen Silverado said, 'You didn't discuss that in between all the face sucking?'"

"Whatever," I muttered. It was one kiss, not a one-night

stand. And I'd written Christy off the minute Silas had caught her kissing me. Yeah. *She* kissed *me*.

Had I kissed her back?

Yes. Because as my fourteen-year-old niece Anna liked to say, I'd caught feelings. A rare occurrence in my world and something I always steered away from. But when Christy— who is extremely attractive, and smells like berries and honey, I might add—had grabbed the back of my head and smashed her lips against mine, my primitive manly instincts took over and I "leaned into it" for a minute. Or fifteen. Sue me.

I laughed at my lawyer pun. But then I scowled. Because the minute Silas had arrived, Christy had steamrolled right over our situationship—as Anna called it—to get to him.

And that was that.

I'm pretty sure Silas thought The Christy Kiss had happened the other way around. That I'd put the moves on *her*. But I didn't care. Christy had been through enough, so I'd quietly take one for the team.

You're not a team, noob. And you need to stop thinking you are.

I shrugged at the shoulder angel trying to steer me in the right direction. Whatever. It didn't matter. Besides, people had thought a lot worse things about me in the past. I was used to being the scapegoat. Pile it on.

Tessie once more. "Sullen Silverado said, 'Would've been nice to know before they named me assistant principal. But once again, you weren't thinking with your head, were you?'"

My fingers clamped down on the steering wheel. "Okay, d-bag." Then I exhaled. Silas was just stressed right now. He didn't usually act like this, I reminded myself.

Not sure how having Christy as his boss was my fault, but that's what happens when you make out with your brother's former fiancée. You get to be the bad guy for a while.

I clamped my jaw, determined to be the bigger man, and pressed the button to reply. "Just told you I didn't know. Haven't talked to her since the last time you saw her. Don't care if you believe me. Congrats on the new job, though."

Truth was, I couldn't be mad at him for acting like a brat. I'd done him dirty, and I knew it. I was single for life. I knew that too. A confirmed bachelor, as my mom had called it ever since watching a particular Dr. Phil episode—even though I'd tried to tell her it wasn't the sixties anymore and it didn't mean what it used to. She said it as more of a joke anyway. She made it clear, always with a pat on my cheek, that my time was coming.

My family thought I played the field because I was on the hunt for a wife. It was easier to let them believe that. But I knew. Had known for years. Happily ever after was not in the cards for me.

I swore as Tessie announced again, "Sullen Silverado said, 'Thanks for coming to the wedding too. Nice to know you supported me throwing away a fiancée, but not marrying the love of my life. Ulterior motives, clearly.'"

A string of expletives came out now. I *was* happy for him and Lemon. Ridiculously. And I'd thought gifting them three nights at a fancy cabin on the Skyline Drive would've shouted that loud and clear. Should've known Silas wouldn't care about that. He could not be bought off, even if I was smack-dab in the middle of the biggest case of my career.

I'd wanted to be at the wedding. Really, really wanted to. It killed me not to see him finally get *the* girl. But they'd given me three days' notice. And my boss, Wellington Sipsby, had made it clear that if I'd come down last weekend, I wouldn't have been able to come this weekend to do what needed to be done. Hopefully, by tomorrow night, Silas would be pounding me on the back, forever in my debt.

An incoming call rang through the speakers. I smiled at

this number and pressed the green call button on the touch-screen instrument panel.

"What's up, Anaphylaxis?" My current nickname of choice for my niece.

"Please, please, *please* tell me you're on your way." The tremble in her voice said she was in no mood for joking around. "We've got this, right?" Her mom, my sister, Sophie, had passed away three and a half months ago and the court date for the ruling on who would be Anna's guardian was tomorrow morning.

"Kiddo," I softened my tone. "Yes. You can stop stressing. I'll be there by the time you're done with volleyball practice. I promise. Granny and Gramps are expecting me to bring you home after."

There was a tiny exhale of relief. "I just really want this to work, you know? It's killing me that Uncle Si and Aunt Lemon are over there, living their best lives without me." Yes, I knew. She'd called me every day since Silas and Lemon had announced their three-day whirlwind engagement and every day since they'd tied the knot.

I sighed. "Anna. I can promise you, if you're not with them, they aren't living their best lives. It is killing them." Lemon had told me as much when I'd called to let her know I wouldn't be able to make it to the wedding.

"What if the judge doesn't care? What if she only sees the mistakes that were made?"

I didn't want to tell her what she didn't want to hear, but I also needed her to be realistic. I was a lawyer. Not a miracle worker. "Then you live with Granny and Gramps. Silas and Lemon will still be a big part of your life."

After a few seconds of silence, she said, "I know. I'm just... I'm having really bad FOMO. Brooklyn says I shouldn't use that word anymore. It's *cheugy*." I swear I could hear her eyes roll. I wanted to roll *my* eyes. Cheugy? So Gen Z was just making up words now.

"Did you talk to Granny and Gramps yet?" I didn't try to keep the hope out of my voice.

"No," she said sharply. "And we're not going to." It was an adorable threat. "If Granny knows, she might try to stop us."

I wasn't sure Anna knew the hurt it was going to cause if my parents weren't aware that she was planning to fight to the death for Silas and Lemon to be her legal guardians. But if I didn't let Anna do this her way, and it turned out badly, she'd never forgive me or my parents. It was her life. She was the one who had to live with whatever happened tomorrow. As her lawyer, it was her interests I had to be committed to. Even if I was working pro bono. And, if I was honest, I felt a duty to Sophie. She'd wanted Anna to be with Silas and Lemon.

I scrubbed a hand over my face. "Okay. If you're sure. You go ahead to practice or you'll be late."

"And you be on time, too. No stopping for snacks." Her stern bossiness sounded just like her mom, and I had to bite the inside of my cheek not to laugh out loud. She knew me too well. I was already planning where the next Sheetz gas station was. I loved their milkshakes. "There's a short parents' meeting at the end of practice, and I need you to sign a form before we leave."

Just then, another call came in.

"Yes, ma'am." I saluted.

"You just saluted. Didn't you?"

"I would never." I chuckled. "See you soon, Annaconda."

I pressed end and accepted the next call from my summer intern, Audrey. I let out a large exhale as the call switched over. If there were a picture for the term "ball of nerves," it would be Audrey. I usually didn't let other people's anxiety bleed over into my life, but Audrey was a quick-witted, filterless, shaky chihuahua. When she was around, tension was inevitable.

"Hello?" I answered, forcing calm and confidence into my tone. Maybe if I kept shoveling it in her direction, some of it would stick.

"I'm so sorry to bother you, Mr. Dupree—"

"Just Holden, Audrey." We did this every time we talked. And we'd do it again next time. Not sure why calling me by my first name like everyone else in our office was so intimidating, but it made her twitchy. Literally. Whenever I said my first name, her left eye would start flicking in quick upward movements, reminiscent of someone about to have a grand mal seizure.

"H-Holden." I heard her swallow through the speaker. "Sir, I really think you should come back. I don't think...no, I *can't* run the meeting tomorrow with Senator Bromhorst. He's been calling here—"

"Audrey, we've already been over this." I pinched the bridge of my nose. Sometimes dealing with this woman was like trying to nail jelly to a wall. "Trixie is covering the meeting tomorrow. I need you to defer to her." I spoke distinctly and slowly. "I have to focus on my niece for the next twenty-four hours."

"But, Mr. Dupree—"

"Holden, Audrey." I cut her off, maxed out. "You've got this. Trixie's got this. Chill." Finally, there was silence. "You *are* capable. You are going to be a great lawyer." Once you go to therapy and get on some medication. "If you have concerns, I need you to go to Trixie. And Audrey?"

"Yes, sir." Her tone was ashamed, like a puppy who'd been caught ripping open a bag of trash.

"Repeat in your head after me: *The meeting will be fine. The world will not end while Holden is gone. Everything will be all right.*" Before she could try to counter, I added, firmly, "I don't want to see your name pop up on my phone again until Monday. Are we clear?" I hated talking to her like a toddler, but this girl was going to sabotage her future career if she couldn't get it under control. And I could not deal with her while I was trying to solidify Anna's future.

"Yes, sir." Again with the puppy guilt.

"Good. And one more thing. After the meeting tomorrow, I want you to do something to de-stress. Whatever that looks like for you. You've got a big bonus coming next week before you head back to school. So go splurge, all right?" My eyebrow was kissing my hairline. I wasn't asking.

"Okay." Her laugh was quivery. "Thank you, Mr.—"

I cleared my throat.

"Thank you, Holden."

We hung up.

Sometimes, I wondered if I'd picked the right field. Honestly, it was no wonder Audrey was an anxious mess at the moment. We were currently representing Senator George Bromhorst from Iowa. According to the press and Jolie Mansfield, the accuser, four years ago Bromhorst had paid her two thousand dollars for one night together. And he'd filmed the two of them in a skeezy motel, off the beltway in Maryland, without Mansfield's knowledge.

But now that he was a famous politician, the videos had magically come into Mansfield's possession and she was suing for three million dollars. One million for each hour he'd filmed her. But, once others had heard about the case, more women had stepped forward. To date, eight women were telling similar stories and had the videos as proof. If it had been up to me, I wouldn't have taken the case. I didn't agree with most of Bromhorst's politics and he oozed shadiness. But Caldwell, Caldwell, Sipsby, and Anderson hadn't built up one of the biggest firms in the metro area by turning down high-profile cases.

I cracked my neck from side to side and let out a big breath. For the next twenty-four hours, I would let it go. For the next twenty-four hours, my biggest and most important client was Annaleise Nicole Dupree.

I cranked up a country song, recommended by my youngest brother, Ford, pressed down the gas pedal, and flew over the green, rolling Virginia hills toward my hometown, Seddledowne.

two

CHRISTY

My head fell onto the wooden desk with a thunk.

Silas was married.

A half-crazed cackle teased my vocal cords. I stifled it. Of course he was. He and Lemon had only been together for a total of...I actually didn't know. According to him, he and Lemon had kissed the day before Beach Week began. So, less than a month.

Who drops the anchor that fast?

No man I'd ever known.

I groaned, lifted my head a few inches, and let it crack against the desk again.

A man who'd been pining over a woman his whole life, that's who. Two people who'd known each other for years and already lived together for three months, that's who. A couple who couldn't wait to kick the bedroom door closed whenever they wanted, *that's who!*

I was such an idiot.

My phone rang, and I lifted my head to see who it was. I squeezed my eyes closed for a second before putting it on speaker. "Hi, Mom."

"Hello, Christianna. How did your first day go?" she asked, but not in the concerned or hopeful tone of a normal mother who wants her oldest daughter to succeed at her new job. Though I'm sure a tiny part of her wanted that. My mother loved me. I knew that. But right now, she was still angry that I'd taken a serious detour from her life plan for me. If I replied that there had been four fights, three drug busts, and the entire school had burned to the ground, she would've given me a fat "I told you so," and a "that's what you get for leaving Laramie," and hopped on the next plane to pack me up and move me home.

I pressed my palms against the cool wood of the desk and ran my hands over the top, trying to calm myself. "It was fine. Everything's great. The teachers and staff are very welcoming." I left out the part where the cafeteria oven had caught fire, burning the pizza that was supposed to feed every kid on the first lunch shift. And I skipped over the two boys who'd been caught smoking weed in the bathroom during second period. I'd had to expel them. On my first day.

"And Silas? How'd he take the news that you're his boss?" Her tone was a touch proud that somehow I'd wrestled the job out of the school board's hands before he could get to it, and a touch hurt that the cowboy she'd grown to love was not going to be her son-in-law. I actually hadn't confirmed that yet. Only that our relationship was on the rocks. And technically, I wasn't his boss. The Seddledowne School Board was. But there was no point in arguing with her.

"It was okay...I think. His first day isn't until Monday. But he seemed fine with it." It was a lie. I mean, yes, he'd acted unruffled. But there was a terrifying fire in his expression too.

"Maybe now that he sees you're a force to be reckoned with, he'll come to his senses." It was almost a question and I hated the hope in her voice. "Tell him your dad is still willing to cut him in on the ranch if he'll reconsider."

I rolled my eyes. Mom could've lived in the eighteenth century, no problem. Love? Romance? Sure, if you happen to find that, great. But to her, marriage was a contract. A negotiation where two people used each other for whatever they most wanted. For her, it had been children. For my father, it had been a ranch.

My mom's family, the Lawsons, owned more land in Wyoming than the next three richest families combined. More than five hundred thousand acres broken up into three parcels. Yup. I was Laramie royalty—if that were a thing. Silas could've been a proprietor in one of the biggest ranches in Wyoming. As a matter of fact, my dad had tried to basically bribe him into the family the first time I brought him home to meet them. Because no way could Christy land a decent man without some kind of strings attached. Silas had simply lifted an eyebrow, slid his arm around my waist, and said, "I'd live with Christy in a trailer by the creek." Then he'd shrugged. "My family has a ranch in Virginia." It's one of the things I loved about him.

Had loved about him. I rubbed my temples. Silas was past tense and the sooner my brain remembered that, the quicker my heart could do the same.

"Christianna?" Mom nudged.

May as well swallow the bitter pill. "Silas is out of the picture for good."

Mom scoffed. "Surely, you can work things—"

"He's married," I yelped and barreled on before she could comment. "He and Lemon are together now. And he looks really happy." He had. Even after finding out that I was the principal, there'd been a gleam in his eye that I'd never seen before. A sparkle that said he'd live in a trailer by the creek with Lemon if he had to. If this job didn't work out. No. He'd live in an un-air-conditioned tent.

Lemon had gotten my "trailer."

I resisted the urge to crack my forehead on the desk again.

"Miss Thornbury?" A teenage girl called from the main office adjoining my smaller one. School had ended an hour and a half ago. The only people left in the building were the janitors and the girls' volleyball team.

"Principal Thornbury?" A second female student called.

"Mom, I have to go." I pressed end, knowing she'd shoot me a text telling me how hurtful I was being. I may have been avoiding her more than usual since I left Laramie.

I walked to the door and poked my head out. Oh, it was Anna, Silas's niece, and another girl about the same age.

I waved even though they'd already seen me. "I'm here."

I smoothed my hands down the front of my faux leather pencil skirt. Normally, I wouldn't be nervous about two teens approaching me, but I'd practically had a nervous breakdown in front of Anna at the beach. There was no telling what she'd told her friend. Or what they'd spread to other students. So yeah, my nerves were on high alert.

Anna strode through the office with more confidence than I felt at that moment. More confidence than I'd possessed as a freshman in high school. If there were any residual hard feelings from the beach, she hid them well.

"Hi, Anna," I offered her a gentle smile.

She studied me for a moment with a quizzical brow, as if my presence answered a question for her. I'd seen her earlier in the cafeteria, but I was pretty sure she hadn't noticed me. At what point in the day had she realized I was the new principal?

Gathering from both of their tiny, tight spandex shorts, they were on the volleyball team.

"I'm Principal Thornbury." I offered my hand to Anna's friend.

She eyed it like I might give her some kind of disease, but gave me a dead-fish handshake. "Brooklyn."

Okay.

Anna's phone was in her hand and she glanced at it as if to gain courage from something on the screen. "I think we have a problem," she said. Then she brushed a stray piece of mocha-colored hair out of her eyes. This girl was the kind of pretty I wish I'd been at her age. Heck, the kind of pretty I wished I were now. Sophie had been a blonde with blue eyes. But Silas had said Anna's father was Italian. I could see Sophie in her— the cheekbones, the smile. But her complexion was tan, and she had dark eyes with lashes most women would kill for. If she never put on a speck of makeup, it wouldn't matter.

I offered her a gentle smile. "What's going on?"

Her chocolate eyes were wide and worried. "Ms. Whorley, our coach, just quit. Like walked right out of practice."

My forehead crunched. "Why would she do that?"

Brooklyn let out a loud sigh. "Because she does nothing. She's the definition of mid. Told us to play Queens and sat on her phone for the first hour and a half of practice. Just like every other day. So when Coach Byrd—"

"That's the varsity coach," Anna interjected.

Brooklyn plowed on. "Got fed up with it, he started coaching—"

Anna lifted a hand but didn't wait for her friend to stop. "Because we're his future pool of talent, you know? In a year or two, we'll be his varsity team."

Brooklyn continued, a geyser of monotone words. "That got Whorley off her phone real quick. But she still didn't start coaching. Instead, she glared at Byrd for like ten minutes. Like how dare he. And of course, he ignored her because, like I said," she shrugged, "she's mid. So then she told him she did not have to be treated this way. She did not get paid enough for this. And stormed out of the building." Brooklyn made duck lips. "Lame AF."

I snapped two fingers and pointed at her. "Watch it. I know what that means."

Brooklyn shrugged. "Sorry." She didn't look sorry though and I couldn't tell if she was an apathetic punk or if it was her personality to be this vanilla.

Whatever emotion Brooklyn was lacking, Anna made up for it—evidenced in every line of her worried face. I couldn't blame her. I knew Silas had worked with these two all summer, trying to get them ready for tryouts. I could imagine the heartbreak, after all that preparation, to think your team was now going to fall apart.

I offered them an easy smile so they'd know I wasn't ruffled. Hopefully, they'd feed off of my energy. "Are you girls alone in the gym?"

Anna shook her head. "No. Coach Byrd is still there...for today. But the rest of the team is freaking out because we don't have a permanent coach. And our first game is Monday." Her eyes darted around my face, hoping for a miracle. Brooklyn still looked unfazed.

"Where's Mr. Alvarez?" This was more of an athletic director situation. I handled the academic side of things. Sports weren't part of my contract.

"Sksksk." Brooklyn fake laughed and immediately went straight-faced again. "Out with the football team, as always. He doesn't care about girls' volleyball."

We stood there for a moment—Anna watching me and Brooklyn staring off into space—and I had to wonder. If the varsity coach was there, why had Anna come to me?

As if she could read my mind, she glanced at her phone screen once more and said, "Silas said if anyone could fix this, it would be you. Because you're really capable and stuff."

I swallowed the lump in my throat and fought back the urge to wrap her in a hug. And Silas too if he'd been here and wasn't newly married. The fact that Anna was willing to overlook, even momentarily, the beach incident, and give me a chance, was more than I could've hoped for. And the fact that, apparently, Silas, only hours after learning I was here and he'd be my right-hand man, had encouraged her to come to me, was boggling. Then again, Silas was a classy guy. Even if he had broken my heart, I could still admit that.

I bit back the grin that wanted to take over my face. "No worries, I got you. We'll figure it out. We'll make sure you ladies are ready for the game. I promise." It was probably just a misunderstanding.

Anna slouched in relief and smiled.

"Let's go see what's going on." I led them out of the front office. As we trudged down the hall, Anna and Brooklyn whispered to each other behind me. I wasn't sure what they were saying, but the tone seemed hopeful. I'd take it.

I pushed open the door to the gym and the three of us stepped inside. Coach Byrd, one of the twelfth-grade history teachers who I'd met for the first time a week ago, was indeed trying to coach both teams. My high heels clacked against the glossy polyurethane floor and most of the girls turned. The bleachers to the left were pulled halfway out and it looked like the parents were beginning to trickle in for the meeting that I knew was scheduled to begin in a few minutes.

Coach Byrd peeked over his shoulder at me, then looked back at the girls and yelled, "Butterfly drills. JV this side." He pointed across. "Varsity on the other. Jasmine and Ming, take charge."

He stepped back to join me but continued watching the girls' progress.

"Coach Whorley quit?" I asked.

"Yup." The P popped. He shook his head. "And before you ask if I can coach both teams, I already tried last year and was told no by Alvarez."

That had been my next question. "There were problems last season?"

His eyes were trained on the drill as he spoke to me.

16

"Whorley coached JV last year, and it was a nightmare. Same thing as now. No coaching, just wasting time. She only cares about the paycheck. The girls and their parents"—he waved toward the adults on the bleachers—"were extremely frustrated. But Whorley is the only teacher in the county besides me who knows anything about volleyball and no one else applied." He shrugged. "Halfway through the season, they hadn't won a single set." He cocked an eyebrow. "Do you know what a set is?"

I nodded. "They play three sets every match. Whoever gets to twenty-five first wins a set." One of my best friends in high school had been the captain of our varsity team. I'd been to some games.

He nodded, pleased. "Yeah, for JV it's something like that. Varsity plays best three out of five. Anyway, JV hadn't won a single set, which is ridiculous. They have talent, just no direction. So I told Alvarez I'd coach both." His jaw clenched. "He said cool, but I'd only get paid for coaching one team since we practice at the same time." He snorted. "That's not right. Varsity football alone has five paid coaches. There's a lot that goes into coaching that doesn't happen during practice. Games, for one. Besides, I went to college like everyone else here. I'm worth more than that. And I'm not talking just money." He rubbed a hand over his jaw. "But as a matter of principle, I told him to forget it. I thought with all the parent complaints, he'd try harder to find a better coach." His lips were pursed, disgusted. "Nope. Just kept Whorley." He threw his hands up. "And now we have no JV coach at all."

I scanned the moms and dads on the side. Some were wearing looks of concern and I wondered if they'd witnessed Whorley's adult temper tantrum. "What about a parent? Could one of them do it?" These girls hadn't made the team without their parents' involvement and understanding of the sport. My guess was that most had at least been in rec volleyball, if not club or travel, in the past. There had to be at least a couple of adults here that knew the game.

He shook his head. "Has to be a teacher or staff of Seddle-downe School District per Virginia State High School rules, according to Alvarez." His hands moved to his hips. "But that's not true. The next county over has a guy who's coached for twenty years and he's a logger. They just won state. Alvarez is just stubborn. Likes to throw his weight around. But he won't listen to me. Trust me, I've tried."

My lips twisted as I thought about what to do. Techni-cally, this wasn't my problem. But emotionally, as a principal who wanted to know these kids—to care about what they cared about—it completely was.

"I'll try to talk to Alvarez." Coach Byrd eyed me, and I could tell he was unconvinced that it would make a difference. They needed a solution. Now. So I lifted my hand like a schoolgirl ready to answer the question. "And I'll help out for the time being."

Byrd snapped around, facing me now. "You'll coach JV?"

That's not what I said. "I don't know a ton about volley-ball. I'm more of a soccer girl myself. But I could—" I was going to say fill in until we found someone.

A grin split his face. He slapped my back like I was one of the guys. "Great. Why don't you stick around for the parent meeting? I'll introduce you." He glanced back at the players. "Good work, ladies. Shag 'em up!"

I grabbed his arm. "I will *help*. I do not have the time to coach this team by myself the entire season." I widened my eyes. "I'm the *principal*." In case he'd forgotten. It was prob-able since I was at least twenty years his junior.

He nodded, his excitement waning a bit. "Okay. Under-stood. We'll take what we can get for now."

As long as we were clear on that.

The girls scattered in all directions, scooping up balls and dropping them into the ball cart. To collect them as quickly as possible, a few girls popped one or two under their shirts, like a pregnant woman. I gulped as I walked toward the parents. I'd never coached a sport in my life.

And then I gulped again.

Because sitting there, in the middle of the group, was Silas's super hot younger brother Holden. The one I'd kissed right after Silas broke my heart. And he was scrutinizing me with his honey-brown eyes. I swear if a gaze could burn, he would've scorched two iris-sized holes right through me. He leaned back and folded his arms across his chest, a slight smirk at the corners of his mouth. I should've looked away, but he was wearing dark slacks and a light blue slim-fit business shirt that hugged his muscled chest just right. I knew it was muscled because I'd run my hands all over it when I'd kissed him. And let me tell you, abs for days.

His dark blond hair was perfectly coiffed in the front as if he'd just walked out of the barbershop two minutes ago. He had the chiseled jawline of an underwear model, and his eyebrow cocked, like, are you going to look away or what? A muscle in his jaw pulsed, hinting irritation at our little interchange, but his lips looked kind of happy about it. Either that or they'd like to take a bite out of me. Heat prickled my cheeks, and I quickly sat on the front row, turning my back to him. But my mind was ablaze, knowing he was in the same room. My hands wouldn't stop mangling each other.

Holden was...my friend. Or, he had been. I'd turned to him during Silas's and my "reset." What had been a moment of weakness on my part had morphed into nightly phone calls, *The Office* watch parties, and truth sessions that had pulled some of my darkest secrets out of obscurity. Like how I was a disappointment to my mother for letting both of my younger sisters find husbands before me. Or how I'd failed to claim the valedictorian spot in high school by two-tenths of a point. Or how I couldn't run for crap because my lungs seized, and I always ended up with my head between my knees, wheezing for air. I told him things that would've made the polish peel right off my mother's manicured nails. "Put up your best front always," Mom said on repeat. "You never know when a man will look at you as something more." And yet, Holden kept coming back every night for weeks.

Yeah, I'd kissed him out of desperation. My heart had felt like it was on the edge of the world, about to drop off into a dark, bottomless abyss. But something unexpected had happened during that kiss. The way he'd touched me, gently but with a torrent of underlying desire. How he'd looked at me between carefully placed pecks on my mouth like I was the most beautiful woman he'd ever seen. The patient slowness of the movement, like he'd stay there all night if that's how long it took to make that kiss perfect. The heat that had hit in ways it never had with any other guy. How my heart had swollen so big I couldn't take a full breath.

I wanted to fan myself just remembering it.

Hands down, it was the best kiss of my life. Not a runner-up in sight. Top of the medal stand, totally alone.

Until Silas showed up and made me feel like a cheap floozy. And I'd played the part just how he wanted me to. Taken all the blame and then turned, tail between my legs, and bolted for my motel room. With weeks to reflect, I shouldn't have done that. Maybe I had kissed his brother, but he'd broken my heart. We were even.

I glanced back at Holden, whose massive biceps were now locked around adorable Anna, listening intently as she animatedly told him, I don't know, probably about her first day of high school. My chest tightened, and I exhaled. Good gosh, he was even more attractive when he was being sweet and interested in his niece.

My heart panged hard. If I was being honest, I missed him

and his friendship. Achingly. He was smart, kind, and hilarious. And yes, I could've reached out. I could've apologized for going after Silas instead of standing firm next to him. I'd started to text him multiple times.

But I wasn't going to.

Because the thing I'd had to remind myself hourly, no minutely, was this...

Holden was a big, fat player.

Silas had told me that, and Holden had admitted it in one of our first conversations. He'd dated over a hundred girls. Well over. To the point that he'd stopped counting. But I felt confident in labeling him a serial dater. So, no wonder the kiss had been so incredible. He had a PhD in perfectly placed hands and the right amount of pressure needed to induce a moan, or how to use those warm eyes to elicit certain emotions...

But it hadn't meant anything to him.

The entire reason I'd first gone out with Silas when he asked wasn't because I was super attracted to him. Even though I'd grown up in Wyoming, cowboys weren't my type. Nope. Players were. Good-looking, cocky ones, just like Holden. In high school and college, I'd been naïve enough to think I could tame a guy like that. Had even brought one home to meet my family once.

But I'd realized after having my heart obliterated that maybe some girls were capable of conquering a ladies' man—like my little sister Gabby—but I wasn't one of them.

So, while Holden might be dreamy and swole—as I'd heard two teenage girls say today—and his rose petal lips might induce a full-body tremble, weaving an exhilarating spell around your heart—one thing was perfectly clear.

I needed to stay far, far away from Holden Dupree.

three

HOLDEN

I loved everything about this courthouse. The orangey smell of the oiled wood, the Jeffersonian architecture of the dome on top of the building, high school memories of clerking for Jedd Pruitt, who was still the District Attorney to this day. This was where I'd fallen in love with the law. Wonderful stuff happened in this building—I'd witnessed plenty of it—and I was feeling hopeful about today's outcome.

Silas was hiding his nerves fairly well. He'd always been pretty good at that. I was probably the only one in the courtroom who could see, but his left foot hadn't stopped bouncing since he sat down. Lemon on the other hand looked as stiff as I'd ever seen her. Even with Silas's arm around her shoulder—which was weird but awesome to see—she couldn't relax. Her posture was taut, jaw clenched. I tried to catch her eye, give her a smile, but her stare was glued to Judge Franklin's face, as if looking away might disqualify them from any chance of becoming Anna's guardians. Silas pressed a kiss to her hair and still her eyes stayed trained on Franklin.

I'd already spent twenty minutes laying out all the reasons

22

why Anna should be allowed to choose who she wanted to live with. She was mature for her age, made good decisions, had straight A's, and had been incredibly close with Sophie before she passed. I'd given the judge a copy of Sophie's letter, proving it was Silas and Lemon she'd chosen for Anna. And I'd had Lemon and Silas bring the letters Sophie wrote to each of them, reiterating that fact. The judge was folding them back up now.

"Let me be clear," said the judge, an older woman with slices of gray running through her jet-black hair. "When I first read through the paperwork of this case, I thought it was the oddest stipulation I'd come across in many years. Ninety days under the same roof to decide custody? I thought to myself, is this a reality show? Am I being pranked?"

I laughed and masked it with a quick cough into my hand. Unprofessional, but she'd caught me off guard. Working in DC, it was like everyone was so busy with the business of running the country that they forgot it was okay to laugh now and then. That it was okay to be yourself. One of the things I loved about this small town was the realness of the people who lived here.

Everyone glanced at me wide-eyed—Lemon, Silas, Mom, Dad, and Anna. Good grief. Clearly, being in a courtroom had them on edge.

Judge Franklin looked down at the six of us Duprees and continued. "The whole clause of residing together is odd, I'll admit. But then, I thought, maybe this Sophie was a genius." I bit the inside of my cheeks to keep from smiling. She looked pointedly at Silas and Lemon. "Maybe she wanted this to be a trial run before she handed over her daughter to you to raise."

Lemon squeezed her eyes shut like she was in actual pain. She was being way too hard on herself.

Judge Franklin shook her head, lips pursed. "Then, it seems, you all went and made a mess of things."

Anna glanced over at me, fear in her expression. I squeezed her hand.

Judge Franklin held up the two baby-blue envelopes containing letters Sophie had left behind—one for Silas and one for Lemon. "Thank you for allowing me to read what Sophie wrote to you." She handed them to the bailiff to return. He walked them over to Silas and Lemon. Lemon tucked them into a leather purse by her feet.

The judge went on. "It's clear Miss Sophie was quite the matchmaker." She shook her head, unimpressed. "But this is not The Bachelor or The Newlywed Game or Farmer Wants a Wife, et cetera. We are talking about a child's life. And frankly," she cocked her head at my brother and his new wife, "I'm appalled that you couldn't make it three months, but now you've run off and eloped? I'm also appalled that Sophie didn't have a firm agreement in place in case the ninety-day experiment fell through."

I stiffened. This was taking a turn that I wasn't comfortable with. "Your honor," I started.

She held up her hand. "In a minute, Mr. Dupree." She leaned forward, her hands folded together, staring down Si and Lemon. "I am very sorry about the miscarriage. That is heartbreaking."

Huh?

Mom and Dad looked bewildered as well.

Not Anna, though. Her face crumpled a bit and her hand went to her heart. Silas looked over at Lemon with intense compassion as she nodded, eyes filling with tears. She'd lost a baby? When? And what did it have to do with today?

Back to business, Judge Franklin straightened in her chair. "But I'm not convinced the two of you have what it takes to raise this girl. If you couldn't make it three months, what're you going to do if she comes home drunk or drops out of school or has mental health challenges, which is highly likely for a child who's lost their mother?" My mouth parted. Yes, Anna had been through things, but I couldn't picture her in any of those scenarios. Then again, I reminded myself that Judge Franklin saw that kind of thing on the daily.

Before I could counter, the judge held that hand up again. "I've talked with the Custody Evaluator and we've discussed who we think Anna should live with. But I'd like to hear from the grandparents before I offer my final decision."

Final decision? I hadn't given a closing statement yet. *It's not a criminal case, idiot.* Still, the outcome felt just as important as any case I'd been on. Again, Anna looked over at me, her brown eyes the size of quarters.

"Let's see how it goes," I whispered.

Dad stood, helping Mom up. They walked, unitedly, to the podium.

"Your honor," Dad started into the microphone. "I just want to say to my family," he looked back, giving us each a second of eye contact, "that we all want the same thing here. We want what's best for Anna. We all love her. She knows that."

The four of us still sitting nodded.

Dad scratched his cheek, looking back at the judge. "Jenny and I decided last night, we're not going to fight about this. Whatever you decide, we'll honor, of course. We just hope you'll listen to Anna."

I nodded, kind of surprised. I'd expected them to really go for it, especially with Mom's behavior toward Lemon over the past few months.

Mom leaned forward to take her turn. "But we also hope you know that we are happy to raise Anna if that's your decision. That said, we know that Silas and Lemon will do an excellent job. They love Anna so much. You only need to be around them for a few minutes to see that."

My head fell back, surprised.

"Oh, Granny," Anna whispered, her hand once again coming to her heart. She knew. It had taken a lot for Mom to concede on this. Silas and Lemon looked as surprised as Anna and me.

Mom turned to my new sister-in-law. "Lemon, honey, I know I've been hard on you." She gestured to Silas. "On both of you." She turned back to the judge. "I don't do well with change. And losing my daughter at the age of twenty-eight—" She choked on a sob, took a big breath, and recovered. "Having to hand over your granddaughter, unexpectedly... well, I didn't roll with it well." She gestured to the judge. "But more than anything, when we walk out of this room, I just want our family to be intact. Whatever happens here today, I —*we*—need it to be something that will bring peace and not more conflict."

Satisfied, Dad and Mom returned to their seats. I was effulgent. This was going to swing our way. Anna was going to live with Silas and Lemon. And Mom and Dad were going to be okay with that.

But then Judge Franklin gave us all a sad smile. "That, right there," she pointed to my parents, "makes me think Anna should go with Bo and Jenny. That is grace if I ever saw it."

My lungs deflated and I wanted to groan. She hadn't seen the grace exuded by Lemon all summer while my mom took all her pain out on her.

Anna shot out of her seat before I could stop her. "Can I say something?"

Judge Franklin nodded. "Of course, darling. This is your show." She gestured to the microphone. Anna, standing there in her navy blue church dress, reached for me. Oh, I was coming with. We walked to the podium, hand in hand.

She gestured to me with her free hand. "Before Uncle

Holden gives his closing statement, I need to tell you some things."

Judge Franklin nodded.

Anna squeezed my hand and closed her eyes for a second before beginning. "My mom...I wish you could've met her." She sniffed, her eyes already watering. "She was the best person I've ever known. She wasn't perfect but she loved people in a way that was different than anyone else." Anna fingered a gold locket at the base of her throat. "She took risks if she thought you were worth it." She looked right at the judge. "And she thought I was worth it. She thought Silas and Lemon were worth it. So you might think her ninety-day experiment was for laughs, but it wasn't. Please never think that about her." She wiped a tear off her cheek. I blinked. "She did this because she knew Silas, Lemon, and Anna were the strongest equation. It made the most sense. It would produce the greatest outcome." A tear dropped down off her chin and spattered onto the wooden podium.

The bailiff walked over a box of tissues and I let go of Anna's hand long enough to grab a few for her.

Anna took one, wiped her face, and gripped my hand again. "The three of us had a great summer together. And no, maybe we didn't make it the whole ninety days, but it wasn't a failure. Not by a long shot." Her words were picking up speed, growing a little too intense. I squeezed her hand. She paused and blew out her breath. "The only thing Silas and Lemon are guilty of is falling crazy, madly, and completely in love with each other." Her free hand curled into a fist against the wooden podium. "*Exactly* how my momma wanted them to. She *knew* they belonged together. She *knew* neither of them would be happy until they found their way back to each other. And she was right." She thrust her arm toward Silas and Lemon. "Look at them. Look at the way they look at each other." She pointed at them again, urging the judge with her eyes. Judge Franklin did as Anna requested. We all did. Anna held all the cards at that moment.

It actually hurt to watch Silas and Lemon right then, gazing at each other, like they had everything they could ever want between them—except for Anna, of course. I would never have that. I rubbed at a knot in the center of my chest.

Anna pointed at them one last time. "I want a love like that someday."

I was done for. I wiped my eyes on the shoulder of my shirt, not even trying to hide the fact that I, a grown man and a lawyer, was crying in a courtroom because of a teenage girl.

Anna pressed on. "My mom *knew*. She knew about them and, your honor, she knew about me. She knew who I should be with. Who would love me and raise me the way she wanted me to be raised. And whose love would be powerful enough to pull me out of the darkness of her passing. " She sobbed. "I *long* to be with them. Granny and Gramps are everything to me. They always will be. But it's with Silas and Lemon that I belong. And I am asking you to let me be with them. *Please.*"

Everything in the room was pin-drop quiet for five seconds. Somebody sniffled. Mom or Lemon, I couldn't tell.

"Do you have anything you'd like to add, Mr. Dupree?"

It took a second to realize the judge was talking to me since she was a blur. My throat was clogged. I wiped my eyes and studied her face for a moment. I shook my head. There was no need. In all my cases, I'd never given a closing statement as eloquent as Anna's. "No, ma'am. I don't think I can top that."

Anna led me back to our seats. I pulled her under my arm and pressed a kiss to her temple. "Dang, girl. You should be a lawyer someday." She smiled and handed me one of the tissues. If this didn't go her way, it had nothing to do with the Duprees and everything to do with Judge Franklin. And I would make sure Anna knew that.

"Well. I feel chastened," Judge Franklin admitted. "I think

the way is clear, here." She leaned forward on her elbows once more and picked up her gavel. "Annaleise Nicole Dupree, I hereby grant Silas Dean Dupree and Clementine Laura Dupree to be your legal guardians." Then she smacked the gavel against the sound block.

It was over so fast, I sat there stunned. Anna jumped up. I thought she'd go straight to Silas and Lemon, but she didn't. She dove right between Mom and Dad, pulling them into a tight hug.

I shook my head, filled with wonder.

And a little child shall lead them.

Just then Jedd Pruitt caught my eye in the back of the room. His gaze was locked on me. He tossed his chin up and I reciprocated, grinning. I owed that man everything when it came to my law career. To this day, I was convinced it was his letter of recommendation that had landed me a spot in the law program at the University of Virginia. He tipped his head for me to join him.

Anna's words were like a cure-all antidote emitted into the air because right then Silas, my normally tough, unemotional brother, made a beeline for me, wet-cheeked. I held up a finger to Jedd and he nodded. I was hardly to a full stand before Silas tackled me in a rib-cracking hug. I laughed and hugged him back even harder. It's what I'd hoped for.

"Thank you, man." He pounded me hard, almost breathless. "Thank you."

"I hardly did anything." I smiled as we stepped back. "It was all her." I gestured to Anna who had pulled Lemon into a four-way celebration. My mom ran a hand over Lemon's hair and they shared a smile. All was right in the world once again.

Silas wiped his cheeks, nostrils flaring with a silent laugh. "You were here when we needed you. You came for this."

I gripped his shoulder, narrowing my gaze. "And I would've been here for your wedding if I could've been."

29

He nodded. "I know, I know. I was just giving you a hard time. Taking it out on you. Stressed out of my mind over this. Sorry, dude."

"It's fine. I get it." I tilted my head. "Are we okay?" Maybe I should've been more eloquent like Anna. Said something like, "Sorry you have to have a brother who's such an out-of-control headcase that he has to put his lips on every pretty girl he meets, even your ex." But Silas was a man of few words and I was confident he knew what I meant.

He nodded, understanding in his eyes. "Yeah. We're good." A smile lit up his face and he glanced over at Anna, bursting with pride. "We got our girl. Everything is fantastic."

"Yeah, you did."

Just then, Lemon motioned at Silas to leave. He grinned and held up a finger to indicate he needed a second. "We were thinking of heading to Lucy's to celebrate. We'd love for you to come."

Lucy's Italiano was one of three restaurants in town, and the only one that was any good. I didn't love going into public in Seddledowne, but there was no way I was missing this celebration. "Heck yeah. Just let me catch up with Jedd real quick. I'll meet you there."

He squeezed my shoulder one more time before hurrying toward Anna, Lemon, and our parents.

I walked the other way, to my old mentor. Since the last time I'd seen him, his hair had gone white. But he still wore his corduroy slacks and sock ties just like always.

"Man, what's up?" I offered my hand and he gripped it, crushing my bones.

Jedd was in his early sixties, but he'd always made me feel like his equal, even when I was a hot-headed teenager who thought I knew everything. "Same old," he said. "The question is, what are you up to?" His eyes sparkled like a proud father. "You don't need to tell me. I follow every case you're on." He bomb-whistled. "But Bromhorst. Dupree, you have guts."

I blew out my breath in an O. "Wasn't my first pick of cases. But the older guys were already tangled up, so I took it." And most days I wished I hadn't. "What about you? Any interesting cases you're working on?"

He snorted. "Interesting? A literal time suck would be more like it?"

I crinkled my brow.

He expounded. "Last week, I saw an eviction case on a woman who had twenty-seven cats in her apartment. She was allowed two. The owner brought in pictures. I can't even tell you. Crap, literally, everywhere. Carpets were ruined and I can only imagine the smell. But for two hours we had to look at the lady's pictures of every single cat and listen to everything she'd done to take care of them as if somehow that overrode her rental agreement." He shuddered. "And taxpayers are paying my salary for this?"

"Sounds mind-numbing."

He chortled. "Things are really good. That one was just... something else." He cocked his head. "Look, I wanted to talk to you for a minute. Bounce something off of you."

I leaned against the wall. "Shoot."

He ran a hand over his mouth, brows raised. "Denise's been hounding me to retire. She wants to snowbird in Florida for the winters. Her arthritis is getting pretty bad."

I nodded. Denise had had achy joints as long as I'd known Jedd.

He cocked his head and pressed his hands together like he was about to pray. "Thing is, I don't want to step down as D.A. until I know there's someone solid to take my place." All ten of his fingers slowly lowered until they were pointing at me. "Your name is the one I keep coming back to."

I looked at him for a second. "Jedd. I'm in DC—"

"But you could be here. You grew up here. People like you. Dupree is a well-respected name in this town."

I shook my head. "You and I both know there are plenty of people that don't feel that way. And I'd have to win an election."

"Holden." His head bobbled confidently. "Those people are fewer than you think. And the ones who do are simpletons and anyone with any sense knows it. The naysayers will be exponentially outnumbered by people with good old-fashioned common sense."

My mouth opened, closed, and opened again. "I mean, yeah, but...I just...I wasn't planning to come back here."

He scoffed. "That's all you used to talk about. You used to rib me about how, as soon as you took the bar exam, you were going to come put me out of a job."

My hands flew out. "That was before..."

His gaze pinned me and I could feel it coming. The lecture about how I couldn't let the past dictate my entire future. He'd given it to me many times. So had my parents. But coming back to Seddledowne wasn't in the cards for me. Visiting for the weekend was one thing, but living here? Running into people from high school? To this day, I wouldn't go into Food Lion to get my mom a gallon of milk, for fear I might see certain individuals. One individual, really. A lifetime of that? No thanks.

He cuffed my shoulder. "Just think about it, please. DC lawyers are a dime a dozen. I know you, you have to hate the traffic up there. You're a cowboy in your heart. Don't tell me you're happy with your quarter-acre yard." It wasn't even a quarter of an acre, but I wasn't going to tell him that. And yeah, having no land made me crazy. It's one of the reasons I went to the gym so much.

He held his hands up when I started to protest. "Fact is, I'm retiring one way or another and Seddledowne is going to need a good D.A." He smiled. "Bet your momma would like to have you closer."

I ran a hand through my hair. "I'll think about it." I would. But I already knew what my answer would be. No way would I make as much money here as I would in DC. But that wasn't even the real reason. I simply didn't belong in Seddle-downe anymore.

We shook hands and pulled each other into a bro hug, complete with a back slap.

Then I walked to my car, ready for some hot, buttery, garlic-slathered breadsticks, a big plate of Lucy's lasagna, and some family merrymaking like this town had never seen. I pulled my phone out to send my order to Anna so I wouldn't slow them down.

But I stopped dead, in the middle of the sidewalk, in front of the building where all my lawyer dreams had begun. Because there, on my phone, was a text that felt like the end of my dreams.

> Wellington Sipsby: You screwed up majorly by not being here. Your schizo, space-cadet intern completely offended Bromhorst and he fired us. We just lost millions of dollars because you left that lunatic in charge. You're done here, Dupree. Pick up your crap ASAP and leave your key on the counter at the front desk.

My hand shoved into the front of my hair, tugging. "No, no, no, no, no." I speed-dialed Trixie, certain Sipsby was confused. There must've been some kind of misunderstanding. Even if Bromhorst had taken his business elsewhere, this wasn't my fault. I'd covered my butt.

But ten minutes later, it was verified. Trixie had come down with a stomach bug the night before the big meeting. She'd told Audrey to call me. But Audrey, taking me literally, had been too terrified to reach out, and she decided to head up the meeting herself. And she'd bombed it spectacularly. In fact, the meeting never happened.

While waiting for Bromhorst and his wife to arrive, Audrey had left the boardroom door wide open while chatting on the phone with her cousin. The Bromhorsts distinctly overheard her say, verbatim, "That man would hump anything on two legs and some things on four. I wouldn't let him near my dog. I could write his next election slogan, 'Bromhorst's office: Where the men are men and the sheep are scared.'"

Just, wow.

Yup. There was no coming back from that. Audrey had been let go immediately. And I was kicking myself for being too kindhearted to have not fired her months ago. I called Sipsby, but he wouldn't answer. Only sent another nasty text telling me not to bother. And not to bother with the other partners either. They were unanimous in their decision.

I shakily lowered myself to the top of a waist-high red-brick wall. My head dropped into my hands and I forced myself to breathe. If I wasn't Holden Matthew Dupree, Esquire, Associate Attorney at Caldwell, Caldwell, Sipsby, and Anderson, then who was I?

Welp.

Son of a gun.

It looked like I had nothing but time on my hands to figure it out.

four

CHRISTY

I pressed my hands against the edge of the desk and rolled my neck to the right. I'd slept like crap last night. And the night before. Pretty much every night since I'd found out Silas was hired as my assistant principal. Gotten myself all riled up, and lost five pounds from the anxiety for nothing. Because I should've known Silas wouldn't be a jerk about it. He was too classy for that. He'd walked into the front office this morning, wearing khakis, a white shirt, a Stallions blue tie, and an expression that said, "This is gonna suck. Let's do it."

When two pregnant girls had started duking it out in the lunchroom, I'd stepped between them and gotten kicked in the thigh. But Silas had come to the rescue, long legs hauling it across the massive room, pushing through the crowd, and yanking them apart. Why on earth would two expectant females endanger their babies in a brawl? Because they found out they had the same baby daddy. I shook my head just thinking about it.

And when two ninth-graders ended up in my office for drawing male reproductive parts on each other's worksheets, and I thought my mind might explode from the idiocy, Silas, in a moment of genius, made each boy call his mother and explain precisely why he was getting in-school suspension for three days. I'd never enjoyed watching two teenage boys squirm more in my life.

But we were only on the third day of school. If it kept up at this pace, this year might be the death of me. I rolled my head in the other direction, trying to work the kink out.

"Principal Thornbury?" Silas's baritone voice brought me up. He was standing in my office doorway.

"Yes, Assistant Principal Dupree?" I snorted. "That's a mouthful and I hope you don't expect me to call you that all year. Because, just no."

There was a whisper of a smile at the corners of his mouth. He stepped forward, straight-faced, looking down at me. I gulped but forced my neck to crane so I could meet his gaze. Then he lifted his fist and smiled. "Good work today, *Christy*. We might not screw this up after all."

I bumped his knuckles. "Oh, we're going to rock this, *Silas*. Even if it's by sheer willpower."

Our hands dropped to our sides and he stepped back.

He stood there for a second, expressionless, and I held my breath, waiting for the question I knew was coming.

It was in his eyes, the purse of his lips, on the edge of his tongue. He opened his mouth, and I hurled the answer toward him. "I didn't do it for you, okay?"

He bit his lips, staring at me.

I rubbed my temples and closed my eyes. "I mean, yes, originally I applied for a teaching job at the middle school because I hoped we would work out. But things kind of spiraled when they realized I had a master's in administration. Obviously, they were desperate. But I didn't take the job *because* of you."

There was a beat of silence and then he simply said, "Okay."

I opened my eyes to see him standing there, hands in his pockets, waiting for me to go on.

I shrugged. "I needed space from...Laramie." I hated admitting that but he knew all too well what things were like for me back home. "I'm not planning to stay here forever. But the thought of not having to deal with that..." My hand pointed behind me, to the west. "Believe it or not...being here" —*with you married*—"is more appealing than being there." It was true. Living in Laramie, post-Silas, would give me nothing but more heartache. My mom...my sisters...they'd never let me forget that I'd failed to land yet another man.

His head tilted, pity in his expression. "Christy." His voice was full of compassion and I'd never wanted it from anyone less.

I held my hands up. "Don't. Please, don't feel sorry for me. I can't take that."

We stood there for two seconds. Then he nodded and took a step back. "All right. Well, unless you need anything else from me, I'm going to head out." *To see my hot wife.* He didn't need to say the words. They were written in the sparkle of his eyes that he was trying, and failing miserably, to hide. He'd probably been counting the minutes all day.

I scowled. "You're not coming to Anna's game?"

"Not this time. We've got our grand opening for The Upward Dog this weekend and we're scrambling to get the bathrooms finished. We'll be pounding it out every night this week." I'd heard through the grapevine—i.e., Mrs. Ross, the biology teacher—that "The Duprees," as she'd called Silas and Lemon, were opening a new gym here. Maybe I'd get a membership and work out at two a.m. when I'd never run into either of them. "My parents are covering for us this time." He cracked his thumb knuckle. "And Holden."

I choked. On absolutely nothing. I put a fist to my mouth, trying to cough it out. But I choked again. Silas had told me this morning that Anna's custody hearing had been on Friday. Which explained why Holden had been at the volleyball meeting on Thursday afternoon. But I'd assumed he'd be back in DC by now. And now I had to coach a sport I knew nothing about right in front of him?

Silas stood there, watching me gasp for air, wearing an amused expression. I grabbed my water bottle and took a long draw through the straw, my face flaming.

He stepped toward the door. "Anyway. Good luck, Coach." He lifted his hand in a wave.

"Wait." I held up a finger and walked behind my desk to grab the box I'd spent way too much time wrapping ever so carefully yesterday afternoon. I was proud of that flower-bow. It had taken three tries. And I'd shed a tear or two while I was making it. You know, like you do when you're wrapping a wedding gift for the man you thought you'd be marrying.

Most people would say the best gift you could give an ex is your absence. But obviously, that wasn't an option. And since we were going to work in close proximity, daily, I needed to do this. It was my metaphorical burning of the ex-boyfriend's things and a peace treaty, all rolled into one.

And yes, it killed me to hand it to him, but I did it anyway, determined to move past this.

He eyed it like it might grow fangs at any second.

"It's a wedding gift." I gulped. "For you and Lemon."

More silent gaping.

I held my hands up. "Don't worry. It's not a glitter bomb or a defecated litter box with your name on the side or anything."

He shook his head and laughed.

I tugged on the hem of my blouse. "It's something off your registry." An expensive enamelwear dutch oven that I would've liked to own. It had cost a pretty penny, but I'd gotten a signing bonus as principal and thought it only fitting since I never would've heard of Seddledowne if it weren't for Silas.

More staring. And uncomfortable silence.

"Gah." My hands pressed to my cheeks. "You're reading too much into it. Just...congrats...good luck. All of that."

His eyes turned down, a hint of sadness there. "You didn't have to do that."

I held up my hands. "I know, and I didn't do it for a thank-you. I'm not trying to get anything out of you. I just thought since we're going to be working together, living in the same small town..." I clenched my fists. "I know I've invaded your turf here. Put us both in an uncomfortable situation...it only seemed right. And I do hope that you'll have a happy life together." I almost meant that last line. I would get there. Eventually.

He was quiet for a second and then he said, barely above a whisper, "Well. That was nice of you. I'm sure Clem will love it, whatever it is. Thanks." He made no move to leave, like maybe since I'd given him a present, I expected him to hang around and do our nails together, talk about cute boys and all that.

"You're welcome." I nodded. "You can stop standing there, making it awkward." I laughed. He laughed. "Just take your gift and go." My stupid, shaky voice betrayed me.

But he nodded and finally walked away.

I shut the door behind him and fell against it, my hands trembling. One day down. One hundred and seventy-six to go.

I quickly changed from my pantsuit into a pair of black leggings, a blue fitted T-shirt—that was the closest thing to school colors that I owned—and the white and royal blue Seddledowne Stallions athletic jacket Mr. Alvarez had eagerly let me borrow from the athletics closet. Being at the game was just a formality. I wouldn't be coaching on my own today. Didn't know enough yet to lead in any way. Coach Byrd had promised he'd be right there, showing me the ropes, calling all the shots. But he didn't expect me to head anything up at this point. Had I spent my weekend watching match after match of college volleyball? Absolutely. But one weekend of watching videos does not a coach make.

When I entered the gym, the scorekeeper's table was set up. The girls had raised the net and the JV team was practicing their serves. The varsity girls were spread out on the bleachers, braiding hair and working on homework assignments. I scanned the room for Coach Byrd but he was nowhere.

I walked over to Anna and Brooklyn, both with Dutch braids, laughing as they hit a ball back and forth. "Have you guys seen Coach Byrd?"

"He's sick. He's not coming." Brooklyn shrugged as if this was the most boring thing she'd learned today.

I swallowed. Um. "What? Are you serious?" I pulled my phone out of my pocket and sure enough, he'd texted three whole minutes ago, letting me know. I stifled a groan.

Anna grimaced, looking as sick as I felt. "I think he ate the creamed spinach from the cafeteria." She shivered.

My mouth parted. I rubbed the back of my neck, my eyes darting around as if they might land on a solution. The varsity team.

"Okay. Thanks," I said, before walking across the gym to the girls I hoped would be my saviors.

As I approached, they gradually looked up, one by one.

I chewed the inside of my cheek for a second. "Who are the captains for varsity?"

A pretty Asian-American and a towhead blonde hesitantly raised their hands. I rolled my shoulders back. "All right ladies, you're my assistants for the JV game."

Just then, one of the outside doors opened and the

opposing team began filing in. The scoreboard timer was counting down. Sixteen minutes to liftoff. Awesome. My head rolled in the opposite direction when I heard parents coming through the other doors. My stomach tightened. This was getting real. And fast.

The captains looked at each other, wide-eyed, put their books away, and filed down the bleachers.

"Names?" I asked.

"I'm Ming," the Asian offered. "That's Jasmine."

"Nice to meet you." I forced a smile. "Not gonna lie. I know very little about this sport. I've never coached anyone in my life. Don't even know what we do first." I figured if I was humble and honest upfront they might respect me. Either that or devour me for dinner.

"We gotchu," Ming said. "At least for the first set. Then we have to change and stretch for our game."

I'd take it.

Jasmine bounced, excited. "Let me get some paper."

Ming led me across the court to the "bench," which was a row of royal blue padded folding chairs, each embossed with a rearing silver stallion.

"First, we have to figure out who's starting." Ming stuck her fingers in the corners of her mouth and whistled so hard it left my right ear ringing. "Shanaya!"

My eyes moved to the Black girl who snapped to attention.

But then it felt as if someone had lit the gym floor on fire beneath me, because right behind her, standing on the top row of the bleachers, in all his drop-dead swoleness, was Holden, biceps popping as they folded across his chest. And he was deep in conversation with none other than Mr. Alvarez, the athletic director who looked like he couldn't care less that Byrd was MIA and I had no clue what I was doing. Like he wasn't getting paid big bucks for exactly this sort of situation. Alvarez said something and a slow, perfect smile

41

spread across Holden's rugged face. He ran a hand across his bottom lip like he was thinking about something, and the ground tilted a little. Like a pathetic cliché, I dragged my bottom lip between my teeth. I could almost feel those powerful arms around me, those strong lips on mine, those autumn eyes drilling into me, begging for my soul.

And then my gut panged and I thought I might puke. Because in mere minutes I was going to coach his niece's team in their first game of the season and I had no idea what I was doing. I hadn't known him that long, but Holden exuded confidence in a way that only the most capable of people can. He could probably coach this team with his eyes shut and his mouth gagged, and he'd look like he stepped straight off a centerfold as he did it.

I pressed a freezing cold hand to my head. I was pretty sure all circulation to my extremities had ceased. Barring a miracle, I was going to bomb this spectacularly as the one person I'd do anything not to embarrass myself in front of looked on. I would be the topic of conversation around the Dupree dinner table tonight when Anna's team lost. Scrap that. I would be the topic of conversation for every family in the room.

"What's up?" The tall, adorable girl named Shanaya landed right in front of me, snapping me back to the task at hand. Jasmine arrived behind her with a five-subject notebook. Ming motioned for me to sit in one of the padded seats. She sat next to me and the other girls squatted in front of us.

Ming's hands moved as she spoke. "Shay, did Whorley tell you who was starting before she quit?"

Shanaya shook her head. "Uh-uh." Her lips pursed, and she rolled her head in a slow shake. "*Gurl.* You know she didn't."

You have got to be kidding me. I pinched the bridge of my nose.

"Don't you worry, Thornbury. We're not going down like that," Jasmine said, her eyes narrowed in determination.

I had to pull it together. I was the adult. And I needed to instill confidence in these girls. So their JV coach had quit. And the varsity coach was MIA. Principal Thornbury would not leave them hanging.

I clasped my hands together. "Okay. Shay." I pointed to the JV player. "What's your position?" I figured Ming wouldn't have called her over if she wasn't one of the better players. At least, that's what I was hoping.

"Setter. But I can play middle or outside if you need."

Ming shook her head." You want her as setter. She's the best. Not a close second on the team."

"Awww." Shay grinned and made a heart shape with her hands.

"Okay." I looked at Jasmine. "Put her down."

Jasmine wrote setter and Shanaya by the number one. One down. Five to go.

"Alright, ladies." I gave them each a moment of eye contact. "No biases. No picking friends just because you like them. We need the best players to start."

Eleven minutes later, we had a starting lineup and Jasmine had written down when the girls on the bench should rotate in. My confidence level had come up slightly. Four minutes before the game started, I handed in the lineup and called the JV team over. Thirteen adorable jersied girls bounced, ran, and leaped, forming a half-circle in front of me. Their sparkling eyes hit me right in the chest. They'd worked hard to get here and were finally playing their first game of the season.

"Do you guys have a team chant?" I asked.

They glanced at one other, grinning.

Shay put her hand in the middle, and every girl laid theirs over someone else's till all hands were in the pile.

Shay tipped her chin at me. "You too, Coach."

So I added my hand on top. Ming and Jasmine followed.

Shay started the hand bounce, letting everyone's hands drop a couple of inches before lifting them. But this was no ordinary "3-2-1, go team" chant. Because they didn't just stand there, hands moving. Their feet started galloping in place like horses.

Then Shay screamed and everyone followed, "Seddle-downe Stallions, Seddledowne Stallions, if we should win, we fought with passion. Seddledowne Stallions, Seddledowne Stallions, if we should lose, we go down smashin'. Give it our all, leave it on the floor. Seddledowne Stallions, win or lose, we're masters of our fate and we get to choose!" And then they legit neighed like a pack of wild, angry horses. I didn't know whether to laugh or hug them.

But I knew one thing, real coach or not, if they played as well as they made up chants, they were going to kick the Honeyville Eagles' butts.

five

HOLDEN

My gut hadn't settled since Friday when I'd gotten that stupid text from Sipsby. And this volleyball game wasn't helping. If I kept this up, I'd have an ulcer by age thirty. We were five minutes into the first set and the score was already Eagles 14, Seddledowne 3. Christy was giving it her best shot, but I was pretty sure she didn't know anything about volleyball.

Next to me, Dad squirmed and shook his head. Mom sat on his other side, stiffly. "Christy shouldn't be coaching," he grumbled. "Does she even know what she's doing?" He was just being protective of Anna and her love of this sport, but it wasn't Christy's fault they were losing.

"Dad. The JV coach quit. You know that. Anna told you. I'm fairly certain this is not Christy's idea of a good time."

I leaned to my other side, to Gideon Alvarez, who'd planted himself next to me before the game even started. "Man, these positions are all wrong." He had graduated three years before Silas, Sophie, and Lemon, but we were both UVA alum, so we always spoke when we saw each other. "Anna should be playing middle. And number eleven...she should be

45

the libero." A serve from the Eagles landed right between the center and left-back players with zero effort to stop it. They both looked dumbfounded, like "I thought you were going to get that." I groaned and flung my hands up. "They're not talking to each other." I was no volleyball expert, but my minor was in physical education and we'd had to do mock coaching of all major high school sports. I knew enough.

Alvarez shouldn't have been over here by me. He should've been sitting next to Christy, helping her.

He didn't even comment on my comment. Just grunted. And then said, "Man, ain't our new principal smokin'?" He flicked his wrist like he'd been burned. Alvarez had a strange accent. Half Black, half country, like he couldn't figure out his own angle. A surge of protective jealousy roared through me and I stamped it out. *Christy and I are not a thing,* I reminded myself. *Alvarez can check her out if he wants.* But then he sucked his teeth. "Imma try to get with that."

I cleared my throat and laced my fingers in my lap, to keep from punching him in the side of the head. "Pretty sure that'll get you fired." There was no way abstaining from fraternizing with other faculty wasn't in their contract.

Another serve landed in the "campfire" behind our front-row girls. Mom put her head in her hands and Dad blew out his breath, annoyed. A guy in the front row stood up and yelled at his daughter, whose face burst into flame. Anna's shoulders slumped and Christy kept rubbing the back of her neck, looking helpless. I couldn't take it anymore. I slid my phone out of my jeans pocket, praying Christy had her phone on her.

> Me: Don't hate me. Just trying to help. Anna should be middle. She's the tallest and has a strong jump. Number eleven should be libero. And the girl playing outside hitter might do better as opposite. Just a thought.

My thumb hovered above send. She might take this the wrong way—like I was mansplaining the game. But after another point scored for the Eagles, I went for it.

Nosey Alvarez must've been reading over my shoulder because his eyes moved from my lap to Christy, across the court.

I rubbed my jaw, willing her to feel the buzz of the phone that was hopefully in her pocket or somewhere nearby. She jerked a little and I was pretty sure her phone was on her person. Maybe in that jacket pocket. But like a good coach, she was ignoring it.

> Me: Hey.

Again she twitched but left it.

> Me: Christy?

Alvarez leered back and forth. "You know uh?" he asked. Uh, meaning her.

I nodded and chose my words carefully. The last thing Silas, Lemon, or Christy needed was for people to know there was a history there. "She and Silas were in the same master's program. He kind of introduced us. So yeah, we're friends."

I let myself quickly glance over to gauge his reaction.

He said nothing, hopefully rethinking his earlier comments about Christy's hotness.

Christy still wasn't checking her phone. After yet another point, I hissed under my breath, *call a timeout.*

My telepathy game must've been strong because her hands flew up in a T. The ref blew the whistle. I hit call on her name just long enough for her to feel the long buzz of the phone. As the girls gathered around her, she pulled her phone out of her pocket, looked at the screen, and then across at me.

I pointed to my phone, and she nodded. Her eyes dropped, desperately scanning my words. She shoved her phone back in her pocket, rolled her shoulders back, and started barking orders. When those girls walked back onto the floor, every suggestion I'd made had been implemented. I exhaled, hoping they would work.

Christy dropped back into the chair, looking worn out, and picked up her phone.

Ten seconds later, mine buzzed.

> Christy: I'm dying, Holden. I have no idea what I'm doing. The varsity coach just no-showed. He's sick or something.

Alvarez was reading every word, practically straining his neck when I slid the phone to the opposite side of my body.

> Me: It's just one game. It'll be okay.
> Hopefully, things will turn around right here.

Just then, the Eagles' middle spiked on Anna. Anna jumped straight up, her eyes squeezed shut, terrified, but she slapped that ball back down, landing a kill on the other side. I nearly came up out of my seat, I cheered so loud. The stands exploded and her teammates surrounded her, slapping her on the back, shoulder, butt, wherever they could get their hands on her.

Dad sat up taller, grinning. "That's our girl." Mom relaxed

slightly. I only wished we'd been videoing so Silas and Lemon could see later.

Christy kept her focus on the game, but her phone never left her hands, carefully placed in her lap like I was a literal lifeline. Which was fine. Mine never left my hand either.

Our girls came back with a vengeance, but it was too big a divide to close, and the set ended Eagles 25, Stallions 20. At least it wasn't a blowout.

I stood and stretched, trying to pop my back. My phone buzzed.

> Christy: Any chance you want to come hold my hand for the next set?

She followed that with a "gritting teeth" emoji.

I bit back a smile.

> Me: Thought you'd never ask.

Her relief was visible from across the floor.

I leaned over to my parents. "Hey, I'm gonna go help coach."

Dad smiled up at me. "Best idea all night."

I gave Alvarez a, "See ya, man," and bounded down the bleachers, leaving him slack-jawed at missing his chance. I didn't cut across the floor but took my time tracing the perimeter of the court. There was a beautiful, off-limits blonde waiting for me. And she was looking at me like she'd been floating in the middle of the ocean on a driftwood raft lashed together with dried-up vines and I'd just pulled up in my million-dollar yacht.

Christy's brown eyes burned into me as I walked up. "Hey," was all she said. Women should not be allowed to wear leggings. It was just mean. At least when they looked as good as Christy. Her hair was pulled back into a high ponytail, showing off her flushed cheeks, possibly from the stress of the first set.

The same way they'd flushed when we kissed.

STOP.

"Hey." I shoved my hands deep into my pockets.

Anna skipped over, her eyes dancing. "Uncle Holden, did you see my kill?"

I laid my hand out for our low five, sizzle fingers. "So sick." I bumped her shoulder with mine. "Next time, try to keep your eyes open."

She laughed and covered her face with her hands, embarrassed. "I know. I know."

I grinned, not even trying to hide the pride bursting out of me.

Christy watched us, her lips turning up at the corners and her eyes bright. I ran a hand through the front of my hair and looked away. *She's just grateful you're helping. That's all.*

The rest of Anna's team was eyeing me, wondering, I'm sure, what I was doing there.

"He's cute," I heard one girl whisper behind me.

Pretty sure Christy heard it too because heat tickled the top of her ears. I might've preened a little. So yeah, maybe she was still in love with my brother. But I had some kind of effect on her and, not gonna lie, it felt good.

"All right, all right," Christy motioned for them to gather 'round. "This is Anna's uncle, Holden, and he's going to help coach the rest of the game."

They looked at me with expressions varying from curiosity to gratitude to downright suspicion.

"Holden Dupree?" The girl Christy had moved to libero snapped her fingers, eyeing me. "You played baseball with my uncle back in the day. He talks about you all the time. Says you should've played college ball, but you gave it up for law school?"

My eyes narrowed, trying to figure out which of my high school teammates she looked like. Then it hit me. "You're Colby Jones's niece?" The button nose was a clone of his.

She beamed. "Yeah." She pointed to her uncle in the stands. Dude was wearing a GoPro on his hat, filming her. He had glasses now. No wonder I hadn't recognized him. Maybe I could get a replay of Anna's kill to show Silas and Lemon. He tossed his chin up at me and I grinned back. I'd have to say hello after the game.

"Holden is the reason we had a little comeback. It was his idea to move some of you around." Christy smiled at me, eyes sparkling. I bit the insides of my cheeks, not to smile at that. Most of her worry from a few minutes earlier was gone. "Words of encouragement before the second set starts?" she asked.

Every girl's gaze turned to me.

Okay. Yeah.

I rubbed my hands together. "Look. You guys have talent. A lot of it." They probably felt like a ragtag group of orphans with no permanent coach. They needed someone who believed in them. "But talent means nothing if you don't move toward the ball. Some of you look like your feet are stuck in concrete." Brooklyn giggled and pointed to herself. She wasn't the only one. "Your parents haven't spent a lot of money and time on you—and you haven't worked your butts off—only to flop during a game because you're too afraid to move."

"That set is over. Leave it in the past. Time to move on. The great thing about volleyball is you get a second chance." I heard a few girls say "yeah" and "facts." "All the anxiety and frustration you feel during a test, at home, or practice? It comes out on this floor every time you touch that ball. Got it?"

I snapped. "Oh and one more thing. For the love..." I balled my fists. "*Call the ball*. Every single one of them. There should be an insane amount of yelling and talking to each other during this set. Stop caring about looking dumb or what your friends in the stands are thinking. You're a team. Take care of each other." I couldn't stress that enough. "And for every time you don't call the ball when it comes to you, Coach Thornbury's going to make you run a lap in practice tomorrow." I looked at Christy to make sure that was okay. She nodded. The buzzer sounded. "No more nice girls. You hear me? Beast mode." I pointed to the ground. "Starting now."

The setter laid her hand out, and everyone piled theirs on top. I laid mine on Christy's and looked over to catch her watching me, eyes flickering like a smoldering match in a dark night. I really needed her to not look at me like that.

"Beast mode, on three!" The setter yelled.

Once the girls were back on the court, I sat next to Christy on "the bench."

"Thank you," she said, eyes on her team. "You saved me."

"I don't know about that. Don't count your chickens... but...I'm happy to help."

I pulled up the notes app on my phone and entitled a new page: Laps. Whenever a girl failed to call the ball, I shouted their name and the number of laps they were running. Mean? Maybe. But after five minutes, every single ball was being called.

I forced myself to sit back in my chair, settle in, and look relaxed. But it was all an act. Between the game and my body's sonar going off every time Christy twitched, I was a mess inside.

I did not like the effect she had on me.

The girls struggled to get their feet moving for the first few minutes of play. But after an impressive volley that we won, things seemed to snap into place. Pretty soon, we were up 13-10. Everything was okay.

And then the football team rolled in through the locker room doors, fresh off the field from practice. From the number and varying sizes, it looked like JV and varsity had come to support the Lady Stallions. Which would have been good if the air in the room didn't turn a little chilly at their arrival.

I studied the girls' faces and shook my head, not liking what I was seeing. Where there had been confidence and a love of the game a moment before, now there was a mix of dread and insecurity. Anna had told me JV hadn't won a single game last year. Whereas our football program was one of the best in the state. I could almost read these girls' minds. We could've dubbed the gym Intimidation Station right then.

In particular, my niece looked like she'd just fallen into the deep end of a pool with her hands and feet bound. Her eyes doubled in size, and she looked like she was struggling to breathe. What on earth? I scowled, trying to pull her gaze to mine. But her eyes were on the ground in front of her.

And it was her turn to serve.

She'd served once in the first set. Her serves tended to be short, but that was okay, as long as they went over. She'd scored two points, catching the Eagles by surprise, when her ball barely skimmed the top of the net, dropping narrowly onto their side. On the third try it had gone into the net. I knew how anxious serving made her. She'd worked all summer just to get the ball over. The last thing she needed was any reason to doubt herself.

She dribbled the ball double-handed, five feet behind the line, but I did not like the discomfort on her face right then, the already-defeated way she was standing. It was going into the net if she was lucky to even get it that far.

My knee bounced. "Call a time out." I hoped Christy would forgive my bossiness.

Without hesitation, her hands formed a T, and the ref blew the whistle.

I watched Anna, hawk-like, trying to figure her out. Her eyes flicked to a group of three boys in the top left corner of the gym. Two were on their phones, AirPods in their ears. But the third one—a big, buff kid, with guns like logs—was leaning cooly against the cinderblock wall, eyes trained on my niece with an inquisitive, lovesick stare.

Oh, man.

I mean, I couldn't blame him. He had impeccable taste. Not only was Anna too pretty for her own good, but she was witty, brilliant, and kind to her core. The question was, did she like him back? Or did she wish he'd disappear in a cloud of vapor? Either way, he couldn't have shown up at a less opportune time.

I glanced at Christy, who was watching me. I swear she could read my mind because when I grabbed Anna by the elbow, pulling her off to the side, Christy nodded and motioned for everyone else to surround her.

"Hey." I ducked down, looking my niece right in the eye, speaking a hundred miles an hour. We had sixty seconds to fix all her world's problems. "What's going on? You look like someone just peed in your cereal."

She scrunched her adorable nose and let out a breathy laugh. "Ewww. Thank you for the visual." But her eyes flitted for a split second, back to that group of guys. Her hands were trembling.

I grabbed her by the shoulders. "Are those boys making you nervous? Look, you can't let a bunch of jerk guys get under your—"

"They're not j-jerks." Her breath hitched and her cheeks heated.

"Ahhh. Gotcha." I chuckled, causing her cheeks to go from light pink to tomato red. I squeezed her shoulders. "You can't think about that right now."

She put a hand over her eyes and turned slightly to shield her face. "It's this one guy. Blue Bishop. The one in the gray shirt. He's the JV quarterback. I watched a bunch of his high-light reels this weekend." She looked dead ashamed to admit that. "He's like—sheesh—so good. But he's a real athlete. And I'm just..." Her eyes lifted, but they were full of doubt. "I'm just a wannabe."

I shook her slightly. "Don't ever call yourself a wannabe again. Your mom would be so upset if she heard you talk about yourself like that."

Her eyes lifted and she stood a little taller. "You're right."

"This Blue kid is only good because somebody told him he was and he chose to believe it. If he thought he was crap, he'd be crap." Had we not told her enough how amazing she was? It killed me to think that might be true. "You're a freaking Goddess, Anna. Do you hear me? And that guy is looking at you right now like he'd step off a cliff if you asked him to."

"Really?" She crinkled her nose but I could almost see the weight fall off her shoulders and crash like busted concrete onto the floor.

"Yes." My eyes widened. "Really. And you better hope Silas doesn't find out."

She tipped her head back and laughed.

I looked up at the time clock. Fifteen seconds. "We can talk about this Blue kid more later." And we would. "But right now you have five seconds to come up with a mantra you're going to repeat every time you serve the ball. And five more to believe it."

We stared at each other for three seconds and then it came to me. At the same time, we blurted, "All to pieces." It was one of our Dupree family mottos. It meant to do it completely and without reservation. In volleyball speak it was the equivalent of leaving it all on the court. Her mom had said it to her, probably daily.

The buzzer sounded.

I raised my brows, locking eyes with Anna. "You say that in your head when you're dribbling before your serve. You got me? And you don't think about him again until you're done serving."

The ref blew a whistle, warning us.

Determination stole across her face. "Yes, sir." She saluted with a laugh.

I pressed a kiss to the top of her head and left her on the court.

The ref blew the whistle again and Anna dribbled the ball three times. All. To. Pieces. One word for each dribble. She twirled the ball up, her left toe tapping against the court behind her. Then she tossed it up high. Christy's hand shot out, squeezing my knee. Heat exploded up my thigh and I almost forgot what we were doing. My breaths became staggered and my adrenaline surged.

When the ball came back down, Anna reared back and smacked the living daylights out of it. A perfect serve if I'd ever seen one. The ball shot across the court, skimmed three inches above the net, and dropped just this side of the Eagle's serving line. It was so powerful and fast that the libero dove but missed it by a foot. The ball smacked against the ground and flew up behind her, hitting the back wall of the gym.

I did come up out of my seat this time, screaming, "Woohoo!" So did Christy. The entire bench was up. They broke into a chant. "A-C-E, whaaat? A-C-E, whaaat?" As their arms danced in a large circle motion. Then normally expressionless Brooklyn whipped a hand towel over her head like a propeller and screamed, "That's my bestie!"

But Anna wasn't looking at any of us. No, her eyes were

trained on this Blue kid who was offering doublehanded high fives to every teammate in his vicinity, grinning proudly like she was already his.

And she was luminous.

Not even a full week into her high school career and we were already in trouble. Because I knew the look Blue Bishop was wearing all too well. Euphoric, honed in, and half-drunk. This was no crush, passing fancy, or lustfest. It was the expression of someone who'd had an intense love-at-first-sight moment.

I would know. I'd worn the same look when I'd walked these halls.

I shook my head, feeling for the kid. Falling for a girl who was barely a freshman? You may as well throw your hands up recklessly daring Fate to bring it on. There were so many obstacles in the way.

Blue Bishop was magic for Anna. She served six times in a row after that, scoring two more aces. Until her seventh serve, which was so powerful it landed on the outside of the opposing team's serve line. Magic indeed.

We won the second set 25-17. The Eagles were losing their confidence. We were going to win this. I was riding a high, feeling lucky for having been here when Christy needed help. And for Anna's new killer serve. Everything was great. Fantastic.

Until the devil walked in.

Amber "Diabolical" Taylor.

The sole reason I hated going into public in Seddledowne.

My chest tightened and my hands curled into fists. I forced myself to take normal breaths. The last thing I needed was for Christy to notice the panic attack I was about to have. Why had I let my parents talk me into coming? I was so stupid to think this was safe.

I sat on the edge of my seat, head tucked, ready to bolt the second the game was over.

I semi-focused on the last set but my eyes kept drifting, trying to see if she'd spotted me. Seddledowne left it all on the court. When the last serve was tossed on the third set and we'd finally won the game, I exhaled.

"Good work, Coach Dupree." Christy held out her hand for a shake. I hesitated, knowing what any kind of contact was going to do to my insides. I'd let her touch me once before and I'd been regretting it ever since. But how can you not shake someone's hand after you've been in the trenches together? So I slid my palm against hers and squeezed, hating her a little for the tug it put in my gut.

Her eyes were hopeful. "Any chance you can hang around for the varsity game?"

I glimpsed back at Amber. But she was standing there, eyes narrowed, practically licking her lips, fangs bared. I torpedoed a glare right back but it was all show. In actuality, my neck caught fire and I felt a little dizzy. A grown man wigging out at the sight of his childhood plague.

I wanted to stay, desperately. Wanted to help Christy and these girls win.

But I couldn't. I didn't have a choice.

I turned my back to the stands and gave Christy a sad smile. "I can't. I'm really sorry, I promised Silas I'd help him finish his bathrooms at the gym. Varsity should go a lot smoother." It was a lie. I'd promised Silas no such thing. He hadn't even asked. In fact, last minute, he'd called a plumber who was there right now.

Christy's face fell and her cheeks flushed again. "Okay. Well. Thanks for the help." Her words were gracious but her expression was skeptical. But I wasn't going to stand there chatting her up, putting a target on her back by association. I had to go.

Now.

"Hey." Christy stepped closer and put a hand on my arm. "Is everything okay?"

But her hand was like fire now that Amber was watching.

I knocked it off, turned, and jogged from the room. And I didn't exhale until I was outside, in my car, pulling onto the road. I jammed a finger between my neck and the collar of my shirt, trying to get some air.

Every time I came back home, I got my hopes up. This time worse than before with Jedd shoving the D.A. job my way. I'd hoped more than ever that maybe it was time. Maybe I could finally come home for good. I played it off like I was a city boy now. Like I'd outgrown this place.

In truth, Seddledowne was the only place I'd ever wanted to be.

But Amber Taylor was always right there to make sure I knew I could never come back.

Six

T wo weeks after that first game, I couldn't sleep. I hadn't slept well for months. Ever since the night Silas had told me he'd be living with Lemon for three months. The Upward Dog had its grand opening the Friday evening before. I'd slipped in early Saturday morning—when Silas had told me with a wink that neither he nor Lemon would be there—and signed up for a gym pass. And now, I was glad I had. I needed to get some of my anxiety out.

I looked around one more time to make sure there were no creepy men that might sneak up on me—even though I'd been here for forty-five minutes and checked three times already. At eleven thirty p.m., the reception desk by the sliding doors was unmanned and the massive gym was empty except for me and a fellow female gym rat, who was covered in tattoos and had half of her head shaved. She looked buff enough—and tough enough—that she could likely take any perv that walked in here. But as a petite woman, barely five foot three, I could never be too careful.

I straddled the weight bench, looking down at my phone, trying to wrap my head around the fact that Holden's bio information on Facebook had changed. He'd taken down his job at Caldwell, Caldwell, Sipsby, and Anderson. Silas had told me his job there ended but he hadn't said why. The question was, what was he going to do next? Was he moving back to Seddledowne? I scolded myself at how happy that possibility made me.

I tapped on his photos and scrolled until I came to my favorite. Yes, I had a favorite. Shirtless, and muddy from head to toe, Holden stood at the finish of an obstacle course race with a medal around his neck, along with three of his buddies. Were his cut chest, arms, and shoulders nice to look at? Yes. And what I wouldn't give to run my hands all over them. Again. But that wasn't my favorite part. It was the perfection of his dimple, the twinkle in his eyes, the tough, cocky grin that screamed, *I am unstoppable.*

I let out a twitterpated sigh.

Then rolled my eyes at myself.

The other reason it was my favorite was because it was one of the only photos of him without a woman in it. Holden was nothing but a heartbreak waiting to happen. He'd broken it a little when he'd left after the JV game on Monday. And my mangled, barely beating heart did not have it in her for another big one so soon. And I was pretty sure if I let myself fall for him, it would be harder than I'd ever fallen before.

And to prove Holden's chronic playboy behavior, there were over five hundred pictures of him with different women, at bars, baseball games, backpacking, boat rides, the beach. And that was only the B's. The craziest part was, the majority of the pictures were there because he'd been tagged by the women. He wasn't posting them like bragging rights. *They* were. Like he was some unattainable movie star they wanted at least the tiniest connection to. Was he that hard to pin down? The plethora of pictures said yes.

None of it added up, though. Because the guy I'd gotten

to know this summer wasn't an Alpha-hole at all. He was funny and kind, patient and thoughtful. He listened—like really listened—when I was talking. He was a way better listener than Silas had ever been. And he communicated back in a way that left no doubts. Silas would skirt around a topic until I wanted to throw my hands in the air.

But maybe that's why girls liked Holden so much. He paid them perfect attention. Ugh. It was all so confusing. The only thing I knew for sure was that I obviously couldn't trust my gut when it came to guys.

Holden could be my eye candy—my internet vice—to tide me over, but nothing more.

An email notification popped up on my screen.

Subject: Welcome to Small-Town Sweethearts! Let's find your perfect match!

What on earth? It had to be spam. But I opened my app and clicked on the email.

Dear Christy,

Welcome to Small-Town Sweethearts, where sparks fly and hearts connect. We're thrilled you've chosen to join our community...

I deleted it. I'd never joined an online community of any sort but definitely not a dating service.

Back to Holden and his beautiful—

The FaceTime app started ringing, hiding his picture. I groaned.

And pressed the green check button to answer.

"Hi Mom," I said as her video loaded.

"Hi, Christianna."

"Hey there, punkin.'"

"Hey, Christy."

"Whattup, Tink."

My fists curled at the last name. My brother-in-law really needed to stop calling me that. I hated the tangle of emotions I felt at the fact that they were together without me. I'd chosen to move. And I didn't regret it. But still, the FOMO was there.

"Hi." I waved as four faces came into view. Mom, Dad, my younger sister Gabby, and her husband, Rowan. The only ones missing were my youngest sister, Arianna, and her husband, Tyler. "How'd you guys know I was up?"

Gabby shoved her face in front of everyone, her thick, dark, perfect hair taking up most of the screen. "Your active status on Facebook." She pulled her husband, Rowan, into the frame, their heads pressed together. "Guess what?" She squealed, her eyes glowing with excitement.

"What?" I said with almost no emotion, hoping she would bring it down a notch. She didn't. Just gazed into Rowan's eyes for a moment, her shoulders lifted, beaming. The way he looked at her...like she owned every piece of him...even after three years of marriage. It was a punch to the stomach.

"Go ahead," Rowan said in a breathy hush. "Tell her."

My stomach tensed. "Tell me what?"

Gabby's hands curled into fists, pressed against her mouth, her eyes dancing. "We're having a baby!"

It felt like someone shot a confetti cannon.

Two inches from my face.

I sat there for a moment, blinking. "That's...that's so great. Congrats." It was hard enough that my twenty-two-year-old sister, Ari, was now pregnant. Rowan and Gabby had only been married for three years and a half years and this was their *third* pregnancy. Somebody needed to give them "the talk."

"Where's Jonah?" I asked. "Can I talk to him?" Jonah was their oldest. The cutest little two-and-a-half-year-old in existence. I needed to see him right then. Wished I could squish his chubby little cheeks in my hands and kiss him all over his adorable face.

It wasn't that I couldn't be happy for my sister and... Rowan...

Okay.

That was exactly it. I couldn't be happy for my sister and her husband. I'd tried ever since the day they got together. And I definitely couldn't be happy about the fact that they couldn't keep their hands off of each other. Or the fact that I was now three babies behind my sister, who was two years younger than me.

I loved their babies. I really did. And I would love this one too. I just needed time to wrap my head around the news.

Gabby smiled. "Oh, he fell asleep, but we can FaceTime tomorrow if you want."

"Tell her the other thing," Mom sang in the background.

There was more?

I let out an exhale and asked, "What thing?" just to make them happy.

Gabby clapped her hands together and yelled, "We're going to find you a husband!"

My head turned and I looked at them through only my left eye. "What now?"

"Yes. Me and Ari." My baby sister. "We've been brainstorming all week. It's time we take matters into our own hands, don't you think? No more waiting for Mr. Right to show up. We're going to hunt. Him. Down."

Another one of my half-crazed cackles tried to blurt out of my throat. I clamped it down.

"Like a pair of Army snipers," Rowan said and then had the gall to wink at me. "Look out, Tink. They've been scouring social media for every eligible guy within fifty miles of Seddledowne."

My jaw dropped. "Did you sign me up for a dating website?"

"Yes, girl!" She squealed. "Get ready for all the swipes right!"

"No. Absolutely not."

"Oh, honey, it's already done." She leaned over looking at something. "Oh, look at that. You already have one interested customer. A—" She squinted. Gabby had needed reading glasses since middle school but refused. Said they'd leave imprints on her nose and she couldn't have that. "What does that say, babe?"

"Knox Freeman." Rowan read for her.

"Knox Freeman." She grinned. "I think he's good-looking too. I can't tell right now."

"It says he's a firefighter," Rowan added.

Gabby's eyes grew quarter-sized. "Oh, a firefighter." She wiggled her brows. "He can put out all your fires."

"Gabby," I said sharply and then took a cleansing breath. "There are so many things wrong with this. The first being that you made an account without me—"

"Oh, Chris, don't worry. Ari and I did you right. Look." She held up Rowan's phone. For my profile picture, they used a photo from our Maui trip. In which I was wearing a tiny, red bikini.

I gasped, horrified. "What kind of guys do you think that'll attract?"

She shrugged. "The kind that like a pretty blonde with a hot body."

Rowan snickered off-camera.

"No. Take it down now. And not just the picture. The entire profile. I mean it, Gabbs."

"No way." She laughed nonchalantly. "No more messing around. It's time for you to settle down in Seddledowne." Gabby laughed at her pun.

Mom stuck her face in between them. "As long as he's willing to live in Laramie after the wedding,"

My eyes burned and my throat was thick. "Then give me the password and I'll take it down myself."

Gabby waved for Mom to go. "You'll thank us later, Chris. When you're on the front porch, wrapped up in your hubby's arms with a baby on your lap. I promise. And the dating profile isn't all. Ari already made you your own Facebook group too. It goes live tonight, complete with photos. We've got a link to sign up for interview slots and everything. Get ready to vet all the *hotties*." She sang.

My jaw dropped in horror. This had to be a joke. Someone was going to pop out from behind one of these pieces of equipment any second now, cameras rolling. "Over my dead—"

"Mom says she's willing to pay for a conference room too. Ari and I might fly out and run a speed dating night. But you'll be the only woman there. How fun would that be? Hundreds of guys show up, just to meet *you*."

I full-on let the cackle out now. Didn't even try to stop it. "Um. No. Absolutely not."

"Too late." Gabby grinned with a shrug. "It goes live at midnight. We'll update you every hour on the hour. But the dates begin a week from today." She rubbed her hands together. "I can't wait! We're going to throw everything at the wall. Something is bound to stick."

The humiliation at the fact that my sisters thought my life was so pathetic that they needed to do something of this caliber was making my eyes fill up and the end of my nose twitch. "Gabs, that's really sweet." My voice hitched. "But, I'm going to have to say no. I don't have time for that and I-I... I'm ready to be single for a while." A total lie. I'd never been lonelier than I was right now. But this was not the answer.

Gabby pursed her lips and sighed. "Christy, enough is

enough. Your ovaries are drying up as we speak. No more waiting around for God or Fate or whatever. It's time to take the bull by the horns, find you a man, and pop out some babies."

I couldn't speak, only blink. Blink and try to breathe. *Oh. My. Word.*

"Mom." I squeezed my eyes shut. "Mom!" I almost yelled.

Her face popped into view, smiling like wasn't this the best idea they'd ever come up with.

I threw my hand up in frustration. "What on earth? I'm the high school principal. I can't be part of a dating ring like some kind of pimp. Even if I am the only customer. You know what gossip's like in a small town." I hated the way my voice was shaking. "Make them stop."

She pursed her lips like I was complaining about having to eat wheat bread instead of white. "Honestly, Christianna. They're only trying to help. They love you. They're worried you're going to end up an old maid is all."

My mouth opened and closed a few times. And I was about to say I'd rather be alone for the rest of my life than humiliated by this nightmare. But the words choked in my throat as someone plopped down onto the weight bench in front of me. *Right* in front of me.

I gasped and my hand went to my heart, as I willed it to quit trying to buck its way out of my chest.

Holden.

His eyes were scorching and his jaw clenched like he was mad enough to throat-punch someone. I scowled, trying to figure him out. But then I remembered I was on the phone.

My mouth parted and I sucked in air. Had he heard my conversation with my family?

I turned my head, hoping to hide my tears and at least some of the humiliation I felt. But his arm shot out, winding possessively around my waist. Then he pulled me right up to him, so fast I had no choice but to hook my thighs over his. What the...?

His caramel-colored eyes burned into me for a split second before flashing to my lips angrily. I leaned away but his hands came up, gripping my face. His thumb wiped a tear from under my eye. Then his forehead furrowed and his gaze flicked between my eyes and my mouth three times, almost as if he was having some kind of internal struggle.

"I'm on the phone. What are you—" I started to say. But I never got to finish. His mouth crashed against mine with so much force that our teeth clinked.

I froze, dazed. All the noise on the other end of the Face-Time ceased.

Holden's hands slid into my hair, his lips moving hard against mine as if doing compressions to make mine work. He smelled like leather and spicy cologne and his mouth tasted like cinnamon gum. As if his kiss had some magical mind-melding power, my eyes fluttered shut, and I melted into him, completely ruined. Sparks of heat rolled in waves over my chest, down my arms and legs, all the way to my fingertips and toes. I'd forgotten what it was like to be kissed by him. This had to be what heaven was like. Then again, it was tinged with a splash of wickedness, so maybe not. A soft moan purred in my throat and I started to lower the phone. Because my family did not need to see how my hands were about to rove over his awesomely sculpted abs.

But Holden's hand shot out, lifting mine back up so the phone had a perfect face-level view.

Oh.

He wanted my family to see our kiss. He'd heard the conversation, and he was sticking it to them. Saving me. It was sweet. And utterly pathetic. I didn't care.

It was amazing. All heady and breathless and hot.

And if this kiss got my sisters to kill their ridiculous Find Christy A Husband campaign, even better.

In an instant, I slid into character. I was Christy Thornbury, principal of a small town high school who was capable of finding a bodice-ripper-worthy love interest all on her own thankyouverymuch. I slid my free hand up into the back of his hair and tugged him closer, smiling against his lips for a millisecond before diving back in. I inhaled a few times, trying to lock his heavenly smell into my long-term. It was the stuff candles should be made of.

"Christy," I heard my mom say somewhere along the edges of my consciousness. "*Christianna*." Yeah. Ok. We'd made our point. I could stop now. But I really didn't want to.

I hesitantly pulled back but didn't look at the phone. Instead, I gazed "lovingly" at Holden, whose warm eyes were still blazing into me, his lips a little puffy now. He looked down for a second, and I sensed some regret.

Nope. Nuh-uh. He'd started this. I was going to make sure he saw it through.

"Hey, *baby*," I said with a smile, probing his eyes. "How was your day?"

He looked up and smiled, his gaze still holding a touch of fury. "Better, now that I'm with you."

"Um, hello? *Baby*?" Gabby said, with a squeaky laugh like she'd just been delightfully scandalized. "Are you going to introduce us?"

I finally looked at my family. Mom's lips were pursed like she couldn't believe a child of hers would behave in such a way, but her eyes were curious and maybe a touch excited for me. Rowan seemed wholly unaffected. He may as well have been watching a diaper commercial. But Gabby was on the verge of erupting any second, her fists pressed against her mouth as if holding back a thousand squeals.

Holden maneuvered onto the bench behind me, his legs

straddling mine. Then he wrapped his arms around my waist and rested his chin on my shoulder so they could see his face. His underwear model, more-confident-than-any-man-had-the-right-to-be face.

"This is Holden," I said, my smile trying to burst out of my cheeks. I snuggled back against his rock-hard chest. "My sexy lawyer boyfriend."

Gabby looked like she'd swallowed an apple whole. Rowan nodded, slightly impressed. But Mom was shaking her head, full-on shocked.

Holden pushed the hair off my neck and pressed a kiss to the hinge of my jaw. Then said straight to the phone. "No need to find her a man. Christy's already taken."

SEVEN

HOLDEN

I shot up off the bench the second she pressed end. My chest was tight and I couldn't take a full breath. Oh, man. What had I done? Stupid question. I knew exactly what I'd done. I'd just broken the one rule I'd lived by for the last ten years.

Never, ever initiate the kiss. *Ever.*

No matter what.

I pressed on my temples. Maybe Christy was my kryptonite. For years, Silas had been telling me it could happen. Said she might be out there somewhere. Lemon was his.

Kryptonite or not, I didn't have the luxury of giving in. The difference between Silas and me was that he could be a soft place for Lemon to land. But I shouldn't be anyone's landing place. I was all jagged parts and sharp edges that cut to the bone. Loving me came with too many risks. My past was a constant reminder of that.

Why had I let myself listen to her FaceTiming her family? It was none of my dang business. And from the way she was glaring at me right then, I was fairly sure she hadn't wanted my help. I paced the floor, my arms wrapped around my head.

"Uh. What was *that?*" Christy asked.

I stared at her, chest heaving, not sure what to say. "Sorry… your family…they're something else."

"Yeah. I told you that. Did you not believe me?"

I had. But this was even worse than she'd described. What kind of sisters mastermind a humiliating scheme to marry their sibling off *without her permission*?

Her hands flew out. "Why else do you think I took a job across the country in the same town as my ex? Did you think I was trying to get him back? Like some kind of stalker-lunatic person?" Her voice shook. She was going to cry again.

"No. I never thought that." Without thinking, my hands started to lift, reaching out to pull her to me. I snatched them back to my side. Like I said, kryptonite. *Get it together. There's a reason you're a one-man band.*

Shields back up, starting now. Cocky Holden persona engaged. It was the only way to keep this grenade from detonating.

I ran a hand through my hair. "It got under my skin, is all. Sorry." I turned to walk to the leg extension machine, hoping she'd let it be.

"Excuse me? Nuh-no. We're not done here." She grabbed my arm, stopping me. And that tiny contact sent my stupid heart fluttering like I was back in high school. "My family is going to expect to see you around when they FaceTime. They'll want pictures and updates."

I stepped away, shaking her off. "Yeah. That's why I apologized. My mistake." I sat down and pulled the pin out of the sixty-pound slot. Had a toddler used this last?

"Your *mistake*?" She folded her arms across her chest, jaw right, buzzing with irritation. "No."

I chuckled and shoved the pin into the heaviest slot—two hundred and fifty pounds. "What do you mean, no?" Then I hooked my feet under the pads of the machine.

"No. You don't get to kiss me like that in front of my family and then say, "Sorry." She mimicked my deep voice on the last word, adding an arrogance that was probably deserved. Fine. It was fully deserved. But I couldn't go soft in front of her. If she knew how weak I really was I would be the doll and she would be the voodoo master.

I shrugged like a heartless tool. "I mean, I just did."

She called me a name that would've made my mom's toes curl. Then she sat on top of my feet with a glare that said she held me responsible for making her resort to such petulant behavior. "No," she said again. "Sorry isn't going to cut it. They think I have a hot lawyer boyfriend named Holden. That's going to be a problem for me. A big one."

"Sexy," I corrected. She probably weighed around a hundred pounds. Good. Two-fifty wasn't close to enough.

She folded her arms again, lips pursed. "Excuse me? Did you just call me *sexy*?" Her face was twisted in adorable fury.

"You told them I was your '*sexy* lawyer boyfriend.' Not hot." I gripped the machine handles and took a deep breath. Then I heaved, taking her for a waist-height ride. She shrieked, fell forward, and gripped the tops of my knees. *Dag-gone-it.* I did not need her touching my bare skin, causing electricity to thrum up my legs like that.

Her jaw dropped, incensed that I would actually use her to get my sweat on. But she didn't hop off. Simply readjusted her position, eyes trained on me like a scope. "You are unbelievable," she said.

In response, I heaved again, swinging her faster this time. She crossed her arms, lips pressed flat, as I swung her up six more times. I had to give it to her, she had a strong core.

When the set was over, she leaned forward, fingers digging into either side of my knees. "You're going to be my standby boyfriend, Holden. That's the only way I'm forgiving you."

I scoffed. That was a solid nope. Such a bad idea. Hugging

her, holding hands, kissing her like we just had? Nopity, nope, nopers. Not if I wanted her to stay safe. And I did. A deep-rooted need to protect her had burrowed into my chest. Not sure when it started. This summer? Maybe. The minute I spotted Amber Taylor at the game? Absolutely. The urge to tuck Christy against me and use my body as a shield if need be was in full force.

I cocked an eyebrow. "Forgiving me? For what? Saving you from having to star in your own real-life season of *The Bachelorette*? You should be kissing my feet, not sitting on them."

Her jaw clenched. "I had the situation under control."

"Hardly."

Anger permeated her expression. She hopped up and yanked the pin out of the machine, making it useless. Then she tossed it across the room, eyes blazing.

I coughed into my elbow, trying to hide a laugh. I could throw her over my shoulder and run laps if I wanted to. Did she think she was intimidating? I shrugged and walked over to the leg press. But no sooner had I sat down than she yanked the pin out of that one too. She hurled it in the opposite direction. The only other person in the gym, a woman covered in tats, glanced over like we'd lost our minds.

I bit the insides of my cheeks, fighting the guffaws trying to roll through my chest. And it took every ounce of willpower not to pull her in my arms and kiss her again. She was so stinking adorable when she was mad.

I sat down at the hack squat machine. Then the seated arm curl. Seated overhead press. Pins pulled. Back extension. Hamstring curl. Pec fly. Seated dip. Pins, pins, pins, everywhere.

The tatted lady grabbed her bag and headed for the exit, keeping a side-eye trained on incoming pin-missiles as she escaped. Crap. I hope we didn't just cost Silas and Lemon a customer.

Christy threw her hands up after chucking another one. "I can do this all night."

"Me too." I walked to the lying leg curl machine.

She jumped in front of me, gripping my biceps and glaring me down. Up actually. She barely reached my shoulder. "You're going to pose as my fake boyfriend, Holden. Whenever I need you to. I moved all this way so they wouldn't be on me about my love life. And now you've made them think that I actually have one. You have no idea what you've started but you are most definitely going to finish it. Do you hear me?"

I booped her on the nose. "You're so cute when you're mad. Like a little pissed off fairy."

Her eyes narrowed. But then they filled with tears. *No, no, no.* Tears were exactly what I was trying to avoid.

I'd have to Google the chemicals that make up fictional kryptonite because I swear her real-life tears contained all of them. My hands yearned to touch her, to pull her against me and smooth her hair. To tell her I would do anything and everything she ever asked me to.

But I couldn't.

I jammed them down by my side. "C'mon, Chris. Don't cry. I was just teasing you."

"Don't you dare call me that." Her chin quivered. "Only my friends get to call me Chris, and you're being a complete jackwagon." A tear rolled off her jaw and it killed me.

"Trust me." I sighed, almost no restraint left. "I'm the last person you want pretending to be your boyfriend."

That was the wrong thing to say, I guess, because her shoulders rolled back, her eyes turned to red-hot coals, and she jabbed her finger deep into my chest. "I don't care. You're going to be on speed dial or I'm. Telling. Silas."

I huffed but there was a little shake to my voice. "Telling Silas what?"

She poked her finger harder, probably leaving a bruise.

"That you kissed me just now. That you exploited someone in their moment of need just so you could get some lip action."

Was that really what she thought? My face felt like it was hanging from a spit over the world's biggest bonfire. I'd done it for *her*. Did she think I was taking advantage of her?

With the last bit of my reserve, I shrugged like I didn't care. "This conversation just went completely juvenile. You're threatening to *tattle* to my brother."

She stabbed me again, digging in. "More juvenile than objectifying a perfectly respectable woman?"

Had she just gut-punched me? No. But the words stole my air all the same. There was nothing she could've said that would've hurt more. She had no idea how hard I went out of my way not to objectify women.

Her eyes flashed. "I don't go around locking lips for fun, you know. If I kiss someone, I mean it. Unlike some people."

"Oh, really?" Now I was feeling the irritation. "So, you meant it when you kissed me at Sophie's place?"

She straightened and shrugged like our kiss was an annoying bug she was shaking off. "A moment of temporary insanity."

My mouth parted. Oh, wow. That was a fist to the chest. I'd thought it meant something. It had felt like it meant something. To me, at least.

"Stop trying to change the subject." Her eyes pierced straight into me with a sharp slice. "The way I see it"—another finger-poke to the pec—"you have to do what I say. Because if you don't, I'll tell Silas." She shrugged like *not my problem*. "And if I tell Silas, he's going to tell your *mother*. And we all know how Jenny feels about your kissing habits. 'Hot Lips Holden.'" She burst out laughing. So Silas had told her my mom's nickname for me.

Just awesome.

Christy thought I was a man whore.

Learning how she truly saw me caused me to temporarily lose my mind, I guess. Because before I could stop myself, I blurted, "I don't kiss them, Christy. Ever. They kiss *me*, okay?"

A laugh choked in her throat and she took a large step back, horrified.

Holy. Crap. What had I just done?

What was it about this girl that made me a bumbling, out-of-control idiot? I'd never admitted that to anyone. Not Silas, not Sophie. No one.

Just then the sliding glass door opened, and darn it if Silas didn't walk in. Wearing basketball shorts and cowboy boots, looking like he'd just rolled out of bed.

Christy's eyes lit up, victorious. "Ah, *karma*."

"You have got to be kidding me," I muttered.

She backward walked her way to him, eyes trained on me the whole way. "Good evening, Silas," she sang. Every muscle in my body tensed. I'd just gotten things right with Silas again.

"Hi," he said dryly. He scowled at me, shaking his head like I was the biggest a-hole on the planet. I knew what it looked like.

They walked over to me, together. Christy didn't even try to rein in the smug smirk she was wearing. "So, Silas, Holden and I were wondering if you could settle something for us."

His gaze skittered between us, unamused. "What?" His tone said he'd rather be anywhere than here at this time of night, catching us together.

Same, buddy. Same.

Her pointer finger made a sweeping motion around the room. "Are those security cameras on?"

She wouldn't.

His head cocked at me. Not Christy. *Me.* "What did you do?"

Christy waved her hand. "Oh, it's only a hypothetical discussion. We were just wondering." She swung a narrowed glare at me. "Right, Holden?"

I shoved my hands into the front pocket of my hoodie and shook my head. "Un-freaking-believable."

She cupped a hand around her ear. "What was that? I didn't hear you, El Smoocherino."

My nostrils flared as I let out a bitter laugh. *This woman.*

Silas's forehead crunched and his head volleyed between us.

I shrugged, mad enough to chew fire. I was only trying to protect her. I threw my hands up. "Fine. You win."

"Yes!" Her fists punched the air. Then she released a massive exhale and waved a hand over her face. "End scene and goodnight." She bowed dramatically. Then she skipped over to the bench where I'd started the whole mess and picked up her bag. As she skipped back by she hissed, "You might be Lord of the Lips, Holden. But I will always win. *Always.*" And she cackled like a witch as she kept on skipping toward the exit.

As the doors slid open, she paused and spun on her heel, aiming her words right at me. "Oh, and the varsity girls lost their game after you left. And JV and varsity both lost on Thursday. I'm sure Anna told you." She shot me with double-finger pistols. "I blame *you.* And as payback, you're going to help me coach until you find a new job. The girls are 'hyped' to have the guy whose 'grin is fire' as their coach." She made quotation marks with her fingers and rolled her eyes. Then she wiggled all ten fingers. "See you at the game tomorrow, Coach Dupree." Without waiting for my response, she spun and skipped out into the night.

And I just watched her go, speechless at how she'd just outplayed this player.

Silas studied me too closely. "She really does need help coaching. Byrd is out for the rest of the season. They thought he just had bad food poisoning. Turns out he had a duodenal ulcer. He came close to bleeding to death and won't be able to work for two months. Maybe longer."

I whistled. "That sucks. But why don't you help her?"

He looked at me like I'd fallen into a vat of bright green dye. "I just got married, I'm running a new business"—he waved at the room—"and a farm, and I've got a full-time job. What are you doing?"

Well, when he put it that way. "I'm busy searching for a new firm." It sounded incredibly selfish. Even to me.

He cocked his head, his eyes questioning. "So why not help out while you look? Mom said you're begging for stuff to do. You even cleaned out all the horse stalls without asking. If that's true, I don't even know who you are."

I blew out my breath, let two heartbeats pass, and spit out, "Amber Taylor was at Anna's game the other night."

He sunk in his boots a bit. "You gotta let it go. That was almost a decade ago. It's way over."

I shook my head. "Man, I'm not so sure. She was eyeing me like she hoped we met in a dark alley somewhere." I hated that she still had me under her thumb even after all this time.

"You didn't do anything wrong, Holden. You weren't guilty. Of anything. Stop torturing yourself."

I grunted and kicked at the floor with the toe of my tennis shoe.

"Look, man," he said. "The best way to show her that she doesn't have any power over you is to live your life fearlessly. Don't hold back because of what she did."

I nodded. "Yeah. You're right." But it wasn't that easy. I'd been trying for the last ten years.

I glanced at the exit, hoping to change the topic. "What the freak is wrong with Christy Did you see her dance out of here like a devious little pixie? Is she always like that—trying to niggle at you until you give her what she wants?" The memory of her backside skipping into the dark churned my insides in the best way. Everything about her made me want to eat her up, just put my lips all over her out-of-this-world, gorgeous face.

"Yeah. She'll push till she gets her way. But only with people she feels safe with." He chuckled. "But don't tell her she's like a pixie. Her ex used to call her Tink. It was cool until it wasn't."

I scowled. Well, that explained why she'd almost cried when I said she was like a cute little fairy.

"What did she want?" he asked.

"Huh?"

"You said she niggles at you until you give her what she wants. And it sounded like you just agreed to do something you didn't want to."

"Nothing." I shook my head. "Just a stupid conversation."

Silas's forehead furrowed like he didn't believe me. "Were you two on a gym date?"

I rubbed the back of my neck, which was suddenly boiling. "No. We just ended up here at the same time."

"So if I go watch the security footage I'm not going to see you making out?"

I forced a laugh. "No. We just happened to be here at the same time. You can ask that one chick who was here earlier. The one with the tat sleeves." I was protesting too much. If anyone knew what guilty looked like, it was an attorney. And it looked exactly like this. *Get it together, moron. Change the subject.* I eyed his outfit. "What're you doing here this time of night? You look ridiculous, Gomer."

He grinned and did a little jig in his boots. "You're just jealous you can't pull this off."

I snorted. "Shouldn't you be at home in bed with your wife?"

"I was." His brows flicked up and he grinned so wide it

was just mean. "Dumb thermostat app went off saying the heat in Downward is eighty-seven degrees. If I'd known you were here I'd have asked you to go check it and stayed right where I was."

"We've all been telling you to use the Find My Friends app."

He grunted and then studied me. "Are you two a thing?" he asked, wearing a frown. "Because it kind of feels like you are."

My hands shoved deeper into my hoodie pocket. "Nope. Definitely not a thing."

"I mean, you're both adults. You can do what you want. It would just make family dinners awkward, you know?" They were just words. He didn't mean them. If he watched the security footage, I would be dead.

I sighed. "Like I said, not a thing, bro."

"All right. If you say so." He turned on his heel. "Well. I'm gonna head. The faster I do this, the faster I get home." His eyebrows wiggled. Then he turned and strode his stupidly long legs toward the Downward side of the gym. When he reached the leg press, he called, "Why are the pins all over the place?" He bent down and began collecting them.

I snickered. "No idea."

I sat down at the hack squat machine and popped in a pin, the gym all to myself. I inserted my Air Pods and flipped my playlist up full blast trying to get that sexy, blond spitfire out of my head.

But my brain did the opposite, replaying that intense kiss over and over. Her soft lips, the way her hands slid up into my hair.

Stop it.

I exhaled and forced myself to think about the conversation and pin shenanigans afterward. That was safer. Sticking my toe in the water but at least I wasn't diving in head first. Toe dipping never drowned anyone.

"Tink." I snorted, wondering what Silas had meant about it being cool until it wasn't. It wasn't until I was three hundred calories down, according to my watch, that a sick realization slammed into my brain.

Christy's brother-in-law, Rowan, had called her Tink.

eight

CHRISTY

For at least the fifth time that night, I looked across the high school gym and snickered.

Anna, still glowing from the five kills—*five*—she'd scored during the JV game, was now sitting in the student section. Right next to Blue Bishop, our uber-talented JV quarterback. And Silas, on the top row, fifty feet away, couldn't stop glaring at the guy. Lemon kept biting back a smile. I couldn't tell if she was happy for Anna, laughing at Silas, or a combination of the two.

And I was proud of myself.

I didn't hate Lemon for stealing my "trailer." My heart was still a little sad about the loss of what could've been. Silas had been my future, at least for a little while. But I could sit across from them in this gym and it wasn't all-consuming. Even when they were constantly touching—hand-holding, arm around the shoulder, a squeeze of the knee. Most of the time, I forgot they were here.

In truth, it was hard to think about Silas and Lemon while Holden and his cocky, swole self sat right next to me, diverting

83

my attention every few seconds. That and the fact that my varsity girls were killing it.

Holden chuckled too close to my ear, throwing my heart into a canter. "Sophie was right to pick Silas to be Anna's 'dad.' I'm not ready to deal with a teenage daughter, dating."

"Poor Blue. I don't think he even knows that Silas is on the verge of ripping his head off."

"Pretty sure all he sees is Anna." It was true. If I'd ever seen a couple with stars in their eyes, it was those two.

I leaned over and whispered, "What's Silas gonna do when Blue touches her? Like actually holds her hand and stuff?"

"We'll have to hide the guns," he hissed back and I could almost swear he was a little breathless being that close to me. But I must've imagined it. The girls on his social media posts were the breath-hitching kind. Not me.

The ref blew the whistle, declaring the game back in play.

Holden's knee bounced next to me, his hands resting stiffly on his thighs. I didn't know what was up with him tonight, but he was on edge. His back hadn't touched the seat the entire evening. And his eyes were everywhere. On the game, the people in the stands, and me, all at the same time.

Ming tossed up the serve. My hand shot over, gripping the top of Holden's. I'd done this same thing every time one of our girls had served tonight. I kept telling myself to stop but I couldn't. Every time I touched him, he flinched, like he was repulsed. Too bad. I needed something to squeeze in those tense moments.

Ming's ball came down and she smacked it hard. It sailed over the net but it was too far right. And if Highland's player had restrained herself it would've been declared out, tying the set back up. But she went for it, starting a thirty-second volley that tried to give me a heart attack. When Jade, our middle, slammed a kill down onto the other side as if she'd had enough, I exhaled. *Me too, Jade.*

That was the match.

The stands cheered and our girls jumped around, hugging one another. Holden and I smiled at each other, relieved that was over. Coaching is not for the faint of heart.

"Hey, what do you need me to do? I need to hurry. I've got some stuff to get done at the ranch tonight." Holden's hands were stuffed in his hoodie pocket and he was hunched, almost like he was trying to make himself invisible. But to who?

"Balls need to be put in the closet and we've got to get the net down, but the girls can do that."

"Ok. Cool." His shoulders dropped a little, relaxed. "I'll grab the ball cart on my way out. See you tomorrow at practice."

"No, I need you to hang out for a few minutes." I leaned closer and hissed, "Boyfriend duties start now. My sisters are demanding we FaceTime."

He squeezed his eyes shut and groaned. "Fine. I'll meet you out by my car." This man wanted out of this gym for some reason.

"My truck. Your car's back seat isn't big enough."

He cocked both eyebrows. "Backseat stuff, huh?"

I smacked him in the middle of his chest. "Dream on, Lady Killer."

He blew out his breath. "Aren't they going to freak when they find out my last name?"

I snorted. "Trust me. They won't care."

But he didn't respond. He hunched his shoulders and turned for the doors with the speed and shiftiness of someone walking from a courtroom to get into a white van where they'd be immediately hidden in the witness protection program. What was with him tonight?

Once every girl was claimed and the crowd was finally gone, I walked to the door, flicked off the lights, and stepped outside into the cool night air.

"Principal Thornbury?"

My head snapped around to the left. "Oh, hey, Alyssa." It was our very talented varsity setter. And her mother, maybe. But the woman to her right looked about my age. Way too young to have a seventeen-year-old daughter.

"Hey, my aunt, Amber, wanted to meet you." She pointed to the pretty brunette.

I reached my hand out. "It's so nice to meet you. Christy Thornbury."

She shook it double-handed and laughed. "It's my pleasure. Amber Taylor." Her laugh was high-pitched and tinkling, like soothing wind chimes. "Hey, so, we were talking and we just think it's a travesty that the football teams have a five-course meal catered by parents before every game and our Lady Stallions have to eat peanut butter and jelly sandwiches that have been smashed in their backpacks all day."

I nodded, chagrined. "Yeah. We're working on getting a bus driver so we can at least take them to McDonald's before games. It's just been kind of crazy with Byrd out for the season. I didn't realize when I was hired as principal that I'd end up coaching volleyball."

She waved away the idea with a kind smile. "Oh, don't you worry about a thing. Jilly and I will handle it."

"Shanaya's mom," Alyssa offered. "They're besties."

I nodded. "Handle it?" My phone buzzed in the pocket of my Stallions jacket. Probably Holden telling me to hurry it up.

Amber beamed, her cheekbones balling into perfect apples. I wondered how she got them to pop like that. Illuminator? Contour? Whatever it was, she knew how to place it just right. "We're going to make a meal schedule and the parents can take turns signing up. We can probably get some local businesses to sponsor the team as well. Maybe Lucy's would cater a dinner or two."

I shook my head, happily surprised. "That would be amazing. So, I can hand those reins over to you?"

"Absolutely. Jilly and I gotchu." Her smile was bright.

Not gonna lie, it had been lonely moving to a place where the only person I knew was my ex. But people like Amber, and some of the teachers and staff, made me think I might gain some friends while I was here.

Relief bloomed in the center of my chest. I stepped up and pulled her into a hug. "That's the best news I've had all day. Thank you so much."

She patted me lightly with a tiny, "Aww, aren't you lovely?"

I stepped back. Alyssa was beaming, so proud of her aunt.

My phone buzzed again. "Well, I need to get going. The next home game is—"

"Tuesday." Amber nodded. "Like I said. Don't you worry about a thing. It's handled."

I squeezed Alyssa's elbow before she could walk away. "You played an amazing game tonight."

"Thanks, Coach."

I turned and walked to my truck, parked in the front row. But I didn't see Holden in the back seat. As a matter of fact, I didn't even see his car in the lot. Had he ditched? I pulled out my phone and read the two texts.

> Holden: I'm parked on the other side of the school, by the vocational building. Meet me there.

> Holden: You coming?

> Me: On my way.

His white electric vehicle was parked in a dark corner. The second I pulled in next to him, he hopped out and got into my truck. I climbed out of the front and slid into the back next to him.

"Alrighty, lover boy." I slid my phone out. "You ready to be grilled?"

He exhaled like he was mentally preparing to climb K2. "Exactly how cozy are we at this point in our 'relationship?' Arms around each other or just heads together?" But it was clear from the shake in his voice and the tremor in his hands, which he was trying to hide, that he needed a minute.

"Well, after that smokin' hot kiss, I'd say they're going to expect us to be all over each other." I scooted back a couple of inches and turned to face him, resting my knee on his thigh. "Are you okay?"

He blinked but said nothing. Geez. He needed to loosen up. I'd get him laughing. Maybe that would help.

"Am I making you *nervous?*" I sang and forced my right eye to twitch like a weirdo. "Don't want to be in a back seat with Craaaazy Christy?"

He chuckled, but it was quiet. "No. Seddledowne is just..." He blew his breath out in an O. "Something else."

What did that mean? Holden wasn't an introvert. From his normally bubbly personality and his plethora of social media friends—he had more than three thousand on Facebook alone—it was clear he recharged by being around people. But tonight he looked drained.

"Would you like to share with the class? Back seat a.k.a judgment-free zone. Promise." I criss-crossed my heart.

He blinked again and then shook his head.

I pulled out my phone and shot a text to Gabby.

> Me: Give us fifteen minutes.

He read over my shoulder. "No, I can do it now."

I chewed my bottom lip. "No way are you ready for the *60*

Minutes interview that's about to go down. Your hands are shaking worse than my mom's rat terrier, Joanie, when she has to go out and pee in a snowstorm."

He grunted at my lame attempt to make him laugh.

"All right. I'm pulling out the big guns." I scrolled through my apps and searched until I found his favorite episode of *The Office*. "You can't be this stiff when we call. It needs to be believable. We'll relax a little and take some time to get into character." I lifted his ripped arm and wrapped it around my shoulder, tucking myself against his side. And, oh my word, he smelled so good. Hopefully, he wouldn't feel how hard my heart was pounding.

He sat there, his arm stiff as a board, staring at the tiny screen on my phone.

"I still say Dinner Party is the best episode," I whispered, trying anything to take his mind off of whatever was paralyzing him.

"No way." He pointed to the screen. "This one's got so many good parts. Save Bandit, Kevin loots the vending machine, Stanley's heart attack, and stupid Michael not knowing how to do CPR so he shoves a wallet in Stanley's mouth." He threw his free hand out like *C'mon*.

I opened my mouth to respond but he had the gall to shush me.

"Here it comes." His eyes were twinkling with anticipation as Dwight heated the door handle with a welding torch.

Four minutes later, by the time Angela tossed Bandit into the ceiling and the cat fell through the other side, Holden was belly laughing and his hands had stopped shaking. His free hand slid over, picked up mine, and twined our fingers together. I leaned my head against his chest and let the beating of his heart thrum through me like a sound bath. If I'd been in the back seat with any other guy, I would've been finagling a plan to claw my way out of there. With Holden? I'd never felt safer. Once Dwight had cut the face off the CPR dummy and slapped it on his own like Hannibal Lector, Holden was slouched down in the seat, legs stretched, relaxed.

When Rowan and I had started dating, it was the first time I'd realized how good it felt to be touched. A handhold, a tight hug, a soft kiss. With Silas, it was the same. But with Holden, it wasn't just good. Good was a completely inadequate description. Heady, throbbing, deliriously addicting. His skin on mine sparked every nerve ending in my body. His breath, which was grazing the side of my neck, was warm and sweet like a tropical breeze. I closed my eyes, taking it all in. But I needed more. So I scooted in deeper, leaning into the middle of his chest, hoping he'd take the bait.

Holden didn't hesitate for a millisecond. Almost like he'd been waiting for permission, his arm tightened around my waist, and he pulled me into his lap, one hundred percent manhandling me. Our twined hands crossed my stomach and curled around the edge of my waist. Then he lowered his chin to my shoulder. And I swear he let out a small sigh. Yeah, I didn't regret any of this. Not one little bit. He could manhandle me all he wanted here in this dark parking lot where no one was watching.

There was no harm in that.

None at all.

nine

I t was a dangerous game we were playing. Maybe it was Christy's nonchalance about the whole fake-dating charade or the incredible pheromones that were messing with my head, but for the first time since high school, I was letting a woman rule my choices. Twenty times a day I checked my phone, hoping, praying, telepathically willing Christy to text or call. Most days she came through, filling my life with excitement and anticipation. The days she didn't were hollow and dull. In the two weeks we'd been a 'couple,' we'd gotten together nine times at her apartment to take pictures or Face-Time her family. The past two evenings, we'd fallen asleep on her couch, arms and legs tangled up, *The Office* playing in the background. My word, I'd never known cuddling could be such a turn-on.

Flying down the highway, my fingers drummed the steering wheel as I replayed last night's cuddle session while I waited for a text from my law school buddy. It was the third trip I'd made back to DC for a job interview and I was already tired of the back and forth. If it weren't for Christy I would've just stayed at my townhouse. But back to Seddledowne I headed.

Tessie announced, "Albert 'Tripp' Murphy says, 'Sorry, man, I think they've decided to pass.'"

I scratched my jaw, irritation bubbling. Another rejection. I was just arrogant enough to admit that I'd forgotten the sting that it left, it had been so long since I'd experienced it.

I pressed the button to respond. "Any idea why?" Though I was pretty sure I already knew.

Another text came through but this one was from Anna.

"Anaphylaxis says, 'Where are you?'" I picked up my phone to see a picture of her and Silas stuffing massively juicy burgers into their wide-open mouths. Oh man, that looked good.

"Almost there," I murmured to myself.

"Albert 'Tripp' Murphy says, 'They didn't say. I know they were impressed when you walked out of here. But they just got off the phone with your old firm a few minutes ago so I'm guessing that was the deciding factor.'"

I gripped the wheel. *Sipsby.*

How was I supposed to find another job if Wellington slandered me to every potential employer that called? I'd even apprised Tripp's boss in the interview. Given him my side of the story, hoping he'd give me the benefit of the doubt. If this kept up, I'd be blacklisted and have to go back to school and choose a different career path.

"Albert 'Tripp' Murphy says, 'I'm sorry, man. Try Benson. Maybe their office is looking for someone.'"

But I'd already tried Benson Honnely. My best friend from UVA Law was the first person I'd contacted.

I pulled into the Seddledowne High teacher lot, parked, and hurried across the lawn. I'd missed last week's home game for another interview but both teams had scraped out a win. Then I'd ridden with the girls, and Christy, on the bus to their away game. Again, both took the win. But this was the first team dinner I'd made it to. And it was ridiculous.

Christy had told me a couple of the moms were heading things up. I'd expected pans of box lasagnas and prebagged salad. But when I walked up, every team member and the majority of their families were in the mostly empty student lot, tailgating. But instead of beers, there were eight kinds of sodas. Two massive grills were smoking as a couple of men flipped burgers and hot dogs. And there was an entire buffet of chips, condiments, salads, and, most importantly, baked beans. And a whole 'nother table full of cookies, brownies, and lemon bars.

Christy bounded up to me with a soft smile—making my chest tighten—and did a Vanna White flourish at the food. "Can you believe this spread?"

"Uh, no. These girls aren't going to want to play. They'll wanna take a nap. They shouldn't be drinking sodas and eating cookies right before a game."

"C'mon, you're just hangry after your long drive." She grabbed my arm and pulled me toward the food. "Let's get some food in that ripped belly of yours. We wouldn't want our Herculean coach to be cranky when the game starts."

I rolled my eyes. "Fine." She was constantly commenting on my muscles, which was hilarious. But knowing that she was thinking about my body composition made it hard not to think about using said body to shove her against a wall and kiss her until she was gasping for air. I'd never actually do it though.

Over the top of Christy's head, I spotted Silas and Lemon at a table full of Anna and her friends. Silas tipped his chin up at me. Lemon, tucked possessively under his arm, offered me a finger wave and a grin. Silas gave me a tentative thumbs up with a cocked brow and a question on his face. He wanted to know how the interview went. I shook my head, lips pursed, and flipped my thumb down. His face fell and his lips twisted in empathy.

I glanced away, on high alert. No doubt, masked somewhere by this chaos, was Amber Taylor. She'd been at every game and I'd discovered she was Alyssa's aunt. Which made me unable to enjoy the fact that Christy was gripping my arm.

My gaze skittered, searching the crowd. Sure enough, Amber was by the baked beans, ready and waiting with her gigantic serving spoon even though everyone had come through the line a while ago. Almost like she was waiting for me and like she remembered, from when we were boyfriend and girlfriend back in seventh grade, that I loved baked beans. And even though I was now twenty-seven, I was incapable of serving myself. It really was a shame God had wasted such a pretty face on someone whose insides were so ugly.

Jilly Booker was next to her, serving up salads. From what it looked like—potato, macaroni, or fruit. Jilly grinned at Amber, her teeth almost luminescent against her dark skin. My heart panged. I really liked Jilly. Always had. We'd been pretty tight in high school. She was hilarious, brilliant, and a friend to everyone—most especially an underdog. But if she was still slummin' it with Amber, we'd never be friends again. And that was truly tragic, in my book.

I didn't feel that I should have to fight a battle to get a helping. But I was hungry, and I wasn't going to let the Black Plague keep me from it. I couldn't drag Christy through a deadly pandemic to get some stupid beans though.

My amble came to a crawl, immobilized with what to do.

Christy leaned back, trying to drag me. "C'mon, Makeout Maestro. We need to get your strength up."

My eyes shot to Silas but he was laughing at something Anna said. Lemon was the perceptive one—her eyes jutting between me and Amber. In less than a second, with our impressive telepathy skills and facial expressions, my sister-in-law and I came up with a plan. She pushed back and stood. I let my feet move again but I gently shook Christy loose. Her expression turned down, dejected and confused.

I offered her an apologetic smile. "I'll be right there, okay? Save me a seat?" She nodded, still hurt, but turned on her heel and went. My snuggling game would need to be strong this evening.

Lemon met me by the plates. "Hey, sorry about the job. Their loss."

I grunted and grabbed a plate and a set of plastic silverware which some mother had taken the time to roll up inside a napkin and tie with a blue and silver ribbon. Go Stallions.

Lemon picked up a plate as well. "You and Christy are getting cozy," she said quietly as I squirted ketchup on a hamburger bun.

My eyes flashed over to see her reaction to that. Her lips were twitching like she wanted to smile. Would she be okay with it if I dated Christy? Because, if she was fine with it, she could convince Silas. Lemon could probably talk Silas into being okay with almost anything.

But then I chided myself. Silas wasn't the reason I couldn't date Christy. There were much bigger things at play here. The crux of which was guarding the baked beans like a Nazi SS officer.

I shrugged. "I mean, I see her pretty much every day, doing this." I waved my free hand toward the girls. "She's pretty cool."

"Pretty *cool*?" She repeated like that was the lamest thing she'd heard today. "I think you meant to leave off the last word in that statement."

She's *pretty*.

My cheeks flared and heat spread up to the tips of my ears. I held my plate out toward the grillmaster who I recognized as Ming's dad. With a smile, he laid a dripping patty with a slice of melty good old American cheese onto my bun.

I smiled back. "Thanks."

"My pleasure, coach."

It was still weird to hear people call me that. I was just a dude sitting on the side, winging it from the hip.

Lemon leaned in when I moved on. "I'm your sister now. And I owe it to Sophie to really stick it to you when it comes to women. So you may as well admit it. You've got a little thing for Christy, don't you?"

I chuckled and ran a finger between my neck and the collar of my polo. Had a hot breeze blown in?

"C'mon." She gave me an open-mouthed grin. "I promise I won't tell Silas. Tell the truth."

I winked at my sister-in-law. "You know me, Lem. I've always had a thing for pretty girls."

She pursed her lips and scowled. "Fine. Play the emotionally stunted ladies' man. But just know that I see right through that thinly veiled facade. And I know the truth."

"The truth?"

"Mhm. That deep down you're just a sweet but broken man, Holden Dupree. But I'll get it out of you eventually. Wanna know why?"

I grabbed a handful of potato chips and plopped them on my plate, sweat beading along my hairline. "Wow. How much caffeine have you had today?" Lemon loved her coffee.

"None, but nice try at changing the subject." She picked up a carrot stick from a metal platter. "Wanna know *why*?" she asked again, more forcefully this time.

I sighed. "Why?"

"Because you're a terrible actor." She gripped my shoulder, her expression completely devoid of any kidding. Then she gazed straight into me until all my carefully hidden scars were laid bare. "You forget I've known you your whole life. And I've seen how you are when you're in love. It hasn't been since Savannah, and I was starting to think it might never happen again." Her eyes darted over my face. "But there it is. Plain as day. Making an appearance after all these years."

I swallowed hard, eyes on my plate, trying to breathe it out.

She squeezed my free hand. "That's what I thought. But don't worry, I'll handle Silas. I have my ways." She wiggled her brows just like Silas had the other night. Then she bit off a piece of carrot. Her head tipped toward the end of the table. "How about we get this done and get you back to your girl?"

But I couldn't move. I just stood there, staring at my annoyingly perceptive sister-in-law, wondering if Sophie's spirit had possessed her for a few minutes to bring me this message.

"It's okay," she coaxed. "You just say 'All right, Lemon,' and we'll pretend we never had this conversation." She leaned in closer and whispered, "And if you won't be honest with me, I hope you'll at least be honest with yourself...and in time... with her."

I rubbed my neck still reeling that I'd been had. "I don't...I don't know if that's what I want."

She snorted. "I don't believe that for a second. The *want* is all over your face." My cheeks were smarting. I could feel them. She patted me on the right one. "You're a good guy, Holdie. Any woman would be lucky to have you. But you need to believe it yourself." She pressed a hand to my lower back and spurred me forward.

We stepped around the grill and I was uncomfortably aware that Amber had a clear shot of me and Lemon. At least Lemon was safe now that she was married to Silas. Amber wouldn't touch that. But the skin on my left cheek felt like it was melting from her evil stare. I hadn't and I wouldn't make eye contact. But her devious glare was pulling at me like invisible tentacles, trying to make me. I turned away and forked a tomato slice. Lemon took that opportunity to step around me, putting a wall between us.

"You want baked beans, right?" she whispered.

I nodded.

"What about salads?"

"Potato."

"I gotchu." Then she slapped me on the back and gave me a little shove in the opposite direction. Back toward Christy.

"Hey, Lemon," Jilly said. "Congrats on your marriage, girl. I always thought you two would make a cute couple." Her voice trailed off as I escaped.

But when I got to the table, I already knew Lemon was wrong. It wasn't safe for me to love someone again. Because there was gorgeous, petite Christy, barking out orders to the JV team with a confidence that reminded me of another woman I used to know.

A girl, really.

Beautiful, kind, and confident too.

I'd loved that girl with all my heart. And she'd loved me back with wild abandon. But when I'd tried to shake her loose, for her own good, she'd hung on even tighter. And stupid, naive, teenage Holden had thought she was right. The tighter we held to each other, the safer we would be.

But clinging had done just the opposite. And instead of saving us, the darkness had wound and tightened and choked until our light was snuffed out.

I looked back over my shoulder and just as I suspected, Amber was watching me from the food table, eyes narrowed.

No. I couldn't do that to Christy.

I wouldn't.

ten

I t was my fault and mine alone. I knew that. I was the one who'd conned The Kissing Bandit into being my fake boyfriend. And I was the one who'd pushed for more intense snuggling. I wasn't even waiting for my family to ask anymore. I was just making stuff up, cuddling for hours, hands all over each other all willy-nilly like there were no consequences whatsoever.

And now the consequences were here.

I sat at the table, watching Holden go through the food line, chatting it up with Lemon after he'd shaken me off like a spiderweb he'd stumbled into. What did I expect?

It was just like the old scorpion and fox story. The fox knows what the scorpion is but gets talked into letting him ride on his back across the lake anyway. And when the scorpion stings him, the fox has the audacity to be shocked. But the scorpion says, "You knew what I was when you let me on your back."

Yeah. That.

I'd begged Holden to take the ride. So why was I sitting there blinking back tears?

99

Because I'd let myself get attached, that's why. I should've known better. Holden might have the kind of personality where he could get cozy with a woman night after night and it meant nothing, but I, Christianna Juliet Thornbury, was not built that way.

No, I got tangled up hard. It had only happened twice before. But it was always a painful mess to cut myself out of. And this one felt worse than the other two combined. That's what happens when the chemistry is red-hot, I guess.

Then again, was there a woman on earth Holden didn't have chemistry with? He probably had chemistry with a rock. I swear I'd heard a ninety-year-old grandma sigh at our last away game when he walked by.

An embarrassing sob choked in my throat and I cut it off. I was not crying about this man right here in the middle of our team dinner. What was wrong with me? I didn't cry about men unless I was in love with them. And yet here I was, fighting back the tears.

Wait a minute...

No.

No, no, *no*.

Was I in love with Holden Dupree?

The realization was a blow to the chest, causing another silent sob to erupt in my trachea.

But even more painful was the fact that he did not love me back.

I glanced at the tall, dark-haired cowboy at the next table over, hardly remembering any of the feelings I'd had for him. Silas who? If they hadn't shared the same last name, I might've forgotten Silas's altogether. All I could focus on was the jagged, breath-sucking ache in the middle of my chest for the blond hottie who consumed my evenings, and once he was gone, consumed my every thought. Pfft. Lying on my couch alone thinking about someone who wasn't thinking about me.

I was pathetic.

It ended here.

Holden sauntered up, holding his plate, looking a little sick. Probably because he'd realized how embarrassingly attached to him I'd become.

I stood. "JV, time to clean up. Throw your stuff away and go get dressed. Warm-ups start in twenty minutes." I picked up my plate, about to walk away, when he had the nerve to put a strong hand on my forearm, sending tingles across my skin.

"Where are you going? I thought you were going to hang with me while I ate. Discuss game strategy?"

I chewed my lip, eyes on the table. "No. I've got some stuff to do before the other team shows up."

He stepped in closer. "Christy," he said in that low, husky tone that made my heart purr. "I wasn't trying to be mean. I'm just worried that the girls might suspect something is going on between us."

I dared to meet his gaze. It was soft and apologetic, his light brown eyes warm and pleading. And I felt like a fool. Because he was exactly right. Of course, he was. I couldn't be hanging on him, and teasing and calling him names in front of the girls. What was wrong with me?

"Sit with me?" Still in that ultra sexy voice that made me feel like I was the most important person in the world right then.

I nodded. "Yeah. Okay." Gah. I was such a sucker. Fine. Maybe he wasn't the jerkface I'd just made him out to be in my head. But facts were facts. He was a satisfied bachelor with no plans of ever changing. If I didn't want this to go any deeper I had to put a death grip on my stupid, out-of-control heart.

"There you go." Lemon slid a plate of baked beans and potato salad across the table to Holden. Huh? He had room on his own plate. Why hadn't he gotten them himself? But that wasn't the real noggin-scratcher. The real conundrum was Lemon lowering herself to a seat across from us.

She glanced at Silas until she got his attention—which took less than two seconds because he was pretty much honed into her at all times—and curled a finger, beckoning him over. He scowled but hopped to attention, almost tripping over his feet to get to her.

I glanced at Holden, whose mouth was parted, gaze narrowed at Lemon. Okay. So he thought this was as awkward as I did.

Lemon looked right at me, bright-eyed, like we'd never been in love with the same man at all. "Hey, so Holden says your favorite show is *The Office*. I've been trying to get Silas to watch it but he won't. Maybe you can help me convince him."

I wanted to tell her I'd tried to convince him, many times, but I was under no disillusions. This was not a powwow we were having. We were not besties. We would not be comparing notes. And nobody at this table wanted the discomfort of associating the past with the present.

Silas looked at her, puzzled, and almost put an arm around her shoulder before thinking better of it. Then he sat up, put on his Perfect Husband hat, and said, "It's so awkward. I don't know how y'all can stand it. Michael Scott is so...cringy."

Holden chuckled and leaned his hand across the table to Silas. "Hand it over, dingus."

Silas picked up my used knife and stabbed at Holden's hand. "Get back, noob."

But Holden was too fast. He snorted. "Sorry, fartknocker. You can't use the word cringy and keep your man card. It's mine now."

"Shut it, ignoramus," Silas said. "I'm living with two females. They're rubbing off. You get what you get."

I didn't even realize I was laughing until Lemon smiled at

me like she couldn't be prouder that two grown men were neck-deep in a name-calling contest.

Just then Ming ran over, squealing, Alyssa and Jasmine right behind her. Still standing, she leaned her elbows on the table next to Holden, a phone in her hands. "Is this really you? Alyssa swears this is you."

My stomach twisted in a knot before I could even see what they were looking at. I already knew. It was one of his stupid social media accounts displaying him with his harem of women.

His face was sheet white. "Uh, how'd you get on there? My account is private." At least he had the decency to feel bad about it, I guess.

She waved him off as the others giggled behind their fists. "We're logged in using Anna's account."

"Excuse me, what?" Silas said in a rough, gravelly voice. "Ming, don't do that." His tone was scary. "Log out of that right now."

"Mr. Dupree is Anna's dad, remember?" Jasmine hissed and grabbed her phone from Ming's hands.

"Uncle," Silas growled, to let them know he'd heard.

Lemon bobbed her head. "Dad-Uncle. Duncle." She was trying to diffuse a very tense situation. "But yeah."

Alyssa let a swear word slip.

"No ma'am," I barked. "Would you like to sit out the first set?"

"Sorry." She slapped a hand over her mouth and her eyes went repentant toward Holden. "Sorry, Coach Dupree."

Holden's cheeks were bubblegum pink and I thought he might vomit. It seemed a bit extreme, even for the current situation. And if he didn't want people seeing all those pictures, why even have social media? Or, you know, take them down.

"But like, that *is* your account, right?" Ming pushed.

I threw my hands up. "You three are in charge of chairs. Put them away. *Now.*"

"Geez. Okay, okay," Ming whispered as they slowly walked away.

"But did you see how many women?" Alyssa giggled. "Hold 'em, Holden."

"No. Mr. Mono." Jasmine snapped her fingers. "Or Captain Kiss."

My jaw tensed. "*Girls.*"

"We're going," Jasmine waved.

My fists balled. "Not fast enough."

"I mean, he's hot. I'd make out with him. Any night of the week." I'm not sure which one of them said that, but it was the final straw. I was an idiot to like someone like him. If it hadn't been clear before today it was glaringly obvious now.

Their whispering faded as they hurried faster. The four of us sat there, painfully silent for two heartbeats.

"Welp." I stood. "I'm going to head inside."

"Christy," Holden said in that stupid voice, but I couldn't. I couldn't even look at him. "Hey."

"This has been..." I shook my head, avoiding eye contact with all of them. "Just...yeah." I turned on my heel and hoofed it out of there.

Good grief, girl. I guess if you're going to get yourself a fake boyfriend, make sure he's not someone you could fall in love with. But if you can't even be that smart, at least make sure he's not Sir Snogsalot.

Eyes burning, I jogged across the parking lot. I threw the door open and stepped inside. JV already had the net up. A handful of girls were still braiding each other's hair. But two-thirds of the team were practicing their serves. I turned when I realized the door never shut behind me. But Lemon was standing there, bright red hair backlit by the sun, chest lifting and falling, looking like a supermodel all flushed and serious. She must've run to catch me.

"Christy." She stared at me, trying to catch her breath.

Why did everyone keep saying my name as if it had some magical power to fix all things? Clearly, Christy Thornbury was completely unmagical.

Lemon grabbed my elbow and pulled me off the court. Then she sat and patted a spot next to her on the bleachers. Okay, maybe she did want to be besties?

She sighed. "Look, I know we're not friends. And unlikely allies at best. But there's something you need to know about Holden."

I blinked, dreading whatever was coming. It couldn't be good. Maybe she'd tell me he was gay. Or a eunuch. Or the world's first believable AI robot. But there was no way the woman who was now married to my ex would be here on a peace mission. It didn't make any sense.

She turned to face me. "It's not my place to tell you Holden's story. And I think he'd be upset if I did. But you need to know that he's been through some hard stuff. Like really hard."

She paused, gauging my reaction. I sat up a little straighter. My eyes had finally stopped stinging. I nodded so she'd at least know I was listening.

"Something...tragic...happened in high school and it broke him. For a long time, we weren't sure if he was going to be okay. But eventually, he pulled through." There was a look of awe in her eyes. "He's one of the most resilient people I know. He's like Sophie in that way." She chewed her lip for a second. "I guess what I'm saying is...Holden might date a lot of women, but he's not incapable of loving someone. On the contrary, he loves deeply. And I don't think he likes all the dating, actually. It's like that one saying—there's a God-sized hole in every man's soul?"

I shook my head. I'd never heard that or anything like it. And why had she suddenly brought God into it?

"Well, there's a soulmate-sized hole in Holden's soul and he's trying to fill it. He's just going about it the wrong way. I'm not sure he even knows that's what he's doing. But it is."

"Why are you telling me this?" I shook my head, mind reeling. Because this did, in fact, feel like a peace mission after all.

"Just...be patient. It might take him a little time. But he'll be worth the wait. I promise." Then she patted my hand, stood, and walked back out through the doors.

Wow.

Lemon, someone I'd viewed as my archnemesis, had just pep-talked me into not giving up on her brother-in-law. Romantically. I couldn't even wrap my head around it.

My hands pressed against my cheeks. Staggered, I dared to hope that she knew her brother-in-law as well as she thought she did. Because, apparently, my busted, sputtering heart was resting right in the middle of his strong, capable hands.

And the only way I was making it out alive was if I took it back.

As much as I hated to do it, the way was clear.

It was time to break up with my fake boyfriend.

Eleven

HOLDEN

The next Tuesday, I rested my forehead against Tessie's steering wheel, willing myself to get inside for the game. I'd skipped the team dinner, making up an excuse about our horse Maisy having a hoof abscess that I needed to tend to. It wasn't a complete lie but Christy didn't know that. Maisy did have an abscess, but the vet had taken care of it. I'd just helped hold Maisy still.

Truth was, I couldn't handle the look in Christy's eyes ever since the team dinner with the Facebook fiasco. I couldn't even decipher it. Was she embarrassed to be associated with me? Ashamed that she'd asked me to be her assistant coach? I wasn't sure. But it cut like a hot knife.

When I'd asked her after that game if we needed to meet up, she told me she was "good" and she had enough pictures to placate her family for a while. The disappointment I'd felt was downright embarrassing. My arms didn't know what to do without her between them. And the longer she stayed away, the heavier this ache in my chest grew. If this went on much longer, I was going to drive to her place and beg for her to be *my* fake girlfriend, for absolutely no reason at all.

A knock on the glass brought my head up. Silas.

I unrolled my window.

He bent down to talk to me, his left brow in an upside down V. "You missed the team dinner."

"Yeah."

"Christy said you were draining an abscess on Maisy?"

"Yeah."

His head cocked. "But I know for a fact that Dad called the vet out to do that."

"Did you tell her that?"

"No, nimrod. But lying goes against the Dupree creed. You're a lawyer who never, ever lies." He threw his hands up. It was true. As a rule, I didn't lie. Hated it when I caught someone doing it. And I'd lied to the woman who meant more to me than anyone.

I stared at my thumbs.

"The game's about to start," he said. "Don't you think you should go inside and help Christy get the lineup situated?"

"Mhm. Yup." But I just sat there, breathing, gut churning, dreading the disappointment in her eyes.

He sighed, walked around, and got into the passenger seat, closing the door behind him. Great. Here came the big brother lecture about being dependable and responsible.

He tried to face me, but couldn't because there wasn't enough room for the stilts he called legs. He reached down to adjust the seat and then frowned when he rammed his head into the ceiling. He swore.

I laughed. "Wrong way, moron."

He laughed too and finally got himself situated. Then he turned to face me. "Man, I really don't want to have this conversation..."

"Then don't."

"I have to. You're pathetic. You've been stumbling around

for a week, head in a fog, all grumpy and unmotivated. Mom says if she has to walk into Sophie's place and smell your B.O. one more time she's going to start charging you for a cleaning lady to come by." He flicked his hand toward the door. "Just go tell Christy you're in love with her, and get it over with. Put us all out of our misery."

What had he just said?

My mouth fell open. "What are you talking about?" My stupid, traitorous face was on fire. But if I admitted it, he might not ever let me live it down. It takes a fair bit of humbling to admit you have a crush on your brother's ex. I didn't know if I was ready for that.

Silas rolled his eyes. "We don't have time for this. You and I both know you have a thing for her, so stop pretending like you don't. You wouldn't have made out with her at Sophie's if you didn't."

It was the most backhanded compliment I'd ever been given.

My entire head felt like someone had doused it with lighter fluid and lit a match. "Let me get this straight. You want me to go tell your ex that I love her?"

He held his hands up, arrested style. "Don't call her that anymore. She's just Christy. Whatever. She's yours now. Here." His hand formed a sideways C. "It's the Christy Thornbury boyfriend torch. It's not really mine to give but I'm the last one who had it so here you go." He held his hand out, cupped around absolutely nothing.

I cocked a brow. "I'm not taking your dumb imaginary torch so put your hand down."

He shrugged. "Well, if you won't take that, maybe you'll accept this." He lifted an invisible...something...off of his head and put it on mine. "You are hereby crowned as the newest Dimwit Dupree who is so love drunk they can't walk a straight line. You can have it. I'm happy to be done." His hands went up again. "Disclaimer: by accepting this title you are also agreeing to good-naturedly accept all the teasing, well-wishes, and pressure that come along with couplehood."

"You're still love-drunk and a dimwit."

He nodded. "True. But I'm not the *newest* dimwit in the family. And I'm married so I'm ineligible.

I picked the crown up off my head and handed it back to him. "I think that belongs to Anna."

He scowled so deep it looked painful. "Do you know that Blue kid had the nerve to call me up and ask permission to take her on a date?"

"A teenage boy trying to be respectful?" My jaw dropped. "The horror."

"Pfft. Respectful, my eye. We all know that for a high school boy 'date' is just code for let me see how fast I can get this girl into the bed of my truck and *dis*respect her." His jaw clamped. "He ain't doing the hippity dippity with my girl. No way."

"Hippity dippity? Don't use mom's old-lady sex terms. Especially when you're talking about Anna." I shivered. "Dude. I don't want to think about her doing that yet."

"And you're not going to have to think about her doing it because she *won't* be doing it. Till she's thirty and been married for at least two years."

I chuckled. "So you told him no, then?"

His lips pursed and he slunk down in the seat. "No. Clem wouldn't let me. He's coming over for dinner on Sunday. But I did tell him she was too young to go on dates. The only dating they'll be doing is in my living room with me watching." He glanced at the gym doors. "Nice deflecting by the way. The crown is still yours. You have to be a legal adult to wear it, so Anna's out of the running. And yeah, you should tell Christy how you feel. I think you would feel a lot better."

I blew out my breath. "It's not that simple—"

"Sure it is." He gripped my shoulder. "Isn't that what you were telling me a few months ago? 'Just do it, man. Tell her how you feel. It'll be rad,'" he said in an eighties surfer voice. "Yeah," he said, returning to his natural baritone. "You feel like you're gonna puke just thinking about it, huh?"

I rolled my eyes. "No, tool. It's literally not that simple. Amber has been watching me like a hawk, and I don't want to pull Christy into her sights. You know what she did to Savannah."

His head was shaking before I was halfway done. "Holden, I'm not gonna sit here and tell you that Amber Taylor isn't a crazy psycho. She definitely is. But Christy's not seventeen and neither are you. You're a lawyer now, for crying out loud." His jaw pulsed. "But if you don't let Christy in because you're afraid of what Amber will do, then that lunatic still wins." His eyes narrowed as if he had x-ray vision and could see straight inside the gym to where Amber was right now. Then he swung those narrowed eyes at me. "Do you want her to own you until the day you die?"

My head dropped into my hands, but I shook it. I hated how much I let her make my choices for me. But I didn't know how to shake her off.

He cuffed my shoulder. "Look, you had my back this summer and I'll never be able to repay you for making me see what was right in front of my face." He tipped his head toward the gym. "Now it's your turn."

I rubbed the back of my neck. "I don't even know if Christy likes me like that. She doesn't take me seriously at all. She's always joking and calling me stuff like Hot Lips or Mister Kiss-ter." My jaw clenched. "And the other day she left her phone on the bus seat. Guess what she's got me listed as in her contacts? Not Holden or Holden Dupree. Not even Golden Holden, which is usually what people go with." I waved my fingers. "So original."

Silas's nostrils flared and he bit his lip, trying not to laugh. "What?"

"Epstein Barr."

That did it. He belly-laughed for at least twenty seconds and threw in a knee slap for good measure. Then held his hands up. "I mean, that's what you get."

I rolled my eyes. "You're laughing at my unrequited feelings. That's just great. Perfect."

He shook his head, wearing a sly grin. "Nah. I'm laughing because...Mister K-Kis-Kiss-ter." He was gasping for air.

"Ha. Ha." I gripped my hair, feeling like I wanted to claw out of my skin. "Just go back and tell Lemon you did what she wanted you to. It didn't work, but you gave it your best. I'm sure you'll get the Husband of the Year award. Good for you."

His face scrunched. "Man, what are you talking about?"

"I know she sent you out here to pep-talk me, dude."

He scoffed. "You think I'm such a dunce that I needed my wife to tell me my brother and best friend is hurting over a woman?"

I shrugged, feeling a little stupid because that's exactly what I'd thought. "Yeah. Obviously."

"I didn't need to be told anything. It's been obvious you two have a thing going on ever since I caught you kissing." He threw his hand out like duh. "But it was a blaring neon sign when Christy took off after Ming outed your Facebook profile at the team dinner. A woman doesn't react like that unless she's caught intense feelings for someone. Lemon said when she found her, she was trying not to cry." He fake backhanded me. "She loves you, idiot. Or at least, she's headed in that direction. But if you don't take those stupid pictures off your social media, unfriend all those women, and swear yourself to a lifetime of monogamy, you might lose the one woman you've been so desperately searching for."

The backhand was fake, but it felt very real. And very necessary. I was a complete tool.

Silas's lips drew into a hard line. "You deserve happiness, bro. Whatever voices in your head are telling you otherwise? It's time to stop listening. Enough is enough."

My phone buzzed.

Christy: *The first set just started. Are you still coming?*

"Crap." Silas and I said at the same moment. We'd lost track of time.

We jogged across the student lot and into the building. With each step, my confidence grew a little. Maybe Silas was right. Maybe ten years was enough penance to pay. Maybe God or Fate or whoever ran this show was done punishing me.

I pulled the door open and smiled at the blond beauty pacing in front of the bench seats.

twelve

CHRISTY

I sighed and opened my office door. It had been a double loss for our ladies and the air in the building felt heavy, even now that everyone was gone. Being principal and volleyball coach was too much. And my administrative duties had suffered because of it. Thankfully, I had a stellar assistant principal who was picking up the slack.

Silas and I seemed to have come to an unspoken under-standing. We had each other's backs. Pokes Pride and all that. But I was learning that running a high school in a small town meant wearing many different hats. Like tonight. Mrs. Yancy, the guidance counselor, had asked me to review the academic record of a tenth-grade transfer student. Said she was uncomfortable with some of the things her mom had said in their initial scheduling meeting. She just felt like something was off.

As I sat in my desk chair, my phone buzzed. My little sister, Ari. I groaned at the text.

> Ari: We wanna FaceTime with you and Holden right now.

My teeth ground.

> Me: Too busy. Sorry.

I set my phone on the desk. No need to put it back in my pocket. She'd respond any—

Ding.

> Ari: It's been like a week. Gabby and I are dying to hear the story about how Sophie wired his teeth shut the day after he got braces.

I punched back a message.

> Me: It's nine o'clock here and I'm still at school, working. It'll have to be another day. Talk to you later, g'night.

I was never this forceful with my sisters. It had been drilled into my brain to be a peacemaker and give them whatever they wanted. But everything with Holden, our volleyball losses tonight, and the long workday had sapped all my patience.

> Ari: Wait. I wanted to tell you the official name for Baby Girl.

I exhaled, feeling like a jerk.

> Me: Yeah. Okay, sorry. I would love to hear it.

> Ari: Great! Because I think you're gonna love it. You used to talk about this name all the time...

My stomach cinched and my fingers stiffened around the phone. Ari wouldn't...

> Ari: Madeleine Rose. Nickname: Maddie Ro

Someone gasped so loudly that I jumped. And then I realized it was me. I'd gasped.

Because that was *my* baby girl name. The only baby name I'd ever picked out. I'd doodled it across notebooks from fourth grade on. Claimed it any time baby names came up. And I only shared it with family and close friends to prevent a situation just like this.

And *used* to talk about it?

I'd never stopped. She knew full well that name was mine. Once again I was blinking back tears.

Moving to Seddledowne was supposed to have stopped the waterworks, especially when it came to my family, not make them worse. This jerk move Ari was pulling had nothing to do with a town, I reminded myself. No, my family made me cry anywhere and everywhere. They weren't partial to one particular setting.

Two sharp knocks pulled me around, and I spun in my office chair, a scream on the edge of my lips. But it was just Holden.

Just Holden.

Pshaw. Those two words next to each other were a complete oxymoron. He leaned against the doorjamb, all cool and unaffected like he'd invented the suave lean against the doorjamb move.

"Geez." My hand pressed against my chest. "What in the world? I thought you left." At least, I'd hoped. I hadn't raced out of the gym at warp speed for kicks.

"Nope. Right here." His arms folded across his chest and I wanted someone to punch me in the sternum to get my stupid heart to stop reacting to his every movement. It was ridiculous.

I gripped the armrests for emotional support. "I see that." He wanted me to ask him why. It was written all over his smug smile. But I wasn't going to. I just wanted to go home, take some ibuprofen to stop the pounding in my head, and go to sleep. I was done with having my heart flicked into a constant tailspin.

His head cocked and his eyes narrowed.

Dang it. He'd seen my tears.

I whipped around to face the monitor and discreetly wiped them away.

He walked over and sat down on the edge of my desk, right next to the keyboard, looming over me, demanding my attention.

I leaned back and exhaled. "What do you want, Holden?"

"I want you to tell me who I need to beat up to get those tears to stop."

I dropped my head in my hand and pushed the phone in his direction.

While he read the message, I massaged my temples, eyes closed. I doubted he even remembered me telling him about the baby name. It was months ago, during Silas's and my reset.

"Hey." He grabbed my wrists, stopping the massage. "Come here." He pulled me to a stand and into his arms, situating me tight against his rock-hard chest. Something about being next to him, secure in his embrace, made the tear ducts flow. I pressed my face into his neck and cried until his collar was soaked.

Okay. So I could be done with Holden Dupree right after this hug.

He stroked my hair. "Ari is a first-class a-hole," he said once the crying had stopped. "Text her back and tell her no. That's your name and she can't have it."

"It's just a stupid name. There are thousands of others."

He unlocked one arm from behind my back to run his thumb over my cheek. "It's not stupid if it matters to you."

Why did he have to say things like that? What guy cared about a dumb baby name I'd been obsessing over since I was a kid? No wonder women fell at his feet.

My gaze drifted down to his mouth. No man should have lips like that either. Pouty and oh-so kissable. Honestly, they were girl lips. But on him, situated perfectly amid the stubble and almost always present cocky grin, they were...

Unfair. Holden was...too much. Way out of my league. And I needed to stop torturing myself. Now.

I looked up to see him looking at my lips the same way I'd been looking at his. And a surge of desire shot through me. His kisses were powerful enough to steal all the hurt from my chest. At least for a little while. I'd experienced it twice before and I wanted it right then more than I ever had.

But post-kiss? I'd be a blubbering idiot, stuck on my couch alone, drowning my sorrows in a pint of cotton candy ice cream—another obsession since childhood. The last thing I needed was to be another girl he checked off when he was finished. Besides, I was way too old to be macking with some guy for fun. Especially if I ever wanted a chance to have a baby to name for real. I needed a man without commitment issues and Holden was not it.

I tried to step back, to remove myself from his embrace, but his strong arms were locked tight.

His nose nipped mine. "Where do you think you're going?"

I rested my hands on his bulging biceps and stared at his throat. "I just...this was a bad idea...the whole fake dating thing...I think we should be...d-done." The last word caught in my throat and I almost didn't get it out. I was positive he'd let me go then. Probably shove me off and say good riddance to the whole thing.

Instead, his arms tightened around my back and a smile

tugged at his perfect lips. "Yeah. I think so too." But his voice didn't match his words. He sounded almost giddy.

And he was still staring at my lips.

I cocked my head trying to figure out whatever game he was playing. And then, all at once his hands came from behind my back and trapped my face. "Christy," he said in a rough voice. And then he closed his eyes and leaned in.

Oh my gosh.

He was actually going to kiss me.

Holden Dupree who *never* kissed girls first.

I stepped back before his lips hit mine. He stumbled, off balance now that I was gone, and his eyes fluttered open, confused.

I threw my hands out. "What are you doing? We just agreed that we weren't doing the fake dating thing anymore. And since when is kissing part of it?"

He shrugged. "It could be. We're pretty good at it. The kissing part, I mean."

I tucked my hair behind my ear and gulped as I slid back another step. Because his expression was the opposite of what it should've been. Hungry and amused, with an annoying dash of arrogance.

"It's not funny," I said, my temper sparking. "Stop looking at me like that."

He took a small step forward, closing the gap between us. "Looking at you like what?" His stupid, sexy mouth was curled up at the corners, one hundred percent toying with me.

I grabbed the A.P. Government textbook off my desk and swatted it at him. "Get back. It's not funny."

He moved closer, eyes twinkling. "I mean, it's kind of funny. You can't tell me you don't want to kiss me. Be real, Chris. We've been dancing around this for weeks. And now you're going to fend me off with a book?" He said it like, of course every woman he met fell at his feet.

They probably did. But I wasn't going to be one of them. Anymore.

He held his hands out like, *C'mon.* "Our chemistry is ridiculous."

I glowered, steam rolling off my head. How dare he play with me like this? He knew my heartbreak. With each step he took, I took another in the opposite direction. But there are only so many places to go in a tiny box of an office. And, finally, he had me backed into a corner, sandwiched between the wall, the bookshelf, and my desk.

His arms spread open, one hand on the desk and the other on the bookshelf, boxing me in as slyly as if he'd drawn the fourth line in the Dots game I'd let Gabby win a thousand times when we were kids. His expression was still amused, but there was a sprinkle of frustration. Well, good.

He shook his head. "I've never, in my entire life, had a woman run from me."

I shrugged, arms folded. "Happy to be the first, Cocky Butt."

He laughed. "You're out of places to go." His adorable nose scrunched. "Maybe you should ask for a bigger office."

I glared at him. But apparently, in Holden's limited experience with rejection, glaring was an invitation because just then he growled—like a real growl—and lunged for me.

I screamed and jumped onto the desk, sending my pen cup scattering. I swung the book in his direction, but I was laughing now. "Seriously, Hot Lips. Get. Back." Swing, swing.

His jaw pulsed as he craned his neck up at me. "Unbelievable."

I held the book as a shield. "*I'm* unbelievable? Excuse me for not wanting to be another one of your groupies."

Irritation flashed across his face, and his jaw jutted forward. And then he lunged again, quicker this time. In less than a second, his arms were locked around my knees, and I was hanging upside down, butt to the ceiling, tossed over his shoulder.

I whacked his backside with the book. "Put me down!" I yelled like a helpless little girl. But he already was. My feet hit the floor with a thunk and his arm was back around my waist like we hadn't just played a ridiculous game of cat and mouse at all.

"Hand over the weapon," he ordered, and with his free hand, he ripped the book from my grasp. Then he tossed it onto the floor and kicked it away with his foot like it was a gun.

I huffed. "I guess you've never been dumped before so you don't know how this works. But let me tell you, this is the wrong response. Obviously, your massive ego is unable to comprehend the concept. So I'm going to make this perfectly clear." I gripped his shoulders. "I don't want you to be my fake boyfriend anymore. Fake relationship over. The end. So stop wielding your cocky masculinity all over the place and leave me be."

All the joking left his face. It was finished. He'd walk away and that would be that. The thought left me sick. But my heart couldn't keep this up.

His head tilted, eyes serious. "What if I don't want to leave you be?"

"T-too bad," It came out embarrassingly breathy. "I just dumped your fake butt, so..."

But if that was true, I wouldn't have my hands hooked around the back of his neck. And I wouldn't be letting him pull my hips closer to his. Or staring at his perfectly kissable lips. I was so pathetic. And weak. Pathetically weak.

"I'm glad you dumped me as your fake boyfriend." His voice was scratchy like sandpaper. "That guy needed to take a hike so your real boyfriend can take over." His nose brushed against the tip of mine. "That's me, in case you didn't know."

121

I stayed there, noses touching, breathing in his aftershave and cinnamon-scented breath. "You don't do real, Holden. You and I both know that."

"Yeah, well...I'd like to try. With you."

Was he serious? I leaned back to study him.

His eyes were hooded, so soft and vulnerable. "Give me a chance? *Please*?" He ran his fingertips over my cheekbones. "Beautiful Christy."

His gaze was so intense that I couldn't hold it. I had to look away. But then I whispered, "Please don't do this if you don't mean it. I don't have another heartbreak in me."

He tipped my chin up, forcing my gaze to meet his. "I'm fairly confident the only heart that might get broken here is mine." His voice was small, like it had taken everything he could muster to admit that.

"Yeah?"

"Yeah," he said, almost breathless, and a little terrified.

His forehead rested against mine for two heartbeats as we breathed it out, lips hovering. Just when I thought he was going to put me out of my misery, he whispered, "It's a good thing you didn't marry my brother. I think it would've been a real problem for me."

I whimpered, the suspense about to crack me in two. I gripped his shirt in my fists, waiting, willing it to happen.

His chest rose one last time like he was taking a deep breath before jumping into the deep end. And then his lips landed against mine with so much force that it stole my air. It was needy and urgent. Even more than the gym kiss. As if he was desperate for me and maybe he'd been dreaming of this moment for weeks. I knew I had.

My fingers threaded through the back of his hair. Our tongues found each other and he let out a moan. It was so cute. I slid my hands under the hem of his shirt and traced his lower spine. Another moan and then he shuddered. With a jerk, his arms curled around my waist and suddenly my feet were off the ground. Before I knew what was happening, he dropped me onto the edge of the desk, and pushed my legs apart, stepping between.

His lips were moving faster, harder as his hands slid up my thighs, over my hips, and onto my waist. Then his mouth pressed kisses down, down, down until he reached the base of my throat. He slid the neck of my shirt over to peck more kisses onto my collarbone. I shivered in delight, my entire body covered in goosebumps. His thumb brushed down the other side of my neck. When his mouth met mine again, *I* moaned. He smiled against my lips and came back for more.

Every nerve ending tingled, the heat almost more than I could take. My fingers curled around the hem of his shirt, peeling it up and over his head. He laughed as I whipped it across the room where it hit the wall and fell to the floor. Mouths never coming up for air, my fingertips ran over his chest and down his six-pack—no, that was an eight-pack—feeling every dip and curve of his muscles. This was too much, too intense. Why did this man make me lose control of all rational thought?

I dove back in, lips firm against his mouth, roving, memorizing him. I wrapped my legs around his waist in a vice grip, and kissed him with more ardor, verging on frantic.

"Chris." He pulled away, chest heaving.

"Hmm," I murmured but pulled his mouth back to mine.

"Christy," he said against my lips, but I wasn't close to done. I ran my fingers down his muscled back, pressing kisses all over his jaw. "Hey." He laughed. "*Woman.*"

That jolted me out of the delirious fog I was in. I lifted a brow, love-drunk. "What?"

He grinned but shook his head. "Not the place."

I exhaled embarrassingly loud and looked around, remembering where we were. In my office. Holy crap. I was the principal of this school and here I was going at it, in my office, on my desk. I'd discipline a student for this kind of behavior.

My word. Holden might be the death of me.

My hands pressed against my cheeks. "Oh my gosh. I'm so sorry. That was...intense."

But he was beaming, desire in his eyes. "Yeah. With you, it always is." He pulled me to him and rested his head against mine. "I just...I want to be the guy you deserve. It's been a long time since I was in a serious relationship and I want to treat it carefully, you know?" He pressed a soft kiss to my lips. "You're really important to me. And it would kill me if we messed this up by being reckless."

"Yeah. Okay." I tipped my head back and laughed.

I don't know how, and I hadn't even meant to, but by some miracle, I think I'd slayed *the* Holden Dupree. The thought made me giddy. But also in complete awe. Because he was important to me too. If I were honest, the most important person in my life. And the fact that he was here now, in my arms, was mind-blowing. Like heart wide open, full to bursting.

He dropped his forehead to my shoulder, taking a beat. It took all my willpower to hold onto his waist and not run my fingertips over his muscled back. But I restrained myself. When he was ready, he walked over and picked up his shirt. As he was shrugging it back on, a small black tattoo on the inside of his left bicep caught my eye. A fully inked-in semicolon. Nothing else. Just that.

Somewhere in the back of my mind, I recalled that it was the suicide prevention symbol. Had Holden, my strong, confident, name-calling hottie, been low enough to consider suicide? I couldn't fathom it.

He turned to me wearing that victoriously smug smile, and the thought left as quickly as it had come. Because there was no way.

He reached for my hand. "If you don't mind, I'd like to take my girlfriend out for dessert."

I nodded, so full of love for this man that I thought I might explode.

He pressed a kiss to my palm, and we headed out the door.

thirteen

HOLDEN

Over the years, Amber periodically tried to friend me on Facebook, under a new account each time. I always deleted the request and kept my account as locked down as possible. Maybe I got too comfortable being home with her, only watching from afar. I thought maybe with some life behind her, she might've finally felt some remorse and changed her ways. But that's the thing about a sociopath. They don't change.

As I walked into the high school the next afternoon, there was a little bounce to my step, not gonna lie. I pulled the gym door open, expecting to be assaulted by the sound of volleyballs pounding off the floors. But it was quiet. Yes, the girls were there, and the net was up, but they were standing around, looking at each other like they didn't know quite what to do.

Silas, who was never in the gym at that time, walked up to me, lips pursed. "All the balls are gone. Every single one. Christy ran to the store to see if she can grab a couple."

"What? No. I put them away myself, right after the game."

126

He waved toward the open storage closet. "See for yourself."

I stepped inside the dank room. Sure enough, all the usual junk Alvarez had lying around—footballs, basketballs, tennis balls—every kind of ball was there, except our volleyballs. And the weirdest part was that the two ball carts were tucked carefully against the wall, empty, making it obvious someone had taken them.

I swore. "Who would do that?"

"Dude. I don't know. Super messed up. But now that you're here, I can go check the security cameras to see if I can figure it out." He stalked off.

Just then Alvarez came running in. Christy or Silas must've called him. "They gone? Seriously?"

I folded my arms across my chest, dumbfounded. Volleyball wasn't a hot enough sport in the Riverbend Athletic District for this to have been the workings of a rival school. If it had been football or boys' basketball, it would've been more understandable. But I'd never heard of anything like this happening at Seddledowne, regardless of the sport.

"All of them," I said.

He stood there dumbly, hands on his hips, swearing under his breath.

Anna jogged up, dark hair bouncing in a ponytail. "What should we do, Uncle Holden? It's going to take Christy—"

I tilted my head like *c'mon now*. She knew better than to address her principal casually at school.

"Sorry," she corrected. "It's going to take *Coach Thornbury* at least a half hour, and that's if they even sell volleyballs at the hardware store."

She wasn't wrong. And we had a game the next day. I could make them do wall sits or plank holds, but it wasn't the best use of our time.

I cuffed her on the shoulder. "Go grab a TV from the library. We'll watch game footage from last night."

She nodded, grabbed her friend Brooklyn, and they took off.

"Ming! Jasmine!" - My hands cupped around my mouth. "Lead everyone in warmup."

"We already did," Ming yelled back.

"Shuttle runs then. Go!"

"Those were special or-duh balls," Alvarez groaned, running both hands through his hair. "You cain't just pick up navy balls with silver stripes at the sportin' equipmunt store." He shook his head. "We'll be the only team in the district without matchin' balls now."

I snorted in my head. The things Alvarez thought were important. But I guess it was his job to worry about stuff like that.

Like Silas, he stalked off to his office, grumbling about having to order new ones. I texted Christy.

> Me: Hey beautiful, find any balls at the store?

She immediately texted back.

> My Last First Kiss: One. Thank goodness. Be back soon.

Then she sent me a kissy face emoji.

I smiled at the name I'd given her in my contacts. Man, that kiss. All her kisses. Yeah, I was addled. And I wasn't ashamed to admit it. Not even a little.

I stood there yelling out drills until Anna and Brooklyn showed back up with the TV. After a few minutes of wrestling with the Bluetooth, we had game footage up and rolling. The girls settled onto the bleachers to watch. I pointed out where we could improve.

Five minutes later, Silas came back in, a sour expression on his face. He jerked his head to the right, ordering me over. We walked to the other end of the court.

When we were out of hearing distance, he hissed, "I guess things went well with Christy last night."

I stopped walking. "What are you talking about?" I'd already texted him that, yeah, we'd figured things out and were together now. Had he decided he wasn't okay with that?

He leaned closer, voice low. "I didn't find the ball thief because they erased fifteen minutes of footage. But I saw plenty of you and Christy *going at it—you shirtless—in her office.*"

The air seeped out of my lungs in a slow but steady leak. "Uh, there are cameras in her office?"

"Yes, *Randy*. The last principal and assistant principal had an affair, remember? There are cameras everywhere now."

I said a word Mom would've popped me in the back of the head for.

"You better hope whoever stole those volleyballs didn't see you when they were erasing the footage."

My heart was pounding out of my chest. I scrubbed a hand over my face. I might be a hormonal man, but I wasn't normally stupid. There was a reason I never kissed women first. A good one. It was a protection. I would never have to worry that I'd crossed a line that might land me in court. As a lawyer, I couldn't afford that kind of press.

But, if this got out, it wouldn't just make me look bad, it would put Christy in a terrible light. It was hard enough trying to acclimate to small-town life when you didn't grow up there, but if the wrong people got a hold of this information, it could be devastating to her career.

"Do you think they saw it?" I asked, almost breathless.

"Nah. It was two hours before. I think you're fine." He

shook his head, disbelief in his expression. "But you gotta think smarter than that, man."

I ran a hand over the back of my neck. "I know. She just...messes with my head and I can't think straight whenever..."

"Whenever she touches you?" He slapped me on the back. "She's probably your future wife then."

Christy and I spent our evening driving to the city to buy new balls. One wasn't enough. It made scrimmaging doable, but nothing else. Hard to practice setting or serving with one ball when there were twenty-six players.

The next day, we were back in business, with twenty new balls—thanks to the Holden Dupree Spare Volleyball Fund—and a plan. We didn't leave balls at the school anymore. They went into a large netted bag and I took them home every night.

"Settle down," I called to the girls at the back of the game bus who were screaming about some up-and-coming artist's TikTok video.

"Seddledowne, downe, downe, downe." The entire bus yelled, jumping to their feet as they sang the words and did The Twist all the way to the floor.

"You have to stop using those words." Christy smirked. "I think they do crap just so you'll say it." Then she winked.

She was right, but it's what my dad had said—still said—whenever he thought his kids were out of hand. It might take years to break the habit. Besides, it was fun seeing them so happy. Sometimes I looked for reasons to say it just so they'd do their funny dance. It added energy to the group and built up their team spirit.

I made sure the bus driver wasn't watching before I lowered my eyes and gave Christy a hungry smile. She rolled her eyes and mouthed the word, *stop*. Did I want to sit on the opposite side of the aisle? No. Not at all. But it was necessary if we wanted to make it through the season without the scrutiny of the girls.

"Uh, Miss Thornbury," the bus driver, Mr. Tinston, said. "The bus was at a full tank when we left but the empty light just came on."

Christy scowled but got up to check it out. She bent over to get a look, giving me a nice shot of her backside. I grinned wide, happy with my view.

"That's so weird," she said. "How close are we to a gas station?"

"'Bout twenty minutes. Hopefully we'll make..." The words died in Mr. Tinston's mouth as the bus lost power and began slowing down.

The girls started hollering from the back.

"What's happening?"

"What's going on?"

"Did we just run out of gas? That felt like we ran out of gas."

"We're going to miss our game!"

"Are you kidding me?" I scowled and leaned forward, looking for myself. Dead empty. And we were in the middle of nowhere.

Mr. Tinston pulled carefully over to the side of the road. As soon as the bus stopped, I shoved the silver handle to open the door and bounded down the steps. A peek under the engine told me everything I needed to know. The gas line was dripping fast. Either we had a leak or it had been cut. A sick pang took up residence in my gut. Had Amber done this? It was the first thought I had whenever anything went wrong, and it felt reminiscent of her past behavior. But then I thought, *nah.* Because what kind of horrible person cuts the gas line on a school bus with students onboard, one being her niece? I was catastrophizing. It had to be a leak.

When I got back on, I told Tinston. Christy was already

on the phone with Don Smith, the guy who ran the bus garage.

The girls were panicking, so I walked back to calm them. "You guys, it's gonna be okay."

"It's a district match. We can't miss it," Alyssa said, her eyes bulging with worry. "This is a team we can destroy."

I held up my hands. "If they won't push the time back, I'm sure they'll reschedule. It'll be okay."

Ming grunted. "I was ready to whip some Maplewood trash." A couple of more girls agreed.

"You'll get your chance. I promise."

"Oh look," Alyssa pointed out of the back window, maniacally waving at someone who'd pulled up behind us. "It's my Aunt Amber. And she's in her SUV. Maybe she can take JV to the game and we'll get another bus in time for Varsity."

My stomach rolled, and a quick thought burst through my mind. *Did Amber do this? And why? To roll up, looking like the hero?* I eyed Alyssa, trying to decipher if she'd been in on it. But no amount of acting could conjure up her present excitement.

I didn't want to be a buzz kill, but, "Every single player would need a signed permission slip to ride with her. Not happening."

As Amber made her way out of her car, I hurried back to the front of the bus. I did not want Christy anywhere near her without me there.

When Amber got to the top of the steps, she flung her dark hair over her shoulder and smiled. "Looks like you're having some technical difficulties. Anything I can help with?" She roved me up and down and I could see that look in her eye. It was the same one from a decade ago that yelled, Challenge Accepted.

"Nope," I said, shutting that down. "We've got it handled. You should head on to the game." I knew that's where she was going. Why else would she be out here in the middle of nowhere? And she hadn't missed a game yet. As a matter of fact, she came to games that Amber's parents hadn't even made it to. I'd never seen an aunt as dedicated as she was.

Christy scowled. I wasn't sure if she was scowling at me, or if she'd seen the way Amber had just undressed me with her eyes. In a much kinder tone than mine, Christy said, "Don is already on his way with another bus. Thank you for stopping, though."

But then Amber waltzed right past us and down the aisle toward the girls. "Who's thirsty? Anybody want a snack while you wait?"

The girls squealed and yelled that they did.

Christy and I shared a questioning look.

Amber sauntered back up the aisle, wearing a devious smile.

My eyes narrowed, and I had a feeling that the pit in my stomach wasn't going anywhere anytime soon.

"C'mon, Holden. Let's put those big biceps to work." Her voice was seductive. Bile rose in my throat. "I'm going to need help grabbing everything from my trunk."

Christy's eyebrow cocked. "You have enough snacks for twenty-six girls in your car?" Her tone was seventy-five percent disbelief, twenty-five percent jealous. There was no need. I wouldn't be caught dead with this woman.

Amber's expression went stony as she eyed Christy up and down. "And drinks. If you were a better coach and principal, you would've been prepared for something like this."

Christy's head snapped back, shocked.

For a second I wanted to lash back, but Amber was clearly playing a game here. I was going to play harder. "Actually, Coach Christy's the best." I winked at my girl. "And nice to look at too."

Amber's head looked like it might explode for a split

second. Then she slid her flirty smile back on like I hadn't just ogled my girlfriend right in her face and tipped her head at me. "Let's go, hottie." She bounded down the stairs and off the bus.

Christy stiffened, her eyes wide like she did not want me going anywhere with this horrible woman.

"You have nothing to worry about. Trust me." I leaned by her ear. "She's a literal psycho. Don't believe anything she says or does. And don't let her get to you." I needed to get that in, just in case. Amber was a loose cannon, and I couldn't guarantee anything when it came to her. I gave Christy a soft smile to ease her worry. "I'll be right back."

I was going to nip this in the bud, right here, right now. I kept my eyes trained on Amber as she walked ahead of me. Who knew someone in jeans and tennis shoes could master a runway walk on the gravel-strewn shoulder of the highway, but Amber was putting on a show. She was the very last person I should ever be alone with. But we were in broad daylight with a bus full of girls watching. And I had to do this for Christy.

As soon as we were behind her van, I let her have it. "I don't know what kind of game you're playing, but it ends now," I said through gritted teeth.

She looked at me, wide-eyed and innocent as she clicked the lift button on her trunk. "I just thought it would be nice to give the girls some energy for their game. Geez, Holden. Chill." Then she winked. I wondered how many guys had fallen to their deaths because of that wink. Probably way too many. But I couldn't worry about any of them right then. I had one person to protect, and I was here to make sure it happened.

"Don't act like we're friends. We're not and we never will be," I hissed. "And you stay away from Christy, do you hear me?"

She lifted a case of Gatorade from her trunk, bending over way too long. When she turned back to face me, she was wearing a sickeningly sweet smile.

I glared as I let her transfer the drinks into my arms. "I mean it. I'm on to you. You're not going to do to her what you did to Savannah. I won't let you." I should've left it at that, taken the drinks, and walked away. But I needed to make sure we were clear.

She grabbed a case of Goldfish crackers, tucked it under one arm, and smiled sweetly. "I didn't do anything to Savannah but try to be her friend. You're the one who couldn't save her. And no worries. Because I'm on to you too." She trailed a fingertip across my shoulders. I fought the urge to shudder. "And it's only a matter of time until you let me *on* you."

And there it was.

I clenched my jaw, trying to destroy her with my eyes. "Not if you were the last woman on earth."

She shrugged and laughed. "We'll see about that." Her gaze narrowed. "And trust me, I know *all* about you and Christy."

I sucked in a ragged breath.

That one line told me everything. She was behind it all. She'd taken the balls, wiped the security feed, and cut the gas line.

And she'd seen the shirtless kiss.

She grinned, her eyes dark and excited as if to say, "I know you're going to watch me walk away."

And I was. But not like that. Never like that.

I made the biggest mistake of my life in seventh grade when I checked the yes box on a Will You Be My Boyfriend note she'd passed to me in English. But how can a twelve-year-old boy possibly know that the pretty brunette he'd been crushing on all year was a psychopath in the making? I figured it out pretty fast. Took about two weeks to realize she didn't want a boyfriend. She wanted a puppet. My heart, my actions, every second of my time, my entire future, she wanted to rule them all. All I wanted was to walk down the hall together and brag to my friends. Thankfully, my parents figured out I was in over my head and helped me back my way out of that train wreck.

But she couldn't let me go. Ever. Every time I got in a relationship bad things happened. Threatening texts to my girlfriends from random numbers, horrible rumors, flat tires. The last girl I tried to have a relationship with was at the end of my junior year of undergrad at UVA. Margo Finnigan, a sassy strawberry blonde, who was pre-law like me. Lasted three months, long enough that I thought we were in the clear, but then one night when we were chilling at my apartment, a girl I'd never seen before showed up, overnight bag in hand, insisting that I'd asked her to sleep over. Apparently, we'd had an online "relationship" going on for a month. She had screenshots of our "conversations" to prove it. Margo left in tears.

I stopped trying after that. Hadn't had a serious girlfriend since. I'd go out with someone once or twice but that was it. If I moved faster than Amber could find out, they wouldn't get hurt. Not much anyway. I'd been a fool to think at twenty-seven she was any different. Part of the Dupree Family Creed was "Forgive, forget, and let people change." As an attorney, I tried to live by it. In my opinion, the prison system should've been renamed the Reformation System, because that's what it was meant to be. At least, when it worked right and people complied. Not everyone deserves to be remembered for the one stupid thing they did way back when. But over the years I'd also learned that, sadly, some people never change. And that's when you have to set boundaries.

I'd tried to do that with Amber. So many times.

But what can you do when someone takes a jackhammer

to your safely constructed walls faster than you can rebuild them?

As I followed her back to the bus, my shoulders slumped, and the darkness tried to pull me down. My brain, which I'd worked so hard to retrain, flipped my positive thoughts upside down like all the cognitive therapy my parents had paid for never even happened. The voices I'd kept down for so long were neon signs in my head.

You can't stop her. She's too strong and you're just a weakling. You're not up for this. Run. Just go. If you leave, you protect everyone you love. As long as you're here in Seddledowne, you're putting everyone at risk.

But the worst voice of all...

You couldn't protect Savannah from her. What makes you think Christy will be any different?

I'd strode back to Amber's van full of confidence and fire, certain I'd stop her once and for all. But heading back to the bus, I realized I'd been a fool. Amber had taken one look at me, finally with the woman of my dreams, and said, *hold my beer.*

fourteen

CHRISTY

There was something Holden wasn't saying. I mean, yeah, he'd told me Amber was a "literal psycho," but I'd already figured that out by the way she'd sexually assaulted him with her eyes with me watching. And how she'd tried to make me feel inferior. Mean girl vibes were radiating off of her. Obviously, she had a thing for him. Welcome to the club. But also, get a hold of yourself. We weren't besties but up until the bus breakdown, I'd thought we were cordial. She must not have known the sis code. Never trample a fellow queen to get to the top. Empower, not compete. There was more to the story than what either of them were putting off. There was a history there. I could feel it in my bones.

For the rest of the day, Holden was quiet, his mind somewhere else. He could hardly snap out of it to help coach. And when I'd tried to kiss him goodnight once we were back in the high school parking lot and all the girls were gone, he sidestepped me, said bye, and told me to go straight home and lock my doors. I didn't know this Holden, but I didn't like him. Not at all.

The next morning I woke up and Boyfriend Holden was

back, full force. Fifteen different apology texts, three phone calls, and he brought me lavender roses, which I'd mentioned were my favorite only once, back in the summer when we were just friends. And we had a sizzling make-out session that night. The next few days were a back-and-forth between Boyfriend Holden and The Guy I Didn't Know. Some kind of tug-of-war was going on inside of him, eating him up, but he wouldn't talk about it.

I was trying to do what Lemon had suggested and be patient while he worked through it. All I could hope was that Lemon was right and he would be worth the wait. But there were times when I wondered if I was hanging on only to be let down one more time.

Five days later, even though it was Silas's week to open up the school, I arrived early to prepare for the new tenth-grade transfer student, Tallulah Hawkins. It was her first day and I wanted to give her the school tour. Normally, Mrs. Yancy had a fellow student do it, but Mrs. Yancy had been right. Something was off in her records. She'd been pulled out of her previous school for five months during eighth grade and then reenrolled. She was now a year behind in school. I guess it wasn't that weird. Things happen sometimes. But there were also notes from the three previous schools she'd attended about her being withdrawn and one mentioned that she'd come to school with a black eye. No one had been able to prove anything and her mother skirted around any talk of abuse. But if there was even a chance that I had a kid coming in who needed extra help, I wanted her to know from minute one that she could come to me. That I was someone she could trust.

When I pulled into the faculty lot, I scowled. There were three cars parked there already. Mr. Jamerson's, our head janitor, Silas's truck, and Holden's car.

Why was Holden here this early in the day?

139

I hurried across the lawn and into the school. All the lights were on, ready to greet the students. I glanced into the library through the floor-to-ceiling hallway glass. Anna was there, reading a book. She must've ridden with Silas. When she saw me, she shot to her feet, her dark eyes wide and... worried? We looked at each other for two seconds. I waved. She waved back, but it wasn't happy like mine. It was the wave of someone who's worried they may never see you again. Maybe? She turned away and walked to a shelf, studying the books.

Okay. That was weird. And concerning.

I pushed open the door to the central office and immediately paused.

No one was in the first room, which housed both of our secretaries' desks and the counter where late students checked in. But I could hear voices.

"Whoa, whoa, whoa. You need to calm down before you do something that you'll regret," Silas said in a tone that he used whenever someone was panicking. He'd used it on me plenty. It was soft, trying too hard.

"Don't tell me to calm down," Holden hissed. "This is exactly what I was afraid of." He groaned. "I'm leaving. I'm going back to Sophie's to grab my stuff and I'm out of here."

What?

"That is the dumbest thing you could possibly do," Silas said, losing his cool. And it took a fair bit to make him lose his cool. "You have to stand up to her or it will never stop."

Her?

"It's never going to stop, no matter what I do. Seriously. My next job will be somewhere far, far away. Hawaii. Guam. Somewhere tropical. I'm going completely off grid. Maybe I'll get a fake ID and passport. If you get postcards from Epstein Barr, you'll *know it's me.*" It would've been funny if his tone wasn't ripped with pain. That had been his nickname in my contacts. Of course, I'd taken it down once we were together, right after we had a good laugh about it.

My feet were moving before I told them to. For once I was glad my heels clacked loudly against the tile so I wouldn't have to announce my arrival. The guys went silent as I moved in that direction. I poked my head into Silas's office to see my hunk of a man leaning forward, hands on the desk, chest heaving like someone had whipped him with stripes across his back.

I looked at Silas. "What is going on?" He gave me nothing, hands in his pockets, lips sealed. So I glanced at Holden, dressed in joggers and a tight T-shirt that, any other morning, would've made me want to run my hands all over his chiseled torso. "You're moving somewhere tropical?" He may as well know I heard.

Still they said nothing. And that's when I noticed them.

Dozens of crinkled flyers in a messy stack on Silas's desk. I walked over, eyes trained on each Dupree, and picked one up. I dropped my eyes to the paper.

And then I gasped.

It was a picture of me and Holden, in my office, kissing, him sans shirt. With the words *What happens in the principal's office, stays in the principal's office* framing it.

My hand went to my heart.

I dared to glance at Silas, sure he was so disappointed in me. Us. In us. But he was stone-faced. Then he gave me a pity smile. Holden was still bent over, eyes on the ground.

I took off for my office, I don't know why. I knew there were cameras in there but no one ever looked at the night feed. There was no reason to. Had I thought there was a minuscule chance someone could find out? Yes. But I'd quickly talked myself off that ledge. The chances were so remote it wasn't worth giving a second worry.

My eyes checked each camera, a red blinking dot greeting

me. My mind reeled a hundred miles an hour, playing through every scenario of how this could've happened. Nothing made sense. I hurried back to Silas's office. Holden was up now, chewing his thumbnail, eyes trained on the door, as I came through.

"Who?" I asked them.

"We have theories," Silas said.

Holden scoffed. "One theory. And it's the only one we need." But then he clamped back down like he'd said too much and I was met with silence once more.

"Okay?" My hands went to my hips. "Would you like to share with the class?"

Silas deferred to Holden with a glance. But Holden was on lockdown.

Alrighty then.

I turned to my assistant principal with zero patience left. "How?"

He held up his hands. "My guess is the password is old. It's a small town. Probably too many people know it, who knows? I'll call Eddie right at eight o'clock." Eddie was the school district's IT guy.

Holden was staring at me, tight-lipped. I was going to have to pull every bit of information out of them one piece at a time.

I held the flyer up. "These were posted around the school?" It wasn't hard to deduce. There was a piece of tape on the top of each flyer. Where else would they have been?

"Don't worry, we found all of them," Holden said.

"You're sure?" I had to ask. If they'd missed even one...

He nodded. "We ran the entire school three times. Anna helped." Great. Anna had seen the flyers. I'd barely recovered my credibility from my freak-out at the beach. That girl was never going to respect me.

How early had Silas gotten here? Early enough to notice,

give Holden time to drive down and search the school repeatedly. I'd never been more grateful that Silas was an early riser.

I'd had enough of the short answers, it was essay time. "Spill it. I want to know who, why, and why you're threatening to leave the country. *Now.*"

Silas cocked a brow at his brother. "I think I'll give you the room. Just keep your clothes on, please. The cameras are rolling."

My face heated as he walked out and shut the door.

Holden looked up with hooded eyes. "I'm so sorry, Chris."

"Why are you apologizing? Did you spend last night taping these all over the walls?"

"No. But it's my fault. I never should've started this." I didn't understand what was going on, but it was clear from his words and the slump of his shoulders that he thought our being together was a mistake. Dread filled my chest.

Ever since the bus breakdown, Holden had been different, and in the back of my mind, I couldn't stop worrying that my heart would get broken after all. An all too familiar desperation settled in. I was going to get dumped. Again. And this time, I would not recover. Not after Holden.

"What are you talking about?" My voice was shaky. I was angry at whoever had done this and so frustrated with this thick-skulled man. "Because we kissed in my office?" I strode over and cupped his breathtaking face in my hands. "Stop talking like that right now. Just tell me what you know."

His eyes closed but he reached out and wrapped his arms around my waist. My breakup fears sprouted wings and fluttered away. Fleeing the country had simply been him venting. He wasn't going anywhere.

He sighed. And then he told me a tale of Fatal Attraction-worthy psychotics like I'd never heard before, only it was real life. *His* life. Without the homicide, thankfully. But still, stalk-eresque-type behavior from Amber through the years that

143

explained so many things about this man I'd fallen for. No wonder he never wanted to commit.

He tipped his head against mine. "I'm so sorry I pulled you into this."

My fists curled around his shirt. "You didn't pull me into anything. Don't you understand that?" Once again his gaze was down. I tucked myself lower so he had to meet my eye. "You listen right now, Holden Dupree. I am right where I want to be. Nobody pulled me anywhere. I'm a big girl and I can decide for myself. And Amber Taylor isn't going to scare me off." I scoffed at such a ridiculous notion. "Do you hear me?"

"But—"

"No buts. The. End. I'm not going anywhere. And if she and I have to meet out in the parking lot and throw down, earrings ripped out, hair extensions on the asphalt, so be it." We'd had three fights already this year just like the one I described. Girls be crazy sometimes.

A chuckle rumbled in his hard chest. "You have hair extensions?"

"No." I picked up a lock and studied it. "It's all mine. But I'll go get them if that's what it takes for you to understand that I am out-of-my-mind crazy about you."

The twitch at the corners of his lips said he wanted to smile, to let it all go. But there was still too much worry in the rest of his face.

"I don't know, Chris. Maybe it would just be better if I went—"

I put a finger to his perfect lips, stopping him. "You promised me that my heart would not get broken and if you leave Seddledowne, it will crack right in two." I shook my head. "Scratch that. Fissures everywhere, shattered to bits, irreparable. Do you want that kind of tragedy on your hands?"

He sighed. "Definitely not. No more broken hearts." He

dipped his head until our foreheads were touching. "I really want to kiss you right now. But, you know, cameras."

My hands slid up into the back of his hair. "I say we give her a show. Really tick her off."

"I'm not sure that's a great idea."

I pecked his mouth. "She doesn't get a say. This is our relationship. And if we want to kiss, we kiss." I pecked him again, hoping he'd take the bait. He hesitated, lips hovering, our chests inhaling and exhaling in perfect unison. "*C'mon.* You know you want to kiss me. Our chemistry is ridiculous." I laughed.

I willed him to be brave. I don't know if it was metaphysics or magnetic pull but somehow my courage must've flowed into him because finally his hands slid up to my cheeks and he pressed his lips against mine. Slowly and carefully, he kissed me and kissed me and kissed me. Until I was downright breathless. When we were done, his eyes flashed up to one of the cameras.

I pulled his face back to mine. "Keep your eyes on me and everything will be fine."

"That I can do." His fingers trailed down my neck and he gave me a scared smile. "I'm crazy about you too, beautiful."

"Good thing." I pressed one more kiss to his mouth. "'Cause you're not getting rid of me. Ever."

"I hope you mean that." His eyes turned so serious. "Because it's going to get worse before it gets better. I can't even promise that it will get better."

I tapped my forehead against his, once for each word. "Not. Going. Anywhere."

The door popped open. His hands fell from my waist and I stepped back.

"Tallulah Hawkins is here for her tour," Silas said.

I gave Holden a small wave and backed out the door. I shook my hands out as I crossed the office, trying to roll off what Holden had told me about Amber. How could someone be that crazy? I mean, I got that Holden was hot. Like really hot. But have some self-respect.

When I came into the hall, Tallulah and her mom had their backs to me, studying a Stallion painting on the wall that a former art student had done back in Silas and Holden's high school days. All I could tell from this angle was that they looked more like sisters than mother and daughter. They had similar builds—thin and tall like models or professional ballerinas. They probably shared outfits on the daily. And they shared the same long, dark hair.

"Well, hello there," I said with a smile in my voice. They turned and thankfully the gasp that escaped my lungs was miniscule. I immediately wished Mrs. Yancy had been more forthcoming in her information. Because the younger woman, who I assumed to be Tallulah, was pregnant. Possibly seven months along, at least. I wasn't sure but I'd watched Gabby go full term twice.

We had two other girls in the school who were also expecting but, and I hated to admit it even in my mind, they fit the stereotype. Low income, from uneducated and broken homes. I couldn't surmise much just by looking but the leather purse the older woman had slung over her shoulder, along with the quality of their clothing, told me they probably had plenty of money. I knew nothing about her home life yet though.

I stepped forward, my hand out. "Christy Thornbury. I'm the principal. It's nice to meet you, Tallulah."

"Tally," the mother corrected. "She goes by Tally."

I shook Tally's hand and then her mother's.

"I'm Kim," her mom offered.

Tally's dark eyes were wide and nervous, skittering around the hallway, not stopping anywhere more than a second or two. She seemed terrified and skittish.

"Well, we're so happy you're here," I said. But now I was wishing I had a student to introduce her to because she hadn't made so much as a squeak. Extroverts had a hard enough time making friends. But being introverted *and* pregnant was going to make this even harder. She was going to need a friend.

Just then Anna stood up in the library to go put her book back on the shelf and it caught my eye. And I almost laughed. If anyone in this school would befriend a pregnant teen, it would be Anna Dupree who was the product of that exact circumstance.

"Could you excuse me for a moment?" I stepped to the floor-to-ceiling window and knocked. Anna turned, and I waved her over. She hurried toward me, a question on her face. I met her at the door and looked her directly in the eyes. She was still worried about Holden and possibly me. That was evident. "Everything's okay. We handled it," I said, my face prickling with a blush. I could feel it.

She snickered. "It's okay. I get it. Uncle Holden is like, sheesh, *perfection.*" She made the chef's kiss gesture. "No worries. I won't tell anyone. Not even Brooklyn." She zipped her lips.

I bit my cheeks to stop myself from laughing. I needed to be professional in front of this girl, regardless of my relationship with her uncle. I tilted my head and said in a secretive hush, "But his shirt shouldn't have come off. You know that, right?" I raised a brow. I needed to make that clear, especially with her "situationship," as the students called it, with Blue.

Her mouth compressed, annoyed. "Yes. Good grief. Are you going to give me the talk too? Uncle Si gives it at least once a day."

I smiled. "Okay. Good. As long as that's clear." And then I inclined my head in Tally and Kim's direction. "Can you do me a favor? I've got a new student here for her tour and she could use a friend."

Her dark eyes turned curious. I moved out of her way so she could see Tally.

Anna did better than me. Didn't even flinch at the sight of her. Not even a little. She glanced back at me and nodded almost imperceptibly.

"Tally," I said as we approached them. "I want to introduce you to one of our finest students, Anna Dupree."

I turned to Anna whose expression had suddenly shifted from worried and curious to fierce and bright. "Anna, this is Tally. She's a sophomore and today's her first day."

Anna strode over to her. "Hey, girl. Welcome to Seddle-downe High School. Oh my gosh, your hair is *so* pretty and I love your earrings. Are they jade? That's my favorite stone." The adorable half-Italian hooked her arm around Tally's. It worked. Tally's expression went from terrified to slightly excited in less than ten seconds. Then Anna led her down the hall. "Miss Thornbury," she said over her shoulder. "Can we show her the atrium first? It's my favorite part of the school."

"You bet," I said with a grin.

fifteen

HOLDEN

Over the next few days, my nerves never settled, not for a minute. It wasn't that I was afraid of Amber so much as I was afraid of losing Christy—and not just relationship-wise—but mortally. May sound dramatic, but I hadn't given Savannah up and it had killed her in the end. I would not lose Christy because I was too selfish to let her go.

I tried desperately to make the cognitive behavioral therapy techniques work, but nothing was touching the anxiety that riddled my resolve not to break Christy's heart. The only thing I knew for certain was that Amber wasn't done. Something was coming, something big. It was only a matter of time.

Three days later, on a Friday in mid-October, I'd arrived at the school an hour earlier than normal. It was homecoming week and Alvarez wanted to showcase all Seddledowne High School athletes at the pep rally.

Blue Bishop, cocky son-of-a-gun, had just been high-lighted as the starting quarterback in tonight's Varsity game. His stats were just too good and they'd bumped him up from

JV, kicking Amari Chambers from his position. If Blue kept it up, he could play college ball, at the very least.

Blue sauntered off the gym floor, eyes on Anna in the stands. He bounded up the bleachers and caught her as she flung herself at him in a congratulatory hug. Blue grinned like he'd just won the lottery. They stared into each other's eyes for a few seconds and I swear every girl in the gym let out a collective "Awwwww."

My gaze shifted to Silas who was standing by the interior exit doors, his arm around Lemon's waist. He'd invited her for kicks. He squinted, his fists balled, eyes firing poison-tipped darts at Blue's back. I chuckled. That kid had a proclivity for getting under his skin. It was my new favorite thing to rag him about.

Anna sat between her boyfriend and an attractive girl with a pregnant belly the size of a basketball. I'd never seen her before, but it made me happy to see my niece befriending someone who probably very much needed it. Someone like her momma. Brooklyn leaned down from behind Anna and whispered something in her ear. They both laughed. When Anna turned back, Blue pulled her into his side, gazing at her like she was the world's biggest diamond.

"Blupree, still going strong," Christy said under her breath, next to me.

"Blupree? That's their ship name?"

She shrugged. "Apparently."

My mind flew through the possibilities. Banna. Blanna. Dishop. Annalue. Yeah. Blupree was the catchiest and rolled off the tongue best.

Christy pinched my elbow. "We're up."

Alvarez was a real Ian Eagle today. Hamming it up and making his voice super dramatic and announcer-like. "And here we have our illustrious Lady Stallions volleyball teeaaaaammm. With a stellar 11 and 3 record. Let's give 'em a rooooouuuuund of applause."

The gym erupted in cheers as our girls sauntered, galloped, and danced onto the floor from the bleachers.

"And ain't no way Principal Thornbury could've known when she first arrived from her redneck roots in Laramie Wy-o-ming that she'd be wrrrrrangled into coaching our girls vol-ley-baaaalllll team? Let's give it up for Prrrrincipal Slash Coach Thornburrrrry." Yes, he said the word slash. Clearly, he was going with an elongated R theme. The entire gym roared and stomped their feet on the bleachers.

Christy's lips quirked. She laughed and stole his mic. "I think what you meant to say was my rrrrrefined rrrrrroots, not rrrrrredneck." She accentuated the rrrr sound of each word. Another eruption of laughter. "Where I come from—seventy-two-hundred feet in elevation, thankyouverymuch—the air is crisp and clean, the men never tease an upstanding lady, no one has to be asked to repeat what they're saying, and 'ain't' is a swear word. Go Pokes!" She held her arms up in a W, fists clenched. It was the Pokes Pride Symbol.

Silas held his arms up, mirroring her in Pokes solidarity. The students roared at that.

"All right, all right!" Alvarez held a hand up, grinning. Everyone quieted down. "Let's look at some highlights of our Lady Stallions!"

The lights lowered for the third time.

They'd done this for every team so far. Just a one-minute clip. We'd already sat through golf and football. Cross country was up after us. Alvarez pressed a button on the remote and a video began playing on a large portable screen set up at the south end of the gym.

The first was a snippet of Ming's killer serve, scoring an ace. Everyone cheered. Next was Anna's first kill, the one where her eyes were closed. Laughter all around. Anna hid behind Brooklyn which made everyone laugh harder.

And then there was a second of gray static like the feed was broken. It glitched and then started going again. It took a millisecond to realize we were no longer watching volleyball highlights.

There was a shot of Christy and Silas, standing on the top of a Wyoming mountain, in hiking gear, his arms around her middle, his chin resting on the top of her head. The room went quiet for a split second until it broke out in guffaws and catcalls. A surge of jealousy and a momentary urge to tackle my brother ripped through me. Knee-jerk reaction. I shoved it back down, trying to figure out what to do. But then the screen changed and I couldn't force myself to stop watching.

This picture was the two of them at a Pokes football game, matching cowboy hats, bright yellow-orange Pokes shirts, beers in one hand and the other arm punched to the air, fists balled, together forming a W, just like the one they'd both made only moments earlier. Then the pictures started flashing almost faster than my mind could comprehend. Christy and Silas kissing on a porch swing. The two of them asleep on a blanket on a lawn, legs and arms tangled around each other. A professional picture of her entire family at their ranch, zooming in on her and Silas at the end, his arm hooked around her waist.

I felt like I was going to puke.

The students were entranced, jaws open, eyes wide. A few had their phones out, recording. Christy was curling in on herself, panic taking over her face, frozen in place.

I torpedoed toward the screen, no idea what I was going to do, but I couldn't stand there doing nothing. Silas was gone. Only Lemon remained at the door, composed as usual but fingers pressed against her lips.

Just as I reached the screen one last picture appeared.

And all my worst nightmares came true. Me shirtless, leaning into Christy, her fingers spread wide over my upper back, neck bared. It looked like I was sucking her blood, full-on vampire style, and she was one hundred percent in compliance. It wasn't the same picture as the flyers, but it was the same kiss.

Just as my hand was about to rip the screen from its stand, the video died.

One breathless beat of pin-drop silence and then the gym exploded with laughter, utters of shock, catcalls, and shouts of glee. I turned back for Christy but she was already to me, tears streaming down her face. I pulled her under my arm and escorted her out of the gym. Lemon followed us through the door and into the breezeway.

Christy turned to me, and I let her bury her face in my chest. Lemon, who was undoubtedly the classiest and least jealous woman on the planet, rubbed circles on her back. She and I shared a look. Anna flew through the door, tears in her eyes. Blue was right behind her. She flung herself into Lemon's arms.

Before the door shut all the way, I heard Alvarez make a lame joke asking if anyone else's eyes were burning. Idiot. The door snapped shut but through its window, I saw Mrs. Yancy, my old guidance counselor, yank the mic from his hands and silence him with a glare. I always did like that woman.

Silas came jogging up, a scorch in his expression, a slew of expletives burst rapid fire out of his mouth. He called Amber a name she more than deserved. Didn't even care that Anna and Blue heard.

"Christy?" he said. "Did you disclose our relationship when they hired you?"

She stepped out of my arms and faced him. "No. We weren't together. You weren't even an employee yet. The paperwork only asked for people we're related to who were employed by the school district." She pressed a hand to her brow. "Did you?"

"Yeah." He nodded. "Had a long conversation with the superintendent about it. Hopefully, that will be enough."

"What about the rest?" I asked, wondering what that shirtless picture was going to do to Christy's career.

He shook his head, lips clamped. "I have no idea. It won't be good though." Then he turned to Lemon. "I'm so sorry, babe." She said nothing, just wrapped her arms around his waist. He pressed a kiss to the top of her red hair.

Then Anna asked the questions we should have. "How did they get those pictures? And how did they tap into the feed? It comes from the AV room right?"

Silas nodded. That's where he'd just come from. He must've taken off the second he realized what the first picture was.

I turned to Christy. "You took all your pictures of Silas off your social media, right?"

Her hands went to her cheeks. "Yeah. As soon as we broke up. But some of those weren't even *my* pictures."

Huh?

And Silas never posted on social, hardly even got on, so it couldn't have been him. Who else would've had pictures like that?

Then Christy let out a gasp so quiet that no one heard but me. She pulled her phone out of her pocket and flipped through her sister's social media. I looked over her shoulder and groaned in frustration as the pictures rolled by. Every single one of the photos in the video was up on Gabby's wall.

She walked away, jaw clenched, punching at her phone like she wanted to jab holes through the screen.

Silas and Lemon hashed out what the next steps needed to be. He dialed the sheriff's office.

I was torn. Did I stay with Christy and help her figure this out? Or was my being in this school going to make things worse? And what else would Amber dish out before this was over? Thirty feet away, Christy's tears were still falling as she lifted her phone to her ear.

I walked toward her.

"Take them down, Gabby. Right now." Her hand went into her hair, her face so helpless. She paced, listening. "I don't care how good you look in that family picture. If Silas is in it, it has to go." More pacing. She was chewing her fingernails now.

She let out a frustrated groan and punched *end call*. "She says she'll take down the ones of me and Silas but the family picture stays because she *can't even* with how good her hair and makeup look."

I swear I was going to *can't even* somebody's face if her sisters didn't stop being so selfish and hurtful.

And then, just when I thought things couldn't get worse, Mrs. Ross, a buxom blonde with huge blue eyes, threw the gym door open, stepped into the hallway, and bent over, trying to catch her breath.

"Christy," she wheezed, and the way she looked at her told me they'd become friends. Had she sprinted to get out here? "You're gonna wanna check your email right now." She glanced at Silas. "You too, Mr. Dupree. It's from someone named Jane Doe and it looks like spam. I don't usually open stuff like that. But you'll understand when you see the subject line."

Christy's face went pale and she swiped to her email. Then she clicked on the first one at the top of her inbox. Subject Line: *Christy Thornbury, Principal or Pervert?* It was the exact video we'd just watched but this time we finished it. Only forty-five seconds long, Amber must've known she had limited time at the pep rally before someone cut it off. Silas had shut it down before the climactic ending that was now playing.

A picture of Christy alone in a tiny red bikini, standing on a beach somewhere tropical. The water was crystal clear and the sand was almost white. She looked out of this world pretty. Divine, perfectly curved hips, flat stomach, tan and smooth legs. She could rival any swimsuit model. And if I'd ever seen it before this moment, especially as her boyfriend, I would've ogled it. No shame at all. Even with the intensity of the moment, it made me want to carry her away from here and do things I'd told myself I wouldn't.

But her expression in the photo tightened my chest. She might've been smiling, but there was a pain in her eyes that said she wanted to be anywhere but there. There had to be a story behind it but this wasn't the time to ask. My lungs cinched at how beautiful she was. It was a fantastic snapshot.

But it wasn't a photo you wanted six hundred of your students to see.

Then a Stallion blue background replaced the picture with silver words that read:

"Is this the kind of person we want leading our children?"

I looked up when I realized Silas was standing in front of us. "Pretty sure from the names in the email list, she sent it to every employee in the district. School board, teachers, everyone."

Christy's eyes closed for a second and then she shook her head, tears dripping down her face, and walked away.

"The sheriff is on his way right now. We're going to nail her, Holden."

I hoped he was right, but I wasn't so sure. I'd tried turning Amber in after everything went down with Margo, but the cops said there was no way to prove she'd made a fake dating account impersonating me. They couldn't find any trace of it. Amber wasn't stupid. There wasn't going to be a trail here. And I couldn't worry about her right then.

I turned and jogged to find Christy. The hallways were

dead quiet. She wasn't anywhere in the central office or her own. I pounded down the halls, peeking in every open room. Had she left the building? I ran back out the front doors and into the parking lot. Her car was still there. I headed into the grass, planning to search every square inch of this campus if I had to.

I'd just pressed send on a text asking where she was when I rounded the southeast corner to find her huddled against the brick wall, knees pulled up, her head in her hands, weeping.

I sat down next to her. "Oh, man, Chris, come here." I pulled her into my arms. "I'm so sorry," I repeated over and over as my fingers tickled her back. I didn't know what else to say.

After a few minutes, she began, her voice a shred of a whisper, "That's the worst picture she could've chosen." Her hands twisted in her lap. "We were supposed to get engaged. Sunset on the beach and all that. He even had the ring..."

"Rowan?"

She nodded, not even wondering how I knew. I intertwined our fingers, rubbing my thumb over her hand.

"I got up early to watch the sunrise the third day we were there. Went to Rowan's room to see if he wanted to come along but his bed was empty. I kind of panicked because he wasn't answering his phone, but I told myself to chill. I mean, maybe he ran out for coffee." She wiped her cheek. "Or maybe he'd decided to get up early and watch the sunrise too. So I went for that walk and guess what?"

I couldn't say anything. Her pain was so intense I was taking it for my own. And it was stealing my air.

"He'd gone to watch the sunrise all right. Except he was missing the whole thing because he was full-on making out with my sister. Like, on a beach towel, moaning and groaning, rolling around, sand in their hair. My *sister*."

"Gah." It came out like an exhale after a gut punch. "Please tell me you were on the next flight home."

"Nope." She sniffled. "My mom wouldn't let me. Said it would ruin our family trip and to suck it up."

My teeth clamped hard. She'd been living with that right in her face all this time. No wonder she left Laramie the first chance she got.

A tear slipped off her jaw. "I thought coming here would make things better. That if I got away from that, I'd finally be able to relax and just be happy."

Arms wrapped around her shoulders, I leaned my head back against the red brick of the building. This was all my fault. She was right. Coming here should've made things better.

And it would have.

If it weren't for me.

It was time to do the right thing.

Time to make sure Christy was never hurt because of me ever again.

sixteen

What was I doing at Dupree Ranch?

A week ago, I'd had it all. Awesome job, great coaching gig, dream guy. And now it was all gone.

The school board put me on administrative leave while they investigated everything. The only thing in my favor was that I was still getting a paycheck. For now. But who knew if that would still be the case whenever they made their final decision.

Silas was acting principal. He'd covered both our butts when he'd disclosed our relationship. Holden was still coaching the girls because he wasn't an employee of the Seddledowne School District. And there was no one else to do it.

But my behavior was "unbecoming" of someone in such a position of leadership. Though I suspected being an outsider had a great deal to do with it. I got a slap on the hand and a swift kick out the door. If things had been the slightest bit better in Laramie, I would've tucked my tail and gone home.

I sat in my truck, hands shaking, running through every breathing exercise I could think of as I stared at the farmhouse

159

in front of me. I'd been here, parked in this very spot, once before, for a few minutes. The day I'd kissed Holden at Sophie's. But I'd never been inside.

I looked at Holden's last message. He'd sent it the night of the pep rally fiasco, a half hour after the school board had decided I was on leave. A freaking text message breakup.

> Holden: Sorry, I've been MIA this evening. I needed time to think everything through, and now I know that this was a mistake. I never should've started this. If I don't end things now, it will only get worse. I'm so sorry. I hope you can forgive me.

Of course, I'd hurled messages back, like,

> Me: You said you weren't going to break my heart. So much for keeping your promises.

> Me: You suck.

> Me: I hope you get herpes.

> Me: I hate you.

> Me: I'm so sorry, I didn't mean that. I actually think I love you. Please, can we talk about this?

My head hung in shame. I'd told him I loved him *after* he'd dumped me, over a text. It doesn't get any more pathetic than that. And even more pathetic was the fact that he never even responded. Just left me on read.

And here I was at his house like *I* was some kind of stalker. What was wrong with me? And what was I doing here? Holden's white car was parked right in front of me. All I had to do was let my foot slip off the brake and bam! it would put a nice dent in his beloved Tessie. The thought was satisfying. And also heartbreaking. Because that was the opposite of what I wanted. I didn't hate Holden. I loved him. I wanted to hug him, not dent his car.

Silas and Lemon walked down the porch steps and across the lawn to my truck. I shoved my phone into my purse and leaned down, pretending to fix the hem of my jeans. They were both wearing a sad smile and I fought the urge to rev the engine, shove the truck in reverse, and high-tail it out of there. Lemon waved through the window and I reluctantly turned the key. The engine died and I got out.

"Hey." She leaned in and hugged me. "I'm so glad you came." Her words were too eager. She was trying too hard. We weren't friends. We weren't at hugging level yet.

I hugged myself. "Of course."

She'd called me the night before saying they needed extra hands to work cattle today. But I knew better. They were panicked about Holden. I was the first woman he'd tried to have a relationship with in years and they were afraid if I walked away completely that he might be alone for the rest of his life. I knew because Jenny had called me, frantic, after she found out we had broken up and told me exactly that.

Silas nodded toward the house. "We're still waiting on Ashton. He's running a little behind. So we're eating lunch first. Mom made a big roast for everybody."

I nodded. "Cool."

They led the way and I was happy to fall in step behind them. I didn't know how these people dressed for working cattle. I mean, Silas was in Wranglers and his cowboy boots. But Lemon was currently wearing a jade green sundress. I felt kind of weird in my jeans, cowgirl boots, and a T-shirt that said "I'd rather be roping cows." This was what I wore in Wyoming when I helped at our ranch, but I'd never worn it here and it felt like I was trying to be something I wasn't. To make it even more awkward, I was pretty sure, from the nervous glances Silas and Lemon kept giving each other, that Holden didn't know I was coming.

Jenny met us at the door and plowed through Silas and Lemon, arms shimmying them apart to get to me. You would've thought I was the queen of England and not the woman she'd called "a mess" at the beach this past summer.

She pulled me into her arms, not caring one bit that my hands were stiff-straight at my side. "Thank you for coming, Christy. Really. It means so much." Then she cupped my cheeks in her hands. "You just have to give him some time. He'll come around. You'll see."

"Oh my gosh, Mom. Stop. You're freaking her out," Silas said.

Still with my cheeks in her palms, she tsked. "She's not freaked out. See, she looks fine."

All three of them were staring at me, waiting for me to let them know that I indeed was not freaked out. I gave them a quick but stilted smile. That's the best I could do with Jenny smashing my face like a panini press.

Jenny grabbed me by the hand and pulled me through the living room and into the kitchen. Anna and Blue were already at the table, along with Tally. Tally's presence surprised me but also squeezed my heart. Anna had taken the whole friend thing to the next level. Tally's eyes darted around the room as if she were taking everything in. With her sitting at the table, her tummy tucked underneath, you couldn't even tell she was expecting.

My gut tightened to see three of my students. Oh, what they must think of me.

Anna's head snapped up. "Coach!" She jumped up, ran around the table, and smashed me in a hug. "Oh my gosh, I've missed you." And for the first time since I put my truck in park I felt myself relax a little.

We weren't at school. This was a family thing. So I wound my arms around her back and pulled her tighter. "Hey, I've missed you too." She gave me the first sincere smile I'd seen in a week. No sadness, no pity. Just a good old-fashioned "I'm so happy you're here" smile. "How's volleyball?"

"Okay, but we all miss you. Uncle Holden is fine but he's been a little intense with you gone, ifyouknowwhatImean." She hooked her arm around mine and led me to my seat. Were they assigned?

I lowered into the wooden chair, across from Tally and Blue. Blue was grinning, but I think that was just because he was enamored with Anna. And Tally was still taking in the room.

Blue stood, leaned over the table, and offered me a fist bump. "What up, P. Thorn?"

I snorted and shook my head. "Really?" I'd heard a rumor that some of the students referred to me as P. Thorn. But no one had ever done it to my face.

In response, his grin widened.

Anna plopped onto the edge of the chair next to me. "Listen, I know you probably think everyone at school is horrified" —she wiggled her fingers and wobbled her head—"at that picture of you and Uncle Holden, but they're not." She leaned in closer, her eyes darting to Jenny who was mixing up a bowl of mashed potatoes on the counter, and said in a hush, "They think you're fie-uh." She sang the word fire. "Ming said that she wishes she were enmeshed with Uncle Holden so he'd be all over her like that." She waved that thought away. "But she can't because she's jailbait. And because he's at full love-haze level with you."

My mouth was open and I didn't know whether to laugh

or gasp. Silas had walked in at just the right time to hear everything about Ming.

His lips pursed into a bloodless line. "Anna, are you kidding me right now?"

She gestured at me. "She should know we're not freaked out about it." She held her hands up. "I'm just sayin'."

"Well, *just say* your way over to your side of the table. Kids over there. Adults over here."

"Pfft. I'm not a *kid*," she said as she hopped up. She walked around and plopped down in her chair between Tally and Blue. "I have a boyfriend," she chirped and then leaned over and pecked Blue on the cheek. He beamed.

Silas glared at them. Lemon two seats down, snickering, reached out, grabbed Silas's hand, and tugged him to his seat.

Bo, the family patriarch, walked in from the hallway and sat at the head of the table. "Hey, Christy. Good to see you."

I hadn't missed the fact that I was flanked by two empty chairs. The foot of the table to my left and another chair to my right. Was I in no man's land? Or had they invited me over just to banish me during the meal as some weird form of punishment? The thought was almost funny until I realized everyone had gone quiet.

I looked around trying to figure out why.

Oh.

Holden was standing there behind Bo, staring at me like someone had kidney-punched him. Hard.

I hated myself at that moment. Nobody who dumps his girlfriend over text deserves to make her heart flutter the way mine was right then. Once again, pathetic. But he was a sight for sore eyes.

He was straight out of the shower, which made no sense if we were working cattle. Then again, maybe he'd just come in from a run. He was training for a Spartan Race. He'd told me that a few weeks ago. His hair was wild on his head, pointing in every direction like he'd shaken the water off and never combed it, not even with his fingers.

We locked eyes for a few seconds while everyone gawked back and forth. Then irritation flashed across his face. A muscle in his jaw ticked and his nostrils flared. His eyes narrowed to slits, flicking from me to Silas and then to his parents. When everyone pretended like this was totally normal, he stalked over, plopped down next to me, and crossed his arms as if to say *fine, but I don't have to like it.*

"Let us say grace," Bo said and then reached his hands to either side. Jenny slipped hers into his. Blue, who looked momentarily confused and then quickly recovered, slid his into Bo's other hand. Like a chain, around the table, hands linked. I laid mine palm up, waiting for Holden, but he was still slumped in his chair, his right hand in Lemon's but his left balled in a fist on the table.

Everyone turned our way. From the blood rushing to my face, I must've been a nice display of sunset-vibrant pinks and reds.

"Holden," Bo growled.

But even with everyone's eyes on him, Holden still sat, fuming. And in that moment it hit me. I was done being the desperate woman who chased after men while they walked— no, sprinted—in the other direction. It was time to take my own advice and have some self-respect.

"No, it's okay." I pushed back and stood. "Hey, Tally, would you mind trading seats with me?" I hated to make a pregnant girl get up out of her chair but she was the only other person not part of a couple.

She blinked, silent, and I almost thought she hadn't heard. But then she blurted, "Oh. Yeah. Sure."

Once we were settled again, my hand in Anna's, I dared to look at Holden. I shouldn't have. His glare was burning, furious, and if I hadn't known he was really a big teddy bear inside

I might've been a tiny bit terrified. I rolled my eyes as if to say *grow up* and then looked at Bo.

Bo bowed his head and opened his mouth.

The front screen door shut with a bang, stopping the blessing dead in its tracks. Jenny flinched and exhaled.

"Where's my *Mamacita?*" A male voice sang. It must've been Ashton. I'd only met him once, but it sounded like him. Every Dupree at the table broke into a smile. Except for Grumpy Butt Holden. Sure enough, the tall blond, who I realized at that moment resembled Holden more than anyone else in the family, strutted into the room and I couldn't stop from smiling too. He was the sunshine of the Duprees, full of happiness, jokes, and easygoing charm.

When he noticed all the hand-holding he sunk down, a little chagrined. "Oh. Sorry." But he still gave Jenny a quick hug before hurrying to his seat.

As he walked by Holden, he purposely bumped his chair and muttered, "What up, shorty?"

I bit the insides of my cheeks to keep from laughing. Ashton was tall to be sure. Like Silas tall. But Holden wasn't anything to shake a stick at. Probably six foot two. And, yeah, a solid wall of muscle.

Holden shot back, "What up, weenie?"

Ashton sat and reached both hands out, one toward me and one toward Tally. As I laid my palm in his, he offered me a dimpled smile and I couldn't tell how much he knew. Did he know Holden and I were now a thing? *News flash,* my brain interrupted. *You're not a thing. Not anymore.* The bigger question: Did he know about the shirtless kissing and pep rally?

I don't think Ashton even looked at Tally or realized he was holding a stranger's hand until the prayer was done. And if I'd happened to be looking anywhere else, I would've missed the best comedy of the whole day. He glanced at her as he pulled away, and the look on his face was priceless. His eyes flew open and his body jerked like someone had slapped him hard on the back, making him choke on a gobstopper. It only lasted a split second but I knew what had happened. Ashton had a love-at-first-sight moment. And Tally had no clue. And Ashton, who was still goggling, eyes soft, cheeks flushed, didn't know she was fifteen.

I took my gaze off him for a split second to see if anyone else was watching. Holden was. Sitting up in his seat now, the corners of his mouth quirked in a sly smirk. He'd seen exactly what just went down and he was here for it, just like me.

Oh, this was going to be so fun.

SEVENTEEN

HOLDEN

Silas and I were going to wrestle when this was through.

I'd made my wishes extremely clear. I didn't want to discuss the breakup with anyone and I didn't want to see Christy. It was over. Or so I would keep telling myself until I believed it. But for the past week my parents, Silas, and even Lemon had treated my request like a doormat.

"You're going to end up bitter and alone," Mom kept saying.

Dad was a tiny bit kinder. "Don't let a good woman go, son."

Silas was just a d-bag with jabs like, "You're an idiot," and "The amount of jackassery you're emitting right now is embarrassing. You should change your last name," and "Stop being a wuss and running every time things get hard."

Screw him.

It was Lemon's words that had been churning in my head, my stomach, and my heart for the last seventy-two hours. "You love her, Holdie. And she loves you. It's as plain as day. She needs you right now and you're turning your back on her. By the time this is over and the stress has died down and you can think straight again, it might be too late."

But that was the thing. It didn't matter how much I loved Christy—and I'd finally admitted to myself that yes, that was what I was feeling—there wasn't going to be an end to Amber's hate. Not until one of us was in the grave. And if I truly loved Christy, I would not put her through another minute where she was a target for Amber's vitriol. She didn't deserve to be on administrative leave, or not allowed on campus to coach the girls or possibly at risk of losing her job.

I was doing the honorable thing here. My family would see that one day. And Christy would too, ten years down the road when she was married to a better man than me with a couple of kids on her lap. She would look back, wipe a hand across her brow, and say, "Schew, am I glad I dodged that bullet." I just hoped my entire body didn't implode from the pain of it all. Mom didn't need to lose another child.

As she sat across the table, snickering at Ash who had just imprinted on a fifteen-year-old like that gross storyline in *Twilight*, I couldn't take in a full breath. Christy was so beautiful it hurt to look at her. Her blond hair in a braid across her left collarbone, the most stunning smile God ever gave a woman, and eyes so warm I wanted to press a kiss to each lid. To think she was never going to be mine, that I'd never run my fingers over her beautiful face, I'd never kiss those lips again, while she sat mere feet away, was utterly gut-wrenching.

It felt too much like losing Savannah.

My fists curled at the thought. My last therapist told me I had survivor's guilt and the only way to overcome it was to be true to my emotions. And to let myself be okay when I finally let Savannah go in my heart. That's what was happening. I'd felt it over the last few weeks. Christy was settling into the space that Savannah had always occupied. I'd fought it as long as I could. But now, Christy was all I cared about, all I could think about. When I thought of my future, she was what I saw. She and I, a farmhouse on this very ranch, and a houseful of kids that looked just like her. Maybe we'd get a dog. A heeler to help us round those kids up every night. I'd wanted it all. Thought for a split second that I'd get it all.

And then the pep rally happened and she'd been put on administrative leave and I realized Selfish A-hole Holden had struck again. And Christy was dead center in the crosshairs because of it. The point of the breakup was to keep her out of those crosshairs, and yet here she was, enjoying lunch like she was part of the family. I didn't want to think what the repercussions would be if Amber found out.

Yeah, Silas was going down after this. I wouldn't fight him. Mom would kill us both. Maybe I'd just put some Nair in his shampoo bottle. Lemon loved his hair. Was always running her fingers through it. That would definitely cause a stir.

Ashton leaned toward Jailbait and grinned his stupid, cocky smile. "Hey, I'm Ashton. Nice to meet you."

Tally looked over, surprised he was talking to her. She nodded, unimpressed, like *that's nice.* "I'm Tally." Then she looked away, eyes on the roast that Lemon was scooping onto her plate.

How had my idiot brother not noticed that she was pregnant? Or that she was a teenager? Then again, she was sitting on the adult side of the table and her stomach was probably out of his line of sight. And, she looked older than her age, possibly from the unplanned stress of realizing she was going to be a mom while still in high school.

"So are you Christy's friend?" he tried again.

Tally didn't even hear him, she was so fixated on the food headed her way.

Anna opened her mouth but I silenced her with a cough and a knowing look. She smiled but rolled her eyes.

Christy cut in when Tally didn't answer. "You could say that."

I took the platter from Lemon, plopped a large serving on my plate, appreciating the smell of the beef and the buttery potatoes, and passed it to Tally.

Mom glowed at Ashton. "So what boring book are you torturing your students with right now?" Ashton was almost done with his Master's in English lit and he was a T.A. for an honors literature class.

His lips pursed. "Stupid *Jane Eyre*. Shoot me now. If I have to listen to another ditsy freshman fawn over Rochester I will poke myself in the eye with a hot Dupree Ranch brand."

In a shocking turn of events, Tally, who I'd thought might be a selective mute up to this point, glared at him like she might do the branding herself. "You did not just diss my girl, Brontë."

The room went still, silverware stopped clanging, conversation halted, and everyone held their breath. Ashton was normally an annoying ray of sunlight shining right in your eyeball. But disagree with him on a book he felt strongly about, and whoa buddy. And Ashton loathed *Jane Eyre* more than almost any other book in existence. Once, when Lemon was still married to her first husband, Billy, she tried to convert Ashton to the "love story." He almost made her cry, saying that any woman who liked that novel was a masochist and deserved whatever piece of crap man she ended up with. It hit a little too close to home since Lemon's first husband was a piece of crap himself. Hence the near tears. Sophie ripped into him afterward.

The question now was, would Ashton kowtow to his new underage crush? Or would his undying love of literature cause him to die on this hill? Stay tuned. I knew I would.

Ashton leaned back in his chair and sighed the sigh of a haggard man who'd come home from battle only to find his wife in bed with another man and was too tired to care. "Of course," he muttered. "Here we go." He gestured like, *let's get it over with.* "Yeah, I dissed your girl Brontë."

"Are you dead inside?" She held her hands out in a mind-blown gesture. "Jane is a hero for women everywhere."

He folded his arms across his chest and sighed again. "A hero? How so?" Maybe he was going to choose his newfound "love" for Tally over his hatred of Brontë after all?

Tally's face lit up. "She experiences gut-wrenching hardships and continues to be resilient anyway. And she doesn't need a Mr. Darcy to save her. She saves *him.* And she teaches us that just because someone is broken and flawed, it doesn't mean they aren't deserving of love. She's independent and strong but also willing to serve Rochester and take care of him when he needs it."

Ashton cocked a disbelieving brow. "She's independent *and* a servant? Do you even hear yourself?"

Sigh. My guy Ash was going to die on this hill. Christy's eyes were bright but she was biting her lip nervously. It was so incredibly hot.

Tally threw her hands up. "She chooses to love him. Loving someone means you serve them."

Ashton scoffed like he'd never heard anything more absurd. "It's a sick, twisted relationship between a pervy old guy and his child almost-bride. He's a predator who feeds on his prey."

She glowered at him, open-mouthed and horrified. "How dare you say—"

He barreled over her, pounding on the table. "Rochester locks his wife in the attic—"

She jerked back like she was afraid. "He was tricked into marrying Bertha and—"

"*And hides it from Jane,* with every intention of keeping it a secret even as he's standing at the altar." Ash threw his hands up. "And this is the kind of man women everywhere dream of marrying? No wonder the divorce rate is as high as it is." He shrugged, not caring in the least that Tally was leaning away like he'd just crawled out of a sewer. There was a dangerous light in his eyes that said, *this is fun.* "And Jane is annoyingly whiny. Like if I had to listen to her in real life, I'd shove a dirty sock in her mouth. It's a terrible story and anyone who likes it is—"

Lemon shot up, causing the table to screech an inch to the right. Water lopped over glasses, wetting the tablecloth. "Tally, could you help me cut the pies?"

Tally, mouth gaping from watching as Ashton tore her beloved *Jane Eyre* limb from limb, turned to look at her. She blinked.

Lemon nodded toward the refrigerator.

And then—and this is the best moment of the day—Tally pushed back, revealing her basketball-sized stomach, and stood.

Ashton's face went slack as if he'd just been shot in the back.

Christy let out an adorable snort and covered her mouth and nose with her hand.

Once Tally was gone, I leaned over, lifted Ashton's chin to shut his mouth before every bug in Virginia flew in, and hissed, "She's fifteen, dong." I nodded at our niece. "She's Anna's friend."

Christy was silently laughing so hard that a tear leaked from her left eye. Her gaze flicked to me when she realized I was watching. My eyes dashed to my plate as I stabbed a mouthful of Mom's mouthwatering roast.

Anna leaned across the table and whispered at Ashton, "She's about to turn sixteen, though." She shrugged. "If that helps."

Ash's jaw pulsed, his face beet red.

Christy snorted again, another tear escaping down her cheek.

But just then Tally whirled around. "Things were different back then. He wasn't a predator. Men married younger women. If you were half as smart as you pretend to be, you would know that. You shouldn't be teaching a class on a *classic* if you can't even understand the culture of the time period." Then she rolled her eyes and sighed like Ashton's outburst hadn't intimidated her at all. "Also, I've met your mom." She gestured at our wide-eyed mother who looked like she absolutely did not want to be brought into this. "And I'm pretty sure she taught you better than to mansplain your wrongheaded opinions to perfectly intelligent females." She huffed a single laugh. "Completely unimpressive."

Ashton's mouth fell back open but for the first time today, no words came out.

Blue snickered. "Dude. She roasted you." It burst the tension bubble and we all started laughing.

Ashton glared at him. "Who even are you?" His glower swung on Silas like how dare he let Anna bring this imbecile over here.

"This is my boyfriend, Blue," Anna said, proudly.

"Blue?" Ashton guffawed. "You're pulling my leg. Your parents named you *Blue*? Were they high?"

"Ashton!" Mom yelled.

Ashton got his revenge on Blue later when we castrated bulls old-school style down at the barn. Usually, we banded them and let nature take its course. But from the glares Silas kept giving the kid, I was pretty sure we were using a scalpel and our hands for a reason. Poor steers. Or should I say, poor Blue? Belying his name, he looked a little green.

So there Blue was on his knees, in between Dad and Uncle Troy, mid-initiation, hands all over a pair of bull testicles for the first time in his life, when Ashton winked at me and reached into the collection bucket. He pulled out some blood-covered leftovers and flung one onto Blue's cheek. Silas hooted. Blue's jaw pulsed and his nostrils flared but he calmly peeled the dangly bits off his skin and tossed them to the ground. Then he stood, rolled his beefy shoulders back, and just when I thought there might be a barfight in the barn, he picked up the bucket with a sly smile. Before Ashton could take a full get-away stride, Blue hurled the entire contents at Ashton's chest.

Ashton screamed like a little girl and for the first time ever, Silas beamed at Anna's boyfriend. Tally, watching from the railing behind us, cheered her approval. It looked like Blue passed the test. But Ashton had not. Covered in nut juice, he stole a glance at the girl he should not be glancing at.

I cleared my throat and he glanced at me. I shivered and mouthed, *No, man. Stop.* His face went red and he turned away, wiping bloody bits off of his shirt. Bro was having a super off day.

"Si, Holt," Dad nodded toward the field. "Need you and the girls to round up the one that got away. Ropes are on the wall." I didn't miss the wink he gave Silas right before we walked off. What was that about?

Silas grabbed a pair of ropes and we hopped on Fred and Judith, the only two horses still available. Christy, Anna, and Lemon were already in the saddle, chatting as their horses chomped the grass on the other side of the fence.

When we were through the gate, Silas rode up and kissed Lemon on the lips. It was a scene from a wedding invitation both of them wearing their cowboy hats. But he had a worried look in his eye. I was ten feet back but I thought I heard him say, "Please be careful."

Not sure what that was about. Lemon rode on her daddy's lap before she ever learned to walk. But it had taken Silas twenty-eight years to finally win the woman over. It would kill him if anything happened to her.

I glanced at Christy, sitting tall in her saddle like it was second nature, braid trailing down her back, cowgirl hat blocking her face from the afternoon sun. She was a sight to behold. She may have had more hours on a horse than me. The way she held herself, straight-backed, posture long and relaxed, I'd never seen anyone more elegant.

Silas rode around and tossed a rope to Christy. Not me. "Let's round 'em up," he said.

She dug in her heels and rode away.

I threw my hand out. "Dude."

"Nah. You're gonna wanna see this." Then he winked at Lemon. In unison, they squeezed their legs and took off after Christy.

Anna was next. I jammed my hat on my head, clucked my tongue twice, and brought up the rear.

Watching Christy ride was an otherworldly experience. Like I was seeing her in a completely different light. And if I hadn't known I was ridiculously in love with her before, I knew it then. The pain in my chest ratcheted even tighter. I rubbed the middle of my breastbone and forced my breath out slowly, working through the ache.

This was taking way longer than it should've. The cows were nowhere near the barn, even though we'd had them right there earlier. Dad was never careless enough to leave gates open, but all of them were. Wide open. Every single one we came upon.

Of course, the cows had scattered, cutting through every field in between the back of the ranch and the barn. We found them by the perimeter fence, next to the river that divided our ranch from our neighbors. We were about a mile from the work area. Good grief. We could've planned this better.

Once we were all there, Silas nodded for us to go again. We

didn't all need to be here. Not when we had Silas with a rope in his hand. It was more for fun than anything. But it felt good to ride again. I always forgot how much I missed this when I was in DC.

The calf we needed cut hard to the right. Silas held back and let Christy go ahead. She raised the rope above her head, whipped it around three times, and snapped her wrist. The calf came crashing to the ground, knees bent under him, rope perfectly secured around his neck. It was absolute perfection.

"Holden," Silas called.

I shook my head to clear my brain. He nodded for me to get the little guy, who was up on his feet again, bellowing for his momma. I hopped down. The calf kicked in my arms but I clamped down and lifted. Silas, still in the saddle, reached down for the calf. Once we had him situated, I stepped back.

Like a crack of thunder, Silas dug his heels into Fred's flanks and took off, almost knocking me on my butt. I stumbled back, a little embarrassed.

"Okay," I muttered. But when I looked up, I realized everyone was gone but Christy, who seemed as bewildered as I felt. Lemon, Silas, and Anna were galloping away.

And they'd taken my freaking horse.

Anna must've slid a rope around Judith's neck the second I hopped off.

I swore, calling them some names I'd regret later. Maybe.

Christy shook her head, but I could tell from the upturn on her annoyingly kissable lips that she was enjoying this. "Looks like we've been had."

I gritted my teeth. "It would seem so." What was wrong with my family?

She tipped her head, eyes a little sad. "Wanna ride, cowboy?"

I could be really obstinate and walk back, but after my five-mile run that morning and working cows the rest of the day, my legs ached. And my family would laugh even harder if I came sulking back on two legs instead of four. Fine. It would be our first and last ride together.

"Yeah. Okay."

She slid her foot out of the stirrup. I jammed mine in, heaved my body up onto the horse, and settled in behind her. My fists curled for a moment before I reluctantly slid them around her waist. And dang if she didn't let out a little sigh as she settled against my chest. I squeezed my eyes shut for a second. Having her in my arms was the best feeling in the world. It was complete torture.

She clucked her tongue and we were off. We hadn't made it out of the field before I had my nose right next to her hair. Peace tried to swirl in my chest but I kicked it out. Peace was a big, fat liar. But I did tighten my arms, pulling her closer, giving myself one moment. This one right here. Her back brushed against my chest. Desire thrummed through me.

Man, I was so weak. I always was. I hated myself for it. Why couldn't I be like Silas who'd moved nineteen hundred miles to get away from Lemon? The man had a will of iron. But I couldn't even leave Virginia. And with Christy, I couldn't even make myself leave Seddledowne.

Every thought I hadn't let myself think in the last three days, whirled in my mind. Matching gold bands. A future where I got to make love to her every night and wake up next to her every morning. Babies in bed between us. Nights under the stars, watching our kids catch fireflies. Barbecues and floating the river. So much laughter... and hard times too. I knew they'd come. But they wouldn't even be that bad if she was right there with me. Christy made everything better. Easy and light.

I peeled my hat off and rested my nose against the nape of her neck. She didn't flinch at all. Like it was totally okay. Like I hadn't broken her heart with my cowardly breakup text. She was the best woman I'd ever known, even in this. My eyes burned. I knew she could feel my tears on her neck but she didn't even mind. I curled my arms as tight as I could around her waist, melting into her as I cried.

When the horse stopped, I looked up, but everything was a blur. How were we already back at the barn? I wiped my eyes and that's when I realized how hard I'd been crying. Sobbing, actually. I'd soaked the neck of Christy's shirt and she'd just let me, like it was a perfectly normal thing to do.

My family was all there waiting, smiles on their faces like they'd come up with the best scheme of all time. And then they saw my tears. And one by one they looked ashamed.

I heaved myself off the horse without looking at the woman who I could never, ever have.

"I hate all of you," I said with a sob.

Then I turned to Christy but I couldn't meet her eyes. "We're not a thing, okay? We're never going to be a thing. It's over."

And I walked away.

eighteen

CHRISTY

I think I finally got it.

Holden was a deeply broken man.

The way he'd wept into my neck was gut-wrenching. I'd never experienced anything like it before. A full-grown man who could command a courtroom and bench press me three times over, sobbing like a little boy. I hoped I never experienced it again.

Google Savannah Clark was the last thing Lemon said as I got in my car to leave Dupree Ranch. But the look on her face was almost as pained as Holden's had been when he'd walked away. Something terrible had happened. Something way worse than Amber and her stalker antics.

I'd been trying to get up the nerve for the last eighteen hours.

I sat down on the couch and flipped open my laptop. My fingers hovered over the keyboard and I let myself just be for a moment. Finding out about Savannah was going to hurt. There's no way it wouldn't. In my gut, I knew. Holden had loved her. Whoever she was. I didn't know how I was going to deal with that. But I also knew that I had to find out what it was that made him think he was unworthy of happiness.

I held my breath and quickly typed in the name.

Savannah Everly Clark, age seventeen, tragically departed from this world on February 2, 2014, leaving behind a profound sense of sorrow and disbelief among her loved ones. Savannah was a bright, compassionate soul, whose infectious laughter and gentle spirit touched the hearts of all who knew her.

Despite her tender age, Savannah faced insurmountable challenges, battling severe depression and the relentless torment inflicted upon her by a merciless bully. Despite her courageous efforts to persevere, the weight of cruelty proved unbearable, leading to her untimely decision to end her own life.

I sat back, chest tight, eyes burning. There was more, but I couldn't read it right then. I did the math quickly in my head. This would've been Holden's junior year of high school. I'd never seen an obituary call out a bully like that. I opened another tab and typed. *Savannah Everly Clark* and the word *bully*.

Nothing came up except the Suicide and Crisis Lifeline number and another page with her obituary. And a school picture. She was beautiful, but what had I expected? Holden Dupree had dated her. Unless she was just a friend. No. He'd loved her. Desperately and deeply. Enough that her death had ruined women for him. Or was that because of Amber? There was no way for me to know. And from the trail of women he'd benched, I doubted Holden had untangled it all.

I tried using different keywords, hoping to learn more. But there was nothing else. Finally, I finished the obituary.

Savannah is survived by her grandparents, Randall and Dahlia Clark, who raised her, her mother Bethany Clark, her boyfriend, Holden Dupree, and many friends whom she adored.

There it was. A boyfriend beloved enough to be included in an obituary. But why had her grandparents raised her if her mother was listed?

That was it, other than saying when and where the memorial had been held.

I opened Facebook to see if she'd had a page. But there was nothing. She wasn't in Holden's photos. I'd searched every one of them multiple times. I would've remembered her.

After a little wall hopping, I found a photo of Savannah on Jilly's wall. The two were eating ice cream cones, heads together, smiling. They'd been friends? I kept clicking. And then I stopped. A formal dance group photo. There were eight couples all in a line, guys in the back, hugging their date in front of them. Looking dapper, Holden had on a black tux with a pink bow tie and cumberbund to match her dress. Savannah's dress was strapless and sparkly and you could see that she felt like a princess. Hair in a complicated updo, she was stunning. My heart stabbed a little to see Holden with another girl. Even seventeen-year-old Holden. But it wasn't like I'd never dated anyone else. I mean, I dated his brother and he rolled it off like it was nothing. Still, it tugged a little.

I tucked my knee under my chin and studied the picture. Jilly was there with her ultra-white-toothed smile. I balked for a moment when I realized Amber was in the picture. She was down on the end with a guy I didn't recognize. There were plenty of people in this picture I didn't know. But it was her.

I searched like crazy then, through every one of Jilly's pictures. I hopped from wall to wall, scouring photos of people I didn't know, piecing things together as best as I could. The only person's page I hadn't touched was Amber's. The mouse hovered over her name and I studied her profile pic. If you hadn't known she was devious and dark, you might think she was a famous actress. She was that pretty.

I rolled my shoulders and clicked on her profile. Thousands of pictures of her with this person or that, usually with a glass of alcohol in her hand, flashing her perfect smile for the camera. The further back I dug, though, my stomach started to churn. Because once I hit high school, I realized there was a story here. Amber and Savannah had been friends. If the pictures were accurate, close ones. And Jilly too. And a couple of other girls I didn't know.

Holden hated one of Savannah's best friends?

My phone buzzed.

Lemon: Do you think you'll make it?

I sat back for a second and pondered the meaning behind her question. Is Holden worth it? Are you willing to fight for him? Regardless of the bumps and bruises you *will* get, do you have it in you to forgive *whatever* he says and does until this is over?

I thought back to the man weeping into my neck. How could I not fight for someone who loved me so intensely? Who had convinced himself that the only way he could protect me from a deranged woman was to break things off and live his life alone?

I did love him. One hundred percent. I knew that now. That wasn't the real problem here. At twenty-six I was old enough and had seen enough relationships to know that sometimes love isn't enough. And if I thought Amber was the only person I had to face off with, it wouldn't be a question. But to face off with the demons Holden hid deep inside? The demons that were eating him alive?

183

I wasn't sure there was a woman on earth who could win that battle.

I texted Lemon back.

Me: Yes, leaving now.

I quickly changed and headed to an address she'd sent me yesterday.

I was late. I'd taken too long to decide to come and what to wear. I parked my truck next to Silas's, hopped out, and jogged down the trail, wishing I'd worn leggings instead. The wind was chilly for October. But after I got moving, I'd be happy I'd chosen something lighter.

I came up on the group so quietly that no one noticed. Then I smiled, in awe. One of Silas's friends, a guy named Knox Freeman, had an obstacle training course set up on his farm—a spear throw, rings, rope climb, and other things I didn't know the names of. And a running trail that disappeared into the woods. He'd spent a lot of time building this. And it was super generous of him to let everyone practice here.

A quick count told me there were eleven people besides me. Silas was teaching Lemon how to hold the spear. Then, with his hand over hers, they launched it at a hay bale with a spray-painted target. It landed inside the circle and I smiled. It was crazy to think I'd ever been broken up about that man. And now I was totally happy watching him with his gorgeous wife.

It had occurred to me recently that I was no better than my mom when it came to finding reasons to marry someone. I'd liked Silas. He'd been my best friend. But love? Hardly. I'd wanted to get married and he was a great guy. Had I thought I loved him? Yes. Or I'd told myself I had. But important things were missing in our relationship. Passion, for one. And the ability to communicate without us both getting flustered. Two pretty important things needed to make a lifelong commitment work.

You don't get over love as quickly as I had. Not if it's real.

A sick thought pitted my stomach. What if I'd married Silas and we'd never known what real love was? An even more terrible thought—what if I'd watched Holden from afar my whole marriage and felt for him what I do now? It would've been like a bad nightmare, only you wake up every day and it's real.

It was like Gabby and Rowan's cheesy first dance song, "Unanswered Prayers." At the wedding, that song had sent me into a fit, sobbing in the coat room when no one was looking. But now, I got it. Holden was my cheesy love song.

Holden. Who was currently swinging across the rings like Tarzan, biceps popping out of his shirt.

Standing here, my eyes flitting over everyone and the obstacles they were conquering, made me cave in a little. I didn't know how to run an obstacle course race. They made it look easy, but I was certain none of this was in my wheelhouse.

"Hey." Lemon walked up wearing the leggings I wished I had. "Glad you could make it."

Silas was right behind her. I was thankful they were both tall, forming a wall between me and Holden. I wasn't ready for him to see me yet.

"Did you look up Savannah?" Silas asked, studying me.

I scratched my temple. "Yeah. It's..." My hand pressed against my chest. "Heartbreaking. The obituary said she was bullied to death?"

He rubbed his neck. "Yeah. Basically. Suicide isn't murder. She chose to do that to herself. But yes, she was pushed to her limits. No doubt." I wanted to ask who the bully was, but it didn't feel like the time. Or maybe Silas wasn't who I needed to ask.

I hugged myself and rubbed my arms covered in goosebumps. "That must've been so hard. I can't believe he had to go through that."

Silas rubbed his jaw. "It was. And clearly, he's still got scars. And if you're not up for this, that's okay."

I scowled and laughed to cover my smarting cheeks. "You think I can't handle this?"

"I know you can. But do you *want* to? It might be harder than you realize. It probably will be. Like today, he's in a foul mood. That's what he does when he's hurting. He covers it up by being a douche."

I looked past them at all the obstacles. Holden was flying across those rings again, oblivious to me invading his hobby. "If you're talking about this race, I don't know."

Lemon put a hand on my arm. "Don't worry. It's only a 5K and you don't have to run the whole thing. You can walk some of it if you need to. I might have to. I've never done this before."

"Me neither," Silas admitted.

"Hold up. Neither of you have done one of these?"

They shook their heads.

"Why are we doing this then?" I hissed. Even though Silas could probably hop up and run a 5K without ever training.

Silas pursed his lips, eyes wide like *use your head, Christy.*

It was all about Operation Save Holden From Himself. They weren't doing this insane-looking race for fun. They were doing it so *I* would.

I shook my head. "You Duprees are something else."

Silas shrugged. "We fight for each other, is all." He shifted his weight. "But you're not a Dupree. You don't have to do this."

I bit my lip, certain I was going to regret this in more ways than one. "I don't think I have a choice."

"That's what I told Silas," Lemon said, relieved. "You love him too much not to try, right?"

I kind of hated how she saw straight through me.

"There's always a choice. Just because you love him doesn't mean you have to sink with the ship. We all learned that a long time ago." Silas's tone was slightly intense. It was unusual for him, and I wondered if it was the love he had for Holden or because he was frustrated with his brother.

Twenty yards away, the guy who must've been in charge hollered for everyone to line up next to where he was standing. But I was perfectly okay with letting them go on ahead. I didn't need anyone watching me run.

"What's going on?"

Crap. I hadn't seen Holden walk up.

He stepped to the other side of Lemon and groaned. At me. "What are you doing here?"

His stance was taut, like he wanted to bolt, and not because of the race. Once again, I detested my traitorous body that couldn't stop reacting at the mere sight of him. Heart swooshing, electricity pulsing, breath hitching, hands tingling. All of it.

I folded my arms over my chest as he sized me up, taking in my running shorts and tennis shoes.

Irritation flashed across his face and he glared at me before swinging it on Silas. "She's a terrible runner, moron. She can't do this. You're setting her up to fail." Then his hate-filled glower narrowed even more as he aimed it at me and his shoulders rolled back, arrogance dripping off of him. "Seriously? You want me so badly that you'd use a 5K as a ruse just to be near me. Christy, c'mon, you suck at running."

Heat flooded my chest and my blood boiled. My eyes were stinging a little too, I won't lie. I looked at Silas and Lemon. "Oh, game on. I am doing this." Then I stepped past Holden, slapped him on the back of the head, and called him a nasty name.

Silas guffawed as Holden yelled, "Ouch!"

I walked away, straight and tall, faking every bit of confidence I had. They bickered in hushed voices. Silas had been right to grill me and make sure I was up for this because, at that very moment, I was torn: leave this place and never see Holden Dupree again, or kick everyone's butts in this race?

"It's not going to work," I heard Holden hiss at him before I was out of earshot. "You really think I'm stupid enough not to know what you're doing? You're all pathetic."

Big exhale and a neck crack. Kick everyone's butts it was.

I sidled up to the edge of the group. I didn't know a single one of them, but they smiled and welcomed me anyway. The main dude, a tall barrel of a guy with black hair, a beard, and tattoo sleeves, stood on tiptoes trying to see if the Duprees were going to stop bickering and join us. I studied my fingernails.

A gorgeous brunette walked over. "Hey, I'm Peyton Jamerson. I'm one of the instructors at Lemon's Barre studio."

"Hi." I smiled, pushing all the hurt down. "It's nice to meet you. Christy Thornbury."

Her eyes widened and her jaw dropped. Oh crap. "You're Silas's ex." Her hand covered her mouth like she shouldn't have said that. That wasn't what I'd thought she was going to say. I was so far past Silas it hadn't even occurred to me that might be what I was known for around here.

Another lady said, "Keep up, Peyt. Nobody's talking about that part. She's the *principal* at the high school." She said it like that should tell Peyton everything she needed to know about me.

"Was." A short, stocky guy added.

Wow. I blinked. Maybe I wouldn't be able to do this after all.

Peyton's eyes went even wider. "You're the one who was kissing Holden without his shirt on in your office."

I blew out my breath, willing my heart to slow. May as well own it. "Guilty."

Her shock turned to awe like I was some kind of movie star. "Oh my gosh. I can't believe you kissed Holden Dupree without his shirt on." She squealed and danced on her tiptoes.

How old was this woman? Because she was acting like a twelve-year-old girl. She reached out, pressed her pointer finger to my skin, and closed her eyes. Was she humming?

"Peyt, what are you doing? Leave her alone." An almost cute guy walked up and put his arm around her waist, trying to pull her away.

She smacked at him, pried one eye open, and scowled. "I'm trying to learn through osmosis. I need whatever she's got so I can become the kind of woman who's confident enough to date brothers, goes at it on her desk with the town's biggest hottie, the whole world finds out, and she doesn't even care."

Everyone was watching like I was a sideshow freak.

I crossed my feet, wishing I could hide. "I wouldn't say I don't care."

Peyton shushed me and kept her finger right at the inner crease of my elbow and forearm, eyes closed, totally still. I looked around, hoping someone would help. But everyone was too busy sniggering. Except for the big tattoed guy. He was eyeing me like a juicy steak.

"Okay, Peyt." Lemon took her by the shoulders and moved her away from me. "Honey, you have to stop that poking thing you've been doing. It makes people uncomfortable."

The guy Peyton was with had his head in his hand, looking like he wished he could die as he led her away.

Tattoos motioned everyone in. "All right, guys, start your watches. The loop is one mile, so keep that in mind. You might get lapped, and that's okay." His southern accent was so thick, and he spoke so fast that I had to really focus to under-stand what he was saying. "We're all at different levels here. No judgment. Just do your best. And let's encourage each other. Team Who Sparted on three." What was happening? What had he just said? Before I could figure it out, he barked "three" and they all yelled, "Who Sparted!"

Wait? That was the team name? Who Sparted? For real? A snort escaped my nostrils. As everyone took off, I stayed, bent over, belly laughing.

"Aren't you gonna run?"

I looked over to see Holden watching me. I thought he was long gone.

"Yes." I stood, wiped my eyes, and fanned my face. "I am." Another giggle escaped.

He tipped his head toward the trail like he didn't believe me. "Well. Get a move on."

I put my hands on my hips. "*You* get a move on. I'm not running with you behind me, judging how my foot hits the ground or how long my stride is." In his current state, I knew that's what he'd do. I made a scooting motion with my hands. "Go. Get."

He rolled his eyes and took off in a burst, like a freaking cheetah. Okay. So maybe I wouldn't be kicking everyone's butts. Possibly not anyone's. But I was still doing this. If for nothing else than to prove to myself that I could.

Once he was out of sight, I clicked my watch and began jogging.

A half mile in and I was not doing this. My lungs burned and my quads were locking up. What was wrong with my stupid body that it couldn't run? No one else seemed to be having a hard time. I'd hoped maybe Lemon might struggle, but her complete absence said otherwise. I forced myself to keep going until I got to the top of the next hill. When I was finally there, I stopped and dunked my head between my knees, gulping air.

"Coming through," the short guy yelled. I stood up and jumped out of the way as he flew past. What? How could someone with legs that short be that fast? It wasn't physically possible. I was glad I'd jumped left. To the right and I would've fallen down a small cliff. Not deep enough to do damage but it would be hard to crawl out of.

Tattoos was right behind him, already with his shirt off. I had to look away, because his shorts were hanging low enough that it was verging on pornographic. My face lit on fire. He gave me a smug grin and I was pretty sure he thought I was checking him out.

"You okay?" He tossed over his shoulder as he passed.

"Doing great." I gave him a wave. Then he sped up and disappeared through the trees.

Dang it. Holden was coming up the hill. And he was shirtless too. Seriously? Where were they storing them? Was there a shirt fairy around here who magically flew up, took your shirt, and stored it for you until you needed it back? He'd started almost last and he'd passed all those people? How was that even possible? If there'd been a bush to hide behind, I would've dove for it. Instead, I ran faster than I had before, as if it somehow made up for the fact that I was an entire mile behind him.

"Chris." He slowed to my pitiful pace and I hated how much I liked it when he called me that, even and especially in this humiliating moment. "What are you doing? You're a mile behind everyone else. You've never wanted to do one of these races. Why are you killing yourself for this?"

"Just leave me—" Gasp. "Alone—" Gulp. "And run."

But he matched my turtle-like speed, shaking his head and muttering angrily. But I couldn't hear any of it over my thunderous heartbeat whooshing in my ears. Finally, when my lungs couldn't anymore, I stopped, certain there was no way cocky Holden Dupree would stop too. Not in the middle of his all-important Spartan Race training. But he did.

He turned to face me, hands on his stupid sexy hips, which were right there in all their hot, chiseled nakedness, his tattoo making a cameo appearance. My T-shirt was drenched, disgusting, and smelled like Taco Bell, and he glistened like he'd only walked around the block.

He threw his hands up, incensed. "It's not gonna work, okay? We're not getting back together. Ever. So just stop. Go home, eat a tub of ice cream like I know you're dying to, and let me run this race in peace." His tone was even meaner than his words. And they were full of finality.

I stared at him, aghast, for two breathless heartbeats.

We both turned when we heard footsteps. Silas and Lemon were maybe forty feet away and their expressions said they'd heard it too.

I turned back to him, my chest rising and falling, but not just because I was trying to catch up on air. "You're a jackass, Holden Dupree. The biggest one I've ever met. And you're right. It *is* over. I wouldn't take you back if you begged me to." Then I shoved him hard in the chest and took off again.

My tears mingled with my sweat. I wiped frantically. I was coming down the hill now and needed to see where to place my feet. Gravity was my new best friend, I ran down that hill like I was being chased by the mafia or a grizzly bear. And it felt amazing.

But if that was true, why was I sobbing?

I knew exactly why.

Because I'd meant every word I said.

nineteen

HOLDEN

Christy's last sentence would've shot a bolt of panic through me if the very next second I hadn't found myself tumbling, backward, full somersault down the side of a cliff. I hit the bottom feet first but the momentum thrust me back and I landed hard on my butt in a puddle of sticks, decaying leaves, and mud.

Silas leaned over the edge of the cliff, wearing a stern, disappointed expression. "You know, for a guy who lost his first love because of a bully, I'd have thought you wouldn't ever do that to someone else. Especially someone we all know you're in love with."

It felt like my lungs buckled under the weight of his words. One word, really. *Bully?* Had I bullied Christy?

"Holden," he said with intense frustration. "I never would've handed you the crown if I'd thought you were going to treat Christy like this. She's already been through too much. You know that."

"I don't want your stupid crown!" I yelled. But it wasn't true. I just needed him off my back for two seconds so I could breathe. I wanted that damn crown! Wanted to be the next sucker so stupidly in love that he was drunk at the mere touch of the right woman. I mean, I was that sucker, I just couldn't chill long enough to let myself be fully inebriated.

The fear of losing Christy had dug in like a spiral ground anchor and I didn't know how to unwind it without tearing myself apart. The word bully had never been associated with the name Holden Dupree until that day. But Silas wasn't wrong. Bullying her was exactly what I'd just done.

Right next to her ear, I'd hissed words to make her doubt herself and feel worthless, exactly how Amber had worn Savannah down. Like I was Satan himself. In all my misplaced determination to make sure Christy didn't get hurt, I'd just hurt her as much as Rowan or Silas ever had. What was wrong with me?

I could've asked my brother for a hand up but the truth was, I couldn't meet his eyes. And he might've denied help anyway. Christy's words sliced through me. *I wouldn't take you back if you begged me to.* Panic hit, like a life-saving jolt to my stupid, stupid heart. Because that was the moment I realized that a life without Christy, dead or alive, wasn't something I had the strength to face.

Savannah had chosen to end her life. No matter how hard I'd tried. No matter how many times I told her I loved her, she'd chosen to believe the lies Amber fed her. But Christy was here, vibrant and alive. And she'd chosen me. An idiot who didn't deserve her. Heart in her outstretched hands, she'd offered it up, willing me to take it.

And I'd slapped it away.

She'd come to run a race she didn't want to run just to show she cared. And I'd acted like some arrogant tool, throwing it in her face. I had to fix this.

Now.

I turned to the right, away from the cliff and toward the

river. The water swallowed my feet like an arctic plunge but I kept going. Running toward the woman I'd just broken with my selfishness and fears. Once I was waist-deep, I plugged my nose and dove backward to get the muck off of my backside. With a frigid blast, the river covered me in a cleansing baptismal wave. A thousand pinpricks to the skin. I shot out of the glacial water with a gasp, and the cold air forced a blanket of painful goosebumps to appear, head to toe. I emerged, shoes sloshing against the mud on the opposite bank. Head tucked to brace against the cold, I sprinted, cutting across a field, only stopping to grab my dry shirt off the top of the fence post I'd left it on. By the time I reached the grassy knoll we used as a parking area, heat was spreading through my limbs, warming me back up.

Good, Christy's truck was still here. By the look on her face right before she pushed me, I'd thought she might leave and I'd never see her again. For all I knew, her mom had finally gotten into her head enough to convince her to come home. And since she was practically jobless, maybe it was the last straw and she'd go.

I raced toward the obstacle course area. When I arrived my shoulders sank in relief. She was there. But she was leaving. Her phone and keys in hand, she was chatting with Lemon and Knox. Lemon must've taken off after Christy as soon as I went backward off the cliff. The fact that my awesome sister-in-law, who'd known me since I was in diapers, hadn't hung around to make sure I was okay, spoke volumes about my behavior.

I wasn't close enough to hear the conversation, so I stretched my legs and strained to catch whatever I could. Christy's eyes skittered to me, still red, the hurt still raw. She looked away. And it killed me that I'd caused that. As she listened to what they were saying, she pressed her fingers to her lips, forehead creased. Knox, who needed to put his stupid shirt on and pull his freaking shorts up, said something and she nodded. I did not like the way he was watching her, eyes greedy, lips tugged in a smirk.

I stretched my right arm across my body, using my left hand. From the keywords I managed to pick up, they were telling her to go to the doctor and get an inhaler. She probably had asthma and just didn't know it. And from the expression on her face, she looked like she was mid-revelation from God himself. It had clearly never occurred to her.

I'd never run with Christy before today, but I was pretty sure they were right. She lifted a lot of weights. She was toned and strong. And maybe her lungs weren't as seasoned as someone who ran often, but she should've been able to go farther than she had without looking like she might pass out.

"Okay. Thanks, guys. I'll make an appointment. Hope-fully, that will fix things."

Lemon waved and took off for the trail again.

"Hey." Knox caught Christy by the elbow. Um, what was happening? "You should stay and work on the obstacles. I can help you."

Christy's big brown eyes pinged to me and then back to him. But I couldn't tell what she was thinking. "I don't want to keep you. I know you need to finish your laps."

He waved that off. "No worries. I can run anytime. It's my place." He gave a stupid, cocky laugh. It was his dad's place. "I don't mind. And running won't be hard when you get an inhaler. But the spear throw can be kind of tough to get. And the rings. The earlier you get started the better."

She rubbed her neck and I knew that tell. That's what she did when she was nervous or uncomfortable. Her other tell was pressing her hands against her cheeks. But I wasn't sure if she was nervous because of Knox or if she thought I might heckle her again.

"Yeah. Okay." She set her phone and keys down against a

tree and followed him to the rings. So I walked to the spear throw thirty feet away, keeping them in my periphery. I picked up the spear, attached to a broom handle, and let it rest on top of my palm.

Knox climbed to the top of the tractor tires in two seconds. "Okay. Watch how I do it." He leaned out, skipping the first two rings, grabbing the third, and then flew across the rest, skipping every other, so fast, that I doubted it was helpful at all. When he reached the last one, he hung, one-handed and then let his fingers release in a calculated one-by-one maneuver until he was only holding on with the pointer finger on his right hand. She fawned a little, giving him what he wanted. Then he dropped with a grin.

I scoffed under my breath. It was a slick, show-off move but it wasn't going to help Christy in the race. *Moron.*

"All right." She let out a nervous laugh. As she climbed up the tires in her shorts, which were way too short, he watched and I could almost see the dirty thoughts playing in his mind. Man, she did have great legs though. She wobbled at the top and squealed.

He reached out and caught her toned thighs with his ginormous palms, laughing. "I gotcha."

I bet you do, Randy.

I needed to chill. Knox was my buddy. At least he had been until ten minutes ago. Then again, being buddies meant I knew the way he talked about women. And it was not something I'd want my mother to hear. Or my girl to experience.

She's not my girl, I reminded myself.

"Okay." He stepped back. "Let's see what you've got."

But I was pretty sure from the look on her face that Christy had nothing.

She reached for the first ring, wrapped her petite fingers around it, and almost fell before she was ready, only hanging onto the tires by the tips of her tennis-shoed toes. Knox reached up and wrapped his hands around her tiny, flat waist, which was peeking out from beneath the hem of her tank top. And I swear his beefy left thumb rubbed a quick circle on her stomach.

I was going to break his stupid face.

Once she'd pulled herself back up, and got resituated, she dropped off the edge with too much thrust. She never made it past the third ring. But I was pretty sure that's what Knox had been hoping for. He caught her in his arms, right against his bare chest, and set her blithely on the ground.

"Why don't you give it another shot. And this time, don't come off the tires quite so fast. Just let yourself gently drop off." Which is the opposite of what he had done.

Pfft.

After two more spectacular fails, and Knox catching her in his arms, Christy climbed the tires again, looking a little defeated. I'd already figured out the problem, but I wasn't sure she'd want my input. If Knox was actually trying to be helpful instead of using this to make her swoon, he'd know too.

And if his hand slipped up under her shirt one more time, she was going to get a lot more than my input. She was going to get a show. Two idiots fist-fighting like we were in a bar. And I fully intended to come out as the winner.

"Whatcha doing?" Silas whispered, suddenly next to me. I hadn't realized he'd finished his loop. Or that I'd completely left the spear throw and was now standing twenty feet behind Knox like a self-proclaimed obstacle course judge.

I scratched my forehead. "Uh. Knox is teaching her how to do the rings," I said as if it wasn't obvious.

"Yes," he agreed. "And why are you standing here watching when you're supposed to be running?"

I scratched my jaw. "Because."

"Because?"

"I don't want to leave him alone with her, Tweedledee," I seethed. He knew how Knox was with women.

"Well, Tweedledum. You can't have it both ways. You don't get to dump her, treat her like gum on the bottom of your shoe, and then hover like a jealous boyfriend. That's not how that works. You have to pick. And from what she said earlier, I think being her boyfriend is now off the table."

I glared at him. "And you're here talking to me when you should be running, why?"

"Because you look a little dangerous and I want to make sure you don't get your butt handed to you after you tackle Knox to the ground."

I snorted. "Whatever."

"C'mon little brother. Whatdya say you make your first smart decision of the day and we take a lap before you go all fisticuffs and get half your teeth knocked out? Mom and Dad paid a lot for that pretty smile."

"No." My jaw clenched. "I'm not leaving her alone with him."

He sighed and stayed put.

The next time Knox caught her, my fists balled and I blew out my breath, trying to burn holes into his skull with my glare.

"Yo, Knox," Silas called with an under-the-breath chuckle. He tipped his head for Knox to come to us. "I'm going to save you from your stupid self," he muttered as Knox walked over. "Go," he ordered, tipping his head toward Christy who was dangling from the second ring.

I caught her just as she dropped. She looked up at me, surprised and then she shrunk back right before I set her on her feet.

"Hey." I caught her by the hand and pulled her against my chest. Her almond-shaped eyes, which were normally two cupid-arrows, harpooning me and pulling me in, turned to fire. "I'm sorry I acted like—"

"A total jerk?" Her voice shook.

"Yes. Chris, I'm so sorry." I rubbed my thumb over her knuckles and squeezed my eyes shut for a split second. When she didn't move, I slid a hand around her waist and pulled her against me, breathing her in. I needed that honey-scented shampoo to fill my nostrils, and when it did, peace filled my chest. And for once I let it stay.

But just as I was about to square her hips with mine, she stepped out of my arms, her brow puckering. "No. I meant what I said. I'm done. No more yanking me around like a yo-yo. I need a very long break from men." She shook her head, lips pursed like she was puzzling something out in her mind. "The ones I keep picking are always in love with somebody else."

My entire body tensed. "I'm not in love with somebody else. What are you talking about?" Didn't she know she was the first woman I'd loved in...forever?

She crossed her arms, lips twisted. "I'm pretty sure you are."

My mind was blown and my ribcage felt like it was being cranked in a vice. "What are you talking about?"

"Don't you mean, *who*?" She stepped up and put a hand on my arm, eyes boring into me. "*Savannah*, Holden."

I stiffened, feeling like someone had ripped all my clothes off with a hard yank. Completely exposed. "How do you know about her?"

She stared at me for two uncomfortable seconds, but I already knew. Silas and Lemon. Her hand moved over and pressed against the center of my chest. "The question is, why didn't *you* tell me about her?"

I blinked, no words, my heart crawling into my throat.

She held my gaze. "You're in love with her still. And that's okay. But don't you think I deserve someone who loves me more than anyone else? Someone who isn't always keeping me at arm's length because their heart is already taken?"

I opened my mouth but I couldn't talk.

She balled my shirt in her fist. "I wish someone loved me so much that they would give up an entire decade of relationships just to keep me locked in a vault in the deepest part of their heart." Her hands flew out. "Or never kiss another woman first because if they did, it would be a betrayal of that love." Her head cocked, her gaze so intense. "I want that. *All* of it. And I'm going to get it or I want nothing at all. And if that means that I wait until I'm seventy before I find that kind of love, then that's what it means. But I'm not settling. Not anymore. Not now that I know what love actually feels like."

From the first line, her words were a knife, digging deeper and deeper into my chest. But the fact that she now knew real love because of what we'd felt for each other, and I was going to lose her because I'd been such a heel, was the final stab.

Her eyes turned down, full of pity. "Maybe another woman would be okay with sharing your heart. But I'm not. Call it selfish if you want." She shrugged. "Then I'm selfish."

She stepped back, a goodbye in her eyes.

The panic of earlier rushed me like a tidal wave.

"Christy." My hands shot out, cupping the back of her elbows. "I love y—"

Her fingers pressed to my lips. "No. Don't. Don't you dare say that to me right now."

I knew what she meant. Don't say it out of desperation. Or manipulation. At that moment, I hated that I'd almost done that. But I did love her. Deliriously. Shouldn't she know that?

As if she'd read my mind she said, "Actions speak so much louder than words. And yours are deafening." She squeezed my biceps and gave me one last look. "You can't keep us both and you won't let her go. So this is goodbye, Holden."

Then she walked over, picked up her keys and her phone, and disappeared down the trail.

And I stood there watching, like a paralyzed mute. Because she was right. She deserved all of that.

And I wasn't ready to give it to her.

Not yet.

twenty

CHRISTY

'd worn my arms out over the last two weeks, but I'd finally conquered the rings. Holden had texted me every day, begging my forgiveness. And he'd even offered to skip the competitive heat and run the open heat with me. But I didn't know if that's what I wanted. I wasn't even sure I wanted to run the race. But I wasn't a quitter. I was raised to see things through.

If I'd taken Knox up on his offer to meet up during the day, when the rest of the group wasn't there, I might've gotten it faster. I also might've gotten myself scandalized by a very large, tattooed firefighter whose gaze said he had a thousand ideas of what we could do in those woods when no one was around. So no. It was Lemon, of all people, who'd helped me figure things out. I'd been killing my momentum, by letting go too soon. I needed to let myself get as far back in my swing as I could before letting go with one hand and reaching for the next ring.

Honestly, it was a leap of faith the first time I'd done it, convinced I was going to fall. But then when it worked and I realized I was swinging like a monkey, a fire had lit under me. I had no idea how I'd do in the race but I knew I could do those dang rings. And they were really fun.

I drummed my fingers against the steering wheel of my truck, pondering the race as I tried to get up the nerve to walk inside the high school. The school board had let me know that morning that I was allowed back inside, finally. Still not allowed to coach or work. But come inside, yes. And twenty-five of the Lady Stallions had texted today asking if I was coming to the big game tonight. The only one who hadn't was Mari and that's because she didn't have a phone yet. Her parents said she had to be sixteen.

They said it was all over school that I was allowed back in. And it was their last game of the regular season. Ming specifically said she needed *her* coach to be there for her last game, ever. Maybe. Unless they won and went to the Riverbend District playoffs. How could I turn that down?

But the school board was also meeting tonight, in the auditorium, to discuss my fate. Silas was invited to come. I was not. But I was allowed to write a letter of explanation, which I'd given to Silas a few hours ago.

The school loomed in front of me and it almost felt like if I stepped inside, I'd jinx everyone. Me *and* the girls. My luck had not been favorable since moving to this place. Or maybe I was just the unlucky type.

My phone rang and I let out a breath before answering. "Hi, Mom."

"Hi, Christianna. Your father and I just wanted to wish you good luck tonight," she said, a sadness in her voice. "You're on speaker."

"Hey, Dad."

"Hey, darling. How're you holding up?"

A small exhale. "I don't know. Okay, I guess."

"I don't know why you don't just pack up and come

home," Mom said. "No one here would treat you the way they have?"

I rolled my eyes. "I got caught on camera, making out with a shirtless man on top of my desk in my office. Laramie probably would've reacted much worse."

Mom huffed. "Do you really have to put it like that?"

"Like what? Plainly and truthfully? I'm not going to make excuses for what I did. It is what it is."

"Well. I still think it's abominable that Silas was made—"

"How're the cows, Dad?" Rude? Maybe. But I didn't want to argue about how Silas was principal now. Honestly, Silas was ridiculously proficient at administration. And from what Mrs. Ross had told me, he was killing it.

While my dad went on a tangent about cattle prices, water rights, and the drought they'd been in for the past two years, I massaged my temples.

"Dallen," Mom interrupted. "She doesn't actually care. She just gets you off on a tangent so she can say she 'did her time' on the phone, and then hop off without telling us anything that's really going on. You fall for it every time." I heard her smack him with something. A magazine or the newspaper, I wasn't sure. But I didn't like it.

"Mom. Be nice to him. I'll tell you whatever you want to know." But my blood was simmering a bit. Yes, I did those things, but only to keep my nerves from exploding every time she called.

"*Whatever* I want to know?" She asked, disbelief dripping in her tone. "Fine. Did you know Holden was fired from his job in DC and that's why he's in Seddledowne?"

I exhaled through my nose. "Yes, I knew right after it happened. But how do *you* know that?"

"Ari told us. But why didn't you tell us?" she whined.

My fingers gripped the steering wheel. "And how did Ari find out?"

"On Giggle."

A snort escaped but I was too mad to laugh. "You mean, *Google*?"

"She's right," Dad said. "It's Google. Not Giggle."

"It doesn't matter," Mom huffed. "The point is that Christy is dating an unemployed man."

My chest tightened. "So little miss nosey butt Ari decided she's suddenly a detective?"

"Honey," Dad said in a calm voice. "She was just on edge because Holden made her—"

"Shhhh," Mom said in a deafening whisper. "She's not supposed to know he called."

My hand flew out, and I sat up, ramrod straight. "Excuse me, what? Holden called you guys?"

Mom whacked him again. "See what you did now?"

"Mom, if you don't stop hitting Dad I'm hanging up. Did Holden call you guys?"

"Yes," was all she said.

"When?"

"The other day," she said barely loud enough for me to hear.

"Be more specific." I was losing it with the teeth pulling. The game was about to start.

"Sunday, honey," Dad admitted. "A couple of hours after Ari announced on that Facebook website that she was naming the baby Madeleine Rose."

Two days ago. Which was twelve days after I'd shoved him off the mini-cliff. This was becoming more of a head scratcher the further it went.

"Why did he call?" was my next question.

"Well." Mom started. "He had several things to say."

I rolled my wrist, willing her to speed up. "Such as?"

"I can't," Mom said in her prissy voice. The one she got whenever someone found a dead mouse in the basement and she refused to be the one to remove it. "I will not repeat his words."

My brow crinkled. What on earth? "Spill it. My girls are about to play. I want every word, verbatim."

A couple of seconds of undecipherable hissing back and forth and then Dad started, "Basically, he said three things. First, that it was bullcrap—only he didn't use that word—the way we handled things when Rowan and Gabby got together. And that you should've been allowed to come home early and whatever the hell else you wanted." Mom hissed something in the background. Dad continued, "I'm sorry but he definitely used the word hell. I remember that very clearly." My hand was over my mouth. "And secondly, to make sure that Ari knew that she could use the name Madeleine Rose if she wanted—because you can't copyright a name—but if she did, there would be two Madeleine Rose's in this family whenever you two had your first baby girl. And he didn't care if it pissed her off. And to get over it because she *knew* that was your name. And she was just being a jealous...your mom won't let me repeat that one."

My jaw was on the floorboard. "Hold up." My brain was racing. There were so many things I wanted to pick apart. But first things first. "He said the two of us?"

"Like twenty times. Why is that surprising?" Mom finally spoke. I'd never told them we broke up. I didn't want to deal with the fallout. But why would Holden say all of that like we had some kind of future together? "Anyway, that man swears like a trucker. Are you sure you want to marry him? You'll be washing your kid's mouths out on a daily basis."

I never said I wanted to marry him. But her mention of it wasn't a surprise. Mom's brain went straight to marriage no matter who we dated. *Are you sure you really want to marry a future game warden? You'll be poor for the rest of your life.* That had been Gabby's freshman-year boyfriend. *Are you sure you want to marry a guy with the last name Tucker? That could go wrong in so many ways.* Ari's first boyfriend in seventh grade. *Are you sure you want to marry a boy from Virginia? That's so far from Wyoming.* She'd said when I first told her about Silas.

"He only swears when he's really mad," I said. He said *the two of us* like *twenty times?* I was still hung up on that. Had he not heard what I'd said before I walked away? I gazed out the window as people walked into the game. "Okay. What was the third thing?"

"Oh." Dad chuckled. "The third was him threatening us with our lives if we ever told you that he called and said all those things. I guess we kind of botched that."

"I'd say." I smiled for the first time that day. "And what did Ari say when you told her about the baby name?"

Dad laughed loudly. "Oh, well, talk about swearing like a trucker."

"Is she still using the baby name though?" That's what really mattered.

"I doubt it," Mom said. "But Christy, why didn't *you* say anything when she told you she was using it?"

Seriously? The way she said it irked me. Like she was in total shock. Like I was expected to express my feelings in this family. Had she not paid attention all these years? "Because, Mom. I'm Christianna. The oldest. The one who bends to what everyone else wants. I always do the right thing. I always apologize first and bow out of an argument to keep the peace and give up my seat at the table and give up my bed when Grandma visits. I fold the laundry, do the dishes, drive the youngers to all their lessons and I'm the one who had to get straight A's. Even while Gabby and Ari were flunking Biology and Pre-Algebra."

My parents must've been stunned speechless because there was only silence as a response.

I took it as an invitation to continue. "Because that's what you wanted, Mom. When Gabby and Rowan announced they were together on the Maui trip, you made me suck it up. And when I said it was too much and I didn't want to come to the wedding, you made me the Maid of Honor. Because you don't care about my feelings. You never have."

"Oh, honey," Mom said, crying. "That's not true."

I don't know what had gotten into me. Maybe it was something in the water here. Maybe it was because I'd already disappointed them when I got caught on the shirtless kissing cam. But I'd had enough of all the bullcrap. If I wanted to be different, to have a man who respected me, it started with me. I had to respect myself. And today seemed as good a day as any to begin.

"It is, Mom. And you telling me that it's not is gaslighting. You can look that term up later on Giggle if you'd like. But those are the facts. That's what happened. And I'm sorry if it hurts you to hear it but it's the truth."

"So," Dad said with a touch of humor in his voice. That was Dad's way and I usually loved it. But not tonight. "What you're saying is that you're probably not excited to move back here next year?"

"Move back?" I said, shocked. "I'm not moving back. Are you kidding me?"

"But Christy?" Mom sniffled. "This is *home*."

I shook my head even though she couldn't see. "Not anymore. Not for me." I didn't know if I'd stay in this town either. With the way things were, probably not. But I'd gotten a taste of freedom—not placating everyone, being whoever I wanted to be, not having them criticize my every move—and I wasn't ready to give that up. Nothing against Laramie, but my family had a long way to go before I'd ever want to live near them again. If I ever did. "I'll come home for short visits but I'm afraid that's as good as it's going to get. You might want to get used to trips to Virginia. The leaves are stunning right now. I think you'd really like it, Mom." The game had already started. "I need to go and you probably need time to process. I do love you guys. I hope you know that."

Mom was ugly crying. I couldn't see her, but the hiccuping sobs coming through the phone told all.

"Good luck tonight, darling," Dad said over her wailing. "And make sure you let us know what happens?"

"I will."

I hopped out of my truck, lighter. And I smiled.

Whatever happened in that school board meeting tonight, I wasn't going to give it another second of worry. No. Right now, I was going to watch my girls play.

The lightness only lasted until I reached the doors of the school. I didn't know what kind of greeting I was going to get when I walked into the gym. I'd gotten a few nasty emails from parents when everything happened right after the pep rally. And one kind of funny one. A mom who said something similar to Ming. "Holden Dupree is one fine specimen of a man. I feel okay saying that because I'm happily married. Good for you for going after what you want. Just, maybe, next time, do it at home. Lol." Once I'd stopped crying about the other messages, I'd giggled about that one for weeks. But I hadn't heard a peep from any parents or faculty in a long time. Not about the kiss anyway.

As I made my way past the ticket taker, who was also one of our cafeteria ladies, she smiled. "Hey there, Miss Thornbury. It's nice to see you."

That was good. At least one person didn't hate me.

I paused as my fingers curled around the gym door handle. And then I swung it open.

Thankfully, JV was in the middle of an intense volley and I slipped onto the closest bleachers mostly unnoticed. Holden was on his feet, arms crossed, brow hardened, watching the girls diligently. Maybe if I sat really still, and kind of curled in on myself no one would—

"Hey!" Peyton said way too loud, right behind me. It was almost a shout. "Why're you sitting over here alone?" She pointed—yes pointed, arm outstretched for the world to see— up to the top of the bleachers. Most of the Spartan Race group was here. Unfortunately, Knox was one of them and he was grinning like it was his lucky night.

It was not.

But the pull to sit with people who were smiling and waving for me to join them was too strong. I may not know them well but it was better than sitting alone. I followed her up the stairs, eyes on my feet so I wouldn't have to meet anyone else's gaze. People were starting to notice me now.

A woman whispered, "What is she doing here? I thought they said she couldn't come in the building."

Eyes down, feet still moving.

Then a woman called me a name that should never be said on school property and my hackles rose. Because I knew that voice. My gaze skidded to where it came from. Amber was sitting next to Jilly, who looked like she wanted to crawl into a hole. I cut her a glare so she would know that I knew exactly who'd said it.

Then I shook it off and kept going, hushed voices now lighting the room like wildfire.

But then someone squeezed my hand as I walked by. I looked down to see Bo Dupree smiling up at me with his dark hair and blue eyes that looked just like Silas's.

"Hey, fancy meeting you here, stranger," he said like he couldn't hear any of them. Then in front of all the naysayers, one of the most respected men in Seddledowne stood and pulled me into a tight paternal hug. It felt like hugging my dad. My breath caught in my throat, and I blinked back tears.

The room hushed.

I squeezed him back and laughed. "Hey. I'm glad to be here."

Jenny was next. Her hug longer and more desperate. Clearly, she still thought I was Holden's last hope. "Anna's going to be so excited you came. Holden too." She had to get him in there. Then she passed me to Lemon. Her's was quick, but when it was over, she pulled me to the seat next to her. Then she waved over her shoulder for Peyton to join us.

Big sigh of relief. The murmurs had died down. And a potential Knox situation was averted.

"Coach Christy!" Brooklyn waved from the floor. And the heads that had just looked away were turned again. I gave her an embarrassed wave, but then all the girls started waving and then I started laughing because they were so adorable, and oh my goodness, I'd missed them so much.

My gaze fell to Holden because how could it not? Or maybe it was because he was watching me and I'd felt it. Which I had. His expression was neutral but his eyes were bright like it made his night that I was here. Without thinking I shrugged and smiled at him.

Then that cocky smile that won me over from the beginning spread across his face. And my heart sputtered like we were still a thing. He lifted a hand in an awkward wave. Which made me giggle because Holden had probably never been awkward a day in his life. Except right then.

Lemon chortled next to me.

But then the moment was over because the ref blew the whistle. Which was good because I'd just told Holden we were through. And if I wanted to hold my ground, I couldn't be having heart-pounding, stomach-swooping moments like that.

JV won in a landslide and as soon as they were off the court, they stampeded the bleachers. Anna tackled me in a hug. And then Brooklyn. And Shanaya. And then Lemon and

Peyton scooted out of the way because the rest showed up. And pretty soon it was one big pile of squealing estrogen.

"Oh my gosh," I had to touch each one of them on their cheeks or shoulders. "You guys played so well. I'm so proud of you. What a way to end the season. And thank you for all the texts inviting me to come."

Brooklyn made duck lips. "Like we had a choice. Coach D said he'd bench anyone who didn't. He's been a grump-head since you left."

My throat grew thick. Holden had orchestrated all the invites?

Anna groaned. "Seriously?"

"You weren't supposed to tell her that," Shanaya glowered. "OMG, Brooklyn."

"Wait," My gaze ping-ponged between them. "He told you to invite me?" Heads bobbed all around me.

Anna shrugged like now that it was out, all bets were off. "He knew today might be hard with the school board meeting."

"But he didn't have to threaten us," Brooklyn said. "We would've done it anyway. Obvs."

Then, her shoulders dropped and they all looked so forlorn.

"Guys?" I reached out to pat Mari, our cute JV libero, on the shoulder. She looked like she'd been crying. "What's going on? Are you just sad that the season's over?" JV didn't go to the playoffs. Only varsity if they won their game.

Anna's smile was melancholy. "Everybody's just sad because Uncle Holden isn't coaching next year."

My head tilted. "C'mon guys. You knew that was temporary. He's gotta go back to DC and get a real job." I smiled so they'd see I was okay with it. Even though I was so totally not.

Anna frowned. "He's not going back to DC. He's staying here."

I cocked my head. "I think you're confused."

She raised her brows like it was laughable that she, his niece, wouldn't know something like that. "Uh, no. He's definitely staying." Her expression was giddy. "He's running for District Attorney of Seddledowne."

My heart jolted and I sat up straight. "What?" He'd never said a word about anything like that to me. I didn't even know that was on his radar. "When did that happen?"

Anna's eyes rolled up to the ceiling and she ticked off her fingers. "Saturday, he drove to DC to put his house on the market. Sunday, he told the family. Yesterday, he told that Jedd guy who's been bugging him for months. And let me tell you, Jedd was supes happy because now he can retire and he and his wife can spend their winters at Disney World. And then this morning Uncle Holden went to the courthouse and filed some documents for it. The election isn't until next year but Jedd's ready. So in the next couple of weeks, he's going to officially retire so Holden can take over as interim D.A." She was out of fingers and out of breath. She inhaled and plowed on. "He's going to live in me and Mom's old house while he builds a new one on the ranch for you two. It's all part of his big plan to win you back."

I swallowed. "Plan to win me back?"

"I wasn't supposed to say that." Her eyes skittered around the group. "Please don't tell him. He will kill me."

Oh my heart.

Had Holden seen my goodbye as a challenge? I didn't know but I did know that apparently the way to get a guy's attention is to walk away. Who would've known?

Actually, probably a lot of women. Just not Christy Thornbury.

Brooklyn sksksksk'd Anna and the other girls hooted. Anna's face was bright red, her eyes still pleading.

"Anna, of course." I crossed a finger over my heart. "Your secret is safe with me."

A minute later they scurried off to change and go sit with their friends and families.

Holden was staying in Seddledowne to run for D.A.? And he was going to build us a house on the ranch?

Lemon slid over and squeezed my hand. "Pretty cool about Holden staying in Seddledowne, huh? Oh, and since we're all telling secrets, Holden was the one who told me how to fix your momentum for the rings." I looked over at her, slightly shocked. She nodded. Then she leaned closer. "And don't worry about the meeting. Silas has you covered."

Oh my goodness, the meeting. For a few minutes, I'd completely forgotten about it.

I returned the squeeze.

But the joke was on her.

Because Silas didn't have me covered. I'd covered him.

He just didn't know it yet.

twenty-one

HOLDEN

I wiped my sweaty palms on my pants and paced in front of the sideline. Christy was here. Thank God. Literally. For the past two weeks, she'd avoided all the group Spartan training I'd been at. Knox said she was coming over during the day to work on things alone. And it made me sick that she wouldn't show up when I was around. Even sicker to think she might be in those woods alone with Knox.

I'd been praying my heart out that this whole mess could be fixed. Just because she came tonight didn't mean it was repaired, but at least she'd made the effort to be here for the girls. And at least I got to see her for a little while, even just across the court. She looked good. No, that was a complete understatement. Stunning, gorgeous, like something out of a magazine. She shouldn't be allowed to wear those jeans in public, or that form-fitting shirt. Especially when Knox Freeman was around.

But Amber's evil stare had been trained on her from the minute she walked in. I'd have to thank my dad later for stopping the hate that was about to take over the crowd.

I folded my hands on my head, still pacing as Varsity

warmed up. Because now that Christy was here, across the gym floor was not good enough. I wanted her on this side, next to me on the bench.

I marched up to Alvarez, who was slumped down in a chair by the door, chatting with Brad Vickers, one of the football coaches. Anna's boyfriend, Blue, was next to them, leaning against the wall, half listening, half waiting for Anna to emerge from the locker room.

I rolled my shoulders back. "I think I'm gonna make Christy an honorary coach for the varsity game." I didn't ask permission on purpose. A subtle way to assert dominance. I felt okay about it, seeing that Alvarez hardly gave a crap about the volleyball team anyway.

He shrugged. "Sure. Go for it."

But then I walked back to the sideline and started up my pacing again, chewing my thumbnail as I subtly glanced Christy's way.

Blue sauntered over and folded his arms across his chest, watching her too. "It's a dilemma, for sure."

"What are you talking about?"

He shrugged. "If you *ask* her to come coach, she'll probably say no." His hands flipped up, like an old-fashioned scale measuring grain. "You broke up with her." One hand lowered. "And then she broke up with you." The other dropped. "And then there's the fact that the school board said she couldn't coach anymore." His hands fell and he shrugged again. "And, despite the shirtless kissing, Miss Thornbury strikes me as the kind of lady who doesn't like to rock the boat."

I grunted. For an oaf of a teenager, he was pretty perceptive. "Yeah," I finally said, slumping a bit.

A third shrug. "Then don't give her a choice."

I scoffed. "I can't *make* her come over here. You think the volleyball coach should just go manhandle the Principal?"

He clapped me on the shoulder. "Holden, Holden, Holden."

"That's Uncle Holden to you. No, Anna's Uncle Holden."

He rolled his eyes. "Fine." He cuffed me again. "Anna's Uncle Holden?" He cracked his thumb knuckles. "I got this." Then he took off at a jog, sweeping the perimeter of the court and up into the student section where half the football team was chilling. My brow crunched, trying to figure out what he was doing. All of a sudden, five guys popped up, their expressions excited. They swaggered down the bleachers and onto the floor, laughing and goading each other. I couldn't hear their words, but I could see it coming.

Man, I hoped Christy would forgive me for this.

She looked up in shock as they surrounded her. Across the court, I heard them count to three and then they heaved her up over their heads like a crowd surfer at a concert. She squealed and the gym broke out in rumbles, confused guffaws, and cheers from all the students.

"Put me down!" she yelled with a shaky laugh.

I held my breath, praying one of them didn't trip.

Twenty seconds later—the gym a thunderstorm of cheers —they set her on her feet in front of me. The varsity girls screamed their approval.

"Oh my word." She huffed and smoothed out her shirt. And oh *my* word, I wanted to take her in my arms and kiss those pouty, annoyed lips right there in front of everyone. She was so beautiful it put an ache in my lungs.

Then she looked at the footballers who were smiling in deep adoration and shook her head laughing. Probably half of them had crushes on her. I know I did. "We got you, P. Thorn," one of them said. "Always."

Which made her blush. Which made me want to kiss her even more.

I released them from their duties with the tip of my chin. "Thanks, guys."

I even offered Blue a generous fist bump. He walked away proudly. I had to give it to the kid. He took our razzing like it was nothing. If he could hang onto Anna hard enough, they just might make it.

Christy's arms folded and she blew a wisp of hair out of her eyes so I could see her glower. I wanted to boop her on her adorable nose that was crinkled in irritation, just like I had that night in her office. Just run my hands up those thighs and... Good gracious.

But she might slap me if I tried that after my behavior at Spartan training.

"*C'mon,* Coach." I took a playful jab at her shoulder. "You know this is where you want to be." I gestured at the bench seats so she'd know I wasn't talking about with me.

"Fine." She sat down with a huff. But her twinkling eyes said she was thrilled. "But I might get in trouble for this."

I sat next to her and leaned my mouth right by her ear. "We'll blame it on Alvarez. He okayed it."

She let out a little shiver as I pulled away. And I may have preened a little. Then she sat up straight and glanced over. "You're moving here and running for D.A.?"

I swallowed. "Oh. Yeah." I took a shrug straight out of Blue's playbook like it was no biggie. "Nobody will hire me up north so I decided it was time to come home." *And I want to be wherever you are,* I didn't say. "Jedd wanted to retire anyway."

"That's..." She ran a hand over the back of her neck. "That's huge. Congrats."

"I mean, I have to be elected, so it might not happen. But I thought I'd give it a shot. Why not, you know?"

Her brows puckered. "You think there's someone else around here that could beat the great Holden Dupree?"

I was about to point out the fact that she'd just called me great when her phone buzzed. She flipped it over to check but purposely blocked my view with her other hand. Not that I was trying to see. I wasn't. It was just kind of weird. She didn't usually do that.

Throughout the game, she kept flipping her phone over to read what was there, and then she'd scowl. And then it would take a few minutes for her to relax again. And just about the time I could see her getting back into the action, she'd check her phone again and the whole thing would start over. By the third set, she looked haggard, and like she was about to cry.

Who was she texting? And then I remembered. She was worried about the meeting. Had she heard something? I pulled my phone out of my pocket to see if Silas had texted and I'd missed it. Nothing.

"Everything okay?" I asked.

She chewed her lip and grunted an indecipherable response. But the worry on her face was so intense that it took everything in me not to take her phone from her and see who it was. *Hands to yourself, tool. You're not her boyfriend.*

Just as that set ended, which we lost, Silas, in a navy suit and his cowboy boots, came barreling into the gym and bull-dozed the team to get to us. Ming accidentally squirted Alyssa in the eye with her water bottle when she jumped out of the way.

"Christy!" Silas practically shouted, his expression wide-eyed with shock. "Why did you do that? I was trying to get you your job back, not get you demoted."

She stood and put a hand on his arm, not looking at all surprised by his very out-of-character outburst. "Whoa, cowboy," she said in a hush, her lips turning up in a smile. "Let's make this a you and me conversation instead of an entire gym conversation, if you don't mind."

"What's going on?" I felt my right brow crawling into my hairline.

Silas shook his head at the ceiling. "I'll tell you what's going on. I'm the principal. And Christy's the assistant. Permanently." Before I had a second to process the news, he aimed his ire at me, like somehow this was my problem to fix. "I'm standing there reading the letter she wrote to the board and I'm completely sideswiped as the words are coming out of my mouth." Then he thrust his hand at her while still yelling at me. "And it was her idea!"

"To switch positions?" I asked.

"Yes." I thought his head might pop off from the frustration.

She sighed. And then laughed. "Why are you so upset? You're a way better administrator than me and we both know it."

"That is not true." But there was a micro twinge in his tone that said he might agree.

"Yes, it is. You tell the kids to do something and they snap to like it's basic training. I tell them to do something and they're all, 'Yeah. Okay, P. Thorn. We'll get to it if we feel like it.' She sounded just like the footballers when she said it. "They do not take me seriously. And I don't care because I'd rather spend my time listening to what they need or encouraging them in their dreams than disciplining or putting out fires."

"Christy," he said on an exhale. "You went to all that school to be an administrator. You agonized over your master's thesis. You've spent thousands of dollars getting a degree so you could become a principal. Nobody dreams of being an A.P."

"You're right. I did. And I hate it," she said simply. "It's really stressful and honestly, I just want to be around these guys. Not all that extra stuff." She gestured at the girls and then to the student section. "Maybe in a couple of years, I'll go back and get a degree in guidance counseling." She chewed her bottom lip. "If I could just coach I would. I've kind of fallen in love with it. But I have bills to pay."

He really did look sideswiped. And I had to give it to my big brother, he was the most humble guy I knew. He'd come into the job dreading the fact that she'd gotten the position over him and he'd given it his all anyway. Anyone else would've been gloating over the promotion. But not Si.

She cocked her head with a sad smile. "Silas, this should've been your job. We both know that. This is your town and these are your people. And I never meant this to be permanent anyway."

I didn't like the sound of that. Like she wasn't just thinking of changing careers but changing locations too. I forced myself to breathe. She hadn't said she was quitting. She'd at least stay the school year. I had time.

His jaw bulged. "Yeah. Okay." But I could tell it was going to take a while to wrap his head around it.

She put out her hand. "Congrats on your new job, Principal Dupree. I can't wait to work with you."

He rolled his eyes but gave her a hearty handshake. "Yeah. Fine. Looking forward to it," he grumbled. Then he jogged off to sit with Lemon and our parents.

"Wow." I chuckled. "I think he was almost not frowning there at the end."

She giggled, eyebrows raised. "Looks like we're all full of surprises today."

Just then the buzzer sounded and we were back at what would hopefully be the last set. Christy's phone was back on her lap, and the constant checking started back up.

So it wasn't the school board meeting.

Then, after another phone check, she laid the phone on the seat next to her right thigh and straightened, her hands balled in her lap. "That's it." I heard her mutter angrily. And she trained her eyes on Amber straight across the floor. "I've had enough."

Awww crap.

For the next ten minutes, she sat board straight on the edge of her seat, eyes volleying between the climbing scoreboard and the psychopath across the room. And Amber's gaze stayed trained on her like two demon eyes hungry for a soul.

My nerves kicked into high gear and my palms started sweating. "Christy, what is going on?"

"Don't you worry about it."

"What is she texting you?" I reached for her phone.

She jammed it under her thigh so I couldn't get to it. "None of your business."

Her bouncing knee was amping me up even worse, so I put a hand out to stop it. "Are the earrings about to come off?"

"And the hair extensions too."

"Chris."

"And don't you dare try to stop me." She bounced my hand right off her knee and deepened her death glare across the court.

As soon as Ming sent a kill over, ending the game, Christy shot up out of her seat and stormed across the floor. But in her haste, she'd left her phone. I picked it up and typed in her password.

And my eyes were inundated with pictures of me and Amber in bed together. In every sultry position imaginable. And not a single one of them was real. Because I've never been in a bed, dressed or not, with Amber Taylor. And I never would be.

But they looked real. Not photoshopped at all. And if I hadn't known better, I would've believed they were one hundred percent legit.

I hopped up, taking the phone with me, and jogged over to where it was about to go down. As I went, I quickly scrolled. There were at least fifteen different numbers that had sent threatening texts and misleading pictures as far back as...

I didn't have time to find out but weeks, at least. Maybe months.

Amber must've been using burners. Christy would probably block her and then she'd start up with a different number. But why hadn't Christy ever said anything? The sad part was, Amber's stunt didn't even shock me.

This was her token calling card.

I sprinted up the stairs as the argument broke out.

Christy, who was five foot nothing and light as a feather, was standing on top of a bleacher right in Amber's face. "If you're gonna be a psycho, at least be a smart one. If you'd actually seen him naked you might've been able to fool me." Whew. Straight outta the gate. She could've stated that better. My mother was watching. Along with everyone else on this side of the bleachers.

Jilly was leaning back, looking at Christy like she was the psycho. I caught her eye and shook my head. She cocked her head, eyes wide in disbelief, and I nodded.

I had horrific visions of Amber shoving Christy backward down the bleachers, so I put my hands against her back just in case. I don't know if she knew it was me, but she didn't even flinch, which told me she most likely did. All I could see was her backside, which I would've enjoyed any other time. It was a wall between me and Amber and I wished I could hold Christy up and see her face all at once. But the crowd was already pressing in. I'd have to be content with listening.

Amber had her hand on her hip. "Sure. You've been with him. In your dreams."

Christy snorted. "See, that's the difference between me and you. I don't have to dream because I've had my hands all over the real thing." That won her some catcalls. I winced. My mom was going to lecture me after this. "And," she threw her arms out, gesturing at the entire room, "Everyone here knows about it, thanks to you."

At least five people gasped.

"Yes, everybody," Christy addressed the already rapt crowd. "You may as well know it was Amber here who hacked into the security cameras. And then broadcast that picture to your children during a pep rally."

"No way! Alyssa's aunt?" A girl said, beginning the outcry. Murmurs ripped through the bleachers like we were doing the wave.

"Fight, fight, fight!" some students yelled from the back. "You get her, P. Thorn!"

My heartbeat was shooting off alerts to every cell of my body. The last thing we needed was a brawl. And the last thing Christy needed was to lose the job she just got back.

I looked over my shoulder, searching for Silas, praying he'd stop this. But he was next to Lemon and my parents, arms crossed, letting it all unfold. A school security officer was heading this way. He'd stop it. But no, Silas grabbed him and pulled him to a halt. They began whispering back and forth.

"No!" Christy's hands patted down their shouts. "Guys. Violence is not the right way to handle a bully." A hush went over the students that would've been comical if it hadn't felt like the room was about to explode. Then she turned back to Amber. "But calling them out is. And that's what I'm doing. Right here in front of everyone."

Amber's nonchalant facade was crumbling. Her hands shook a little at her sides. "I'm not a bully. And I don't have to listen to this. I'm leaving." She tried to turn to make her escape, but Jilly was there, stopping her. She turned the other way, and Peyton and the Spartan team blocked that direction.

Christy folded her arms. "I'm afraid you're not. At least

not until I'm done telling everyone all the nasty things you've texted me. And Amber, you are a bully. A grown-up 'mean girl,' if there ever was one." She looked over at the students. "Bear with me, guys. It's quite the list. Try not to interrupt or you might miss something." They shushed each other until it was deathly quiet.

I felt her inhale and let it out quick. "I am not going 'back to where I came from.'" Her fingers made quote marks. "I'm not 'ugly.' I don't 'need a nose job,' or Botox, or a facelift. My butt is the perfect size. And my chest is perfectly fine the way it is." Facts. "I don't talk funny. You guys do." There were a few chuckles. "I'm not any of the awful names you've called me that I can't repeat in front of my students. And I'm not, no matter how many times you try to put it in my head, going to *kill* myself." Wide eyes, gasps, hands over their mouths, all the reactions you would expect.

And I thought I might puke. That's exactly what Amber had said to Savannah. Over and over until Savannah had finally done it. Only back then, Amber hadn't texted those words. She'd spoken them when no one else was around.

Amber had said those things to Christy—*my* Christy—all this time, and I hadn't known? I'd thought staying away would put a barrier between them, like a shield. But instead, Christy'd been the target of an open-air attack. And when I should've been right by her side, she'd been deflecting all by herself.

What a fool I had been. And that was the nicest thing I could think about myself just then.

Christy threw her hands out, not done. "And, for the love," she paused for one intense heartbeat, "if you're going to Photoshop someone to appear naked and use it to put doubts in their girlfriend's head—which is a felony, by the way—" Her fists clenched as she let out a controlled exhale. "I mean, if you're going to commit a freaking crime that could get you locked up, the least you can do is Get. It. Right." Her left arm flew straight out and she jabbed her right pointer finger into her bicep. "He's got a tattoo right here. A suicide prevention semicolon. And if you'd ever so much as seen him with his shirt off in the last ten years, you'd know that." I hadn't realized she'd ever noticed the tattoo. Then she hooted. "Slept together, my eye."

Holy. Wow.

"Well, look at that Bo," Mom said. "That stupid tattoo actually saved his butt. Can you believe that?"

Again, wow.

A few students high-fived each other and I glared them back to silence. Then Christy gasped like she'd just figured something out. And the hair on my neck stood on end from the way her body tensed against me. She leaned forward and I glanced around trying to see her face, but I couldn't. "It was *you*," she whispered. Then louder, "*You* bullied Savannah Clark to death."

The room erupted and my stomach plunged to my knees. Jilly's eyes welled up and she looked so ashamed. Of what, I'm not sure. But I guessed it was that she'd chosen to believe Amber's lies ten years ago instead of the truth I'd tried to tell her.

"Savannah Clark?" The rumble started back up.

"Who's that?"

"Oh, I remember her."

"She was a darling girl. So Tragic."

"She and Holden dated in high school, remember?"

"You're a lunatic!" Amber screamed over the noise. "Savannah was my friend. I didn't do any of the things you just accused me of. I'm going to sue you for de-fame-ation!"

I curled an arm around Christy's waist, popped my head over her shoulder, looked Amber straight in her evil eyes, and said, "It's defamation. And good luck with that since she'll be suing you for harassment, copyright infringement, libel, and slander, just for starters." Then I dragged Christy backward off the bleachers. My expression was as hard as I could make it to get everyone out of my way. Because I was not slowing down. Not until she and I were far away from here.

"Holden, put me down," she said, her legs flailing. "Holden!" she yelled as we came through the exit door and out into the parking lot. "Look, I'm sorry if you're mad. But please put me down."

"Mad?" I guffawed. I set her on her feet but latched my hand around her wrist, pulling her along behind me. Once we were finally around the corner, I pinned her against the brick wall, my arms on either side so she couldn't escape. She looked up at me, her big brown eyes so beautiful, but a touch afraid. She didn't need to be.

"Woman, what in the world?" My hands slid up to either side of her neck. Her heartbeat was still firing off like the rat-a-tat-tat of bullets.

Her eyes turned down, ashamed. "I'm sorry if I embarrassed you. But I couldn't take it anymore."

"Embarrassed?" I stepped back, now that I was semi-confident she wouldn't run. "I'm not embarrassed. I'm..." My hands shoved into my hair.

I didn't know what I was. An idiot, for starters. Christy didn't need my protection. She was a heat-seeking missile and I hoped to always be on the right side of that fury. This was no self-deprecating seventeen-year-old girl. That was the moment I realized, all this time, I'd been putting Savannah's struggles on Christy like they were the same person. Whether I'd meant to or not, I'd made her carry Savannah's cross.

I was sick in my soul.

In two steps I was back, my arms around her waist. "Why didn't you tell me?"

"Why, so you'd confront her? That's exactly what she

wanted. And I didn't want to give you any reason to be near her."

What?

She'd been protecting *me?*

This woman was unreal.

I let my forehead fall against hers, breathing her in like I always did. I didn't know what was happening in that gym, but out here, it was nothing but overwhelming peace. *She* was where I belonged. And who I belonged with. She always had been. And if I had stopped listening to my dueling shoulder devil and shoulder angel, maybe I would've realized that months ago.

"I..." *Love you* almost rolled off my tongue, and I had to pull it back. She wasn't ready to hear it. Instead, I went with, "I'm crazy about you. You're nuts." I laughed. "Totally nuts. And I'm ridiculously crazy about you. Just incredible."

But she wasn't sharing in my elation.

Pain was evident on her face. Then she pushed my sleeve up and traced the tattoo I'd gotten a few months into my freshman year of college. These days, I forgot it was there most of the time. She pressed a soft kiss to it, which made my gut purr.

She looked up, her doe eyes so sad. "I'm crazy about you too. But it doesn't change anything."

Then she slipped her phone out of my pocket, dipped under my arm, and walked away.

But she was wrong.

Tonight, she'd changed everything.

twenty-two

CHRISTY

The cool grass was making my legs itch. I needed to get up and get in my truck. I had a billion things to do before I headed to the school to help Holden coach the first Riverbend district tournament game. But I kind of didn't want to leave the peace of this place. My head was clear here.

I'd come to Savannah's grave, at a small Baptist church on a back road on the north side of town, at least four times since Lemon had pointed me to the Google search. I didn't have many friends in Seddledowne, and I knew nothing about the girl who'd died a decade ago, but the fact that we'd loved the same man made me feel connected to her in some inexplicable occult sort of way. Even if he had loved her more.

I sat, legs crossed, next to her headstone. Not on top of her grave, which looked way more comfy. Someone took very good care of it, keeping it fertilized, weeded, and carefully trimmed. I didn't know if it was true, what people said, but I'd always heard that if you walked on a grave, it was disrespectful to the deceased. And this girl deserved all the respect.

My hands cupped my phone, and I groaned in frustration.

"This is what I'm talking about," I said to Savannah as if she were sitting next to me, looking at the screen. "He's so confusing, and I don't know if I can trust him. Is this real? Or will he change it next week when he has another freakout?" I'm sure I looked ridiculous, talking to nobody, and if a stranger saw me, they might want to get me checked out. But my frustration was legitimate. Holden had lavender roses delivered yesterday. And there was a card that said, *I'm sorry I panicked and ruined everything between us. You'll never know how sorry. I hope, in time, you'll trust me again.*

And then there were his social media profiles.

Holden had untagged himself from every one of those stupid date photos back when we officially started going out. For real, not fake. But just yesterday, still one hundred percent broken up, I realized he'd unfriended more than two thousand people until there was nothing left but guys and relatives. He hadn't left a single female other than Anna and Lemon. And me. Which was insane. Sweet, but insane. Because there was no way some of those women weren't just friends. He was making a statement. He knew I'd be checking. And he was right. I couldn't imagine how many of those women had messaged him when he'd disappeared from their feed. I'm sure there had been plenty. A thought I didn't want to entertain.

And then last night, as if that wasn't enough, he'd posted a new profile picture.

I'd taken the picture using his phone. A selfie of me and him that first fake-dating night in the back of my truck. I was snuggled in his lap, his chin resting on my shoulder, his ginormous biceps locked around my waist. We were both wearing a mischievous smile like we had a secret. Because we did. We were pretending to be a thing when we weren't. Present me, looking at past us, smiled. We'd enjoyed that opportunity to put our hands on each other, way too much. If only I'd known then, the heartbreak loving Holden Dupree would bring.

What was he trying to pull? Posting this couple shot for the whole world to see, staking his claim when I'd told him we were done, was...

"So confusing," I said again. "Was he this flip-floppy when you knew him?" I asked ghost Savannah.

"Oh, hello?"

My head shot up with a startle to see an older woman standing there, a bouquet of pink silk tulips in her hand. Shoot. My newfound, weirdo penchant for speaking to the dead was busted. Probably by Savannah's relative. I shifted to stand. "Oh my goodness, I'm so sorry, I—"

"Oh, no, you don't need to get up." The woman smiled and knelt next to me, eyeing me curiously. Her hair was a shock of silvery-gray, cropped at her chin, and her face was pretty but wrinkled in a way that said she took good care of it, but she'd been through hard stuff. "Did you know Savvy?"

I froze, not sure if I should bolt because, who goes to the grave of someone they didn't know and sits there, chatting it up, like they did. Or did I stay? Because her eyes said she had questions and I owed her answers.

I shook my head, chagrined. "No. I just..."

The woman's hand reached down in an offered shake. "I'm Savannah's grandmother, Dahlia. It's nice to meet you." Her last word hung in the air, waiting for me to respond in kind.

"Christy." I shook. "Thornbury."

Her eyes flickered with recognition like she suddenly remembered who I was. But that couldn't be. We'd never met. But maybe she'd heard about the shirtless kissing too. Everyone else in town had. "I'm so sorry, this must seem odd to walk up and find a stranger at your granddaughter's grave."

She knelt, two feet away, and smiled. For an older person, she was impressively mobile. "Not at all. Holden told us what you did at that volleyball game. Calling that horrible woman out. You are most welcome here anytime, Christy Thornbury."

My mouth had parted at Holden's name and was still hanging there. "Holden told you about that?"

She nodded, lips pursed in an almost smile. "He did." So he was still close with Savannah's grandparents? The thought made my heart flutter. It was so...sweet.

But then I felt defeated and my eyes dropped to my lap because I was right. She was the love of his life and she always would be. Maybe this woman could give me closure. Or, and I shouldn't have hoped it, a reason to prove me wrong.

She reached out and put a hand on my knee. "He loves you, you know."

My head jerked up. "He told you we..." What were we?

Another gentle smile. "He did. Came to see us last week." She lowered to a seat, settling in as if she knew this might take a while. "I think he wanted our permission to move on."

I swallowed, letting that settle. "Our?"

"Me and Randall, my husband. He's home mowing the lawn one last time for the year. At least that's what he said. He's kind of obsessive about it. Anyway, we raised Savannah. Her mom..." She shook her head, a wistful sadness in her eyes. "Well, she got caught up in drugs when she was in high school and she just wasn't able to care for Savvy like she should." They'd lost their granddaughter to suicide and had to deal with a daughter's drug addiction too? "I'm sorry, I'm rambling."

"No." I laughed. "Please ramble. I have so many questions." My hands flew out. "Not that you have to answer them. It's none of my business."

"I'm sure you do." She studied me. "You're struggling with this whole thing." It wasn't a question. I didn't want to say anything that might take away from the love Holden had for Savannah, but I also knew if anyone could give me a

233

different picture of who Holden really was and what he'd been through, it was this woman.

I tucked my hair behind my ear. "The whole thing has been a struggle. He's so tightly wound over," I gestured at the headstone. "Her. And then there's Amber Taylor. And I'm not sure what to believe or if..." I bit my lip, hating to admit it. "If I can trust him. I already got burned once."

"Holden's been through a lot. You need to know that upfront."

I nodded, hoping she'd elaborate.

She plucked a blade of grass. "I'm not sure how much he's told you."

I blew out my breath. "Not much. He's kind of closed off about it all."

Her eyebrows puckered. "Then you probably don't know that after Savannah passed, Amber accused him of sexual assault."

If this kind-faced old woman had suddenly punched me in the stomach I couldn't have been more shocked. "I didn't..." Why couldn't I complete a stupid sentence? And why hadn't that come up in a Google search?

She went on. "It was an empty threat. And it never made it to court because," she rolled her eyes and scoffed, "it wasn't true. She had no proof. But it shook him hard. For weeks, he was sick with worry that his future was over."

"Why would she do that?" I asked, horrified.

Dahlia's eyes blazed. "Because she thought with Savvy out of the picture that he'd cave and give in to her. She was patient. I have to give her that. She waited about a year, until about a month before graduation. Then she went after him hard. But instead of turning to her, he ripped her apart. Told everyone he could that it was Amber's fault Savannah killed herself." One shoulder lifted. "I guess it made her mad, so she went for blood."

"So after losing the girl he loved, he had to deal with all that too."

She sighed. "I had no idea that he'd still been dealing with Amber all these years." Her gaze met mine. "I'm hopeful that now, after what you did the other night, she'll finally back off." I hoped so too. Whether Holden was mine or not, he deserved a life free of Amber Taylor.

I chewed my lip, digesting it all. "Can I ask you kind of a hard question?"

She nodded. "Of course."

"Why didn't you take Amber to court for what she did to Savannah?" I tried my hardest not to sound accusatory, but I had to know.

"Oh, we tried. Right after Savvy passed, Randall, Holden, and I spent hours at the courthouse, with the police, and with Jedd Pruitt." Her eyes crinkled at the corners. "That's how Holden met Jedd and fell in love with law and the idea of making it a career." I'd had no idea. "But Amber had been so subtle. A lot less bold than she's been with you. There were no texts or anything online. It was all in-person bullying, getting inside Savannah's head. Trying to repeatedly seduce Holden and then denying it when he called her out. Savannah was so twisted up inside, that she didn't know who to believe. And then the final blow happened." Her chest rose and fell.

"The final blow?"

"Same thing as what she did with you. Slipping Savannah pictures of her and Holden in bed together. Holden told Savvy they weren't real. Amber had doctored them. But," her face went soft, heartbreak permeating every line. "Savannah's mom was on drugs when she was pregnant with her. We're pretty sure it messed with Savannah's brain chemicals, and she struggled with depression. We tried to get her help." She shook her head. "She even spent a couple of weeks in the hospital. But in the end, it was just too much."

I leaned back, my hands propping me up. "That's awful. I'm so sorry you all had to go through that."

She twisted the blade of grass around her pinky finger. "It was. A real-life nightmare that you never wake up from." But then she leaned toward me, eyes serious. "But I'll tell you what I've told Holden many times." She waited like she was making sure she had my full attention before she went on. "Maybe Savannah couldn't live a life of happiness, but that doesn't mean he shouldn't. And last time he came to visit, I reminded him of that." Her head tilted. "We also told him he's not allowed to come see us anymore." I blanched. She patted my knee again. "Not because we don't love him or don't want to see him. But because he's been carrying this torch of guilt for way too long. And I think he's been holding back all these years, and with you, because he didn't want to hurt *us*."

"Oh." Wow.

"Please don't hate me and Randall. We never meant for him to miss out on life just to spare our feelings."

"Of course not."

"We just loved seeing him whenever he came home to visit his family. And it always felt like he brought a piece of Savannah with him. But we should've made it clear long ago that if he met someone else. No." She shook her head, determined. "*When* he met someone else, that we would be nothing but thrilled for him."

"He visits you every time he comes home?"

"He does." She nodded and then shook her head. "He did. But no more."

My hands flew out. "But don't you think that'll hurt him?"

She shrugged but there were tears in her eyes. "Maybe. But he looked a little relieved too. Like we'd lifted a weight off of him." She shifted and smiled. "We told him he can come back once a year, if he really wants, but only to visit. Not to ease his guilt." Then she pinned me with her green eyes. "And not until he's married to the woman he loves. And then, and only then, he has to bring her with him. I think he's been ready to move on for a while now."

My forehead furrowed. "You don't know me and we just met but..." I cocked my head. "Do you *truly* think he loves me?" I mean, she'd seen Holden in love before and she'd known him all these years. And if anyone had a motive to lie, it was her. But there was an honesty in the whole conversation that said she was trustworthy. That she wanted what was best for him. I mean, I knew his family thought he loved me. But they were biased. And they really wanted this for him. "I'm just trying to figure it out because we already tried once and it ended disastrously. I don't know if I can do that again."

"He loves you," she said so plainly. "So much it hurts. I've never seen him like this over another woman before. Not even close." I thought she'd preclude that with Savannah but she didn't. She squeezed my hand. "I don't have any right to ask this of someone I just met a few minutes ago, but Holden is dear to my heart. I truly hope you can find a way to love him for who he is, and who he's become with all that he's been through. After all this time, he deserves happiness." Her last sentence reminded me of what Tally had said about Rochester. *He deserves love.* The memory of Ashton and Tally arguing furiously made me smile. Maybe I'd have to read *Jane Eyre* again soon.

But right now, I needed to go get ready for the big game. And to fix things with Holden. He'd been through enough.

twenty-three

HOLDEN

Once again, I paced the floor. The school board hadn't just given Christy her job back—correction, Silas's job—they'd okayed her to coach again. Seddledowne was hosting the first tournament game and it started in an hour. Christy still wasn't here and it had been her idea to arrive early and decorate the cafeteria for an end-of-the-season party. Mom, Dad, Lemon, and Silas had done their best. But now that the girls were arriving, it was taking all of us just to keep them out.

"Bro, she'll be here," Silas said, in his horse-whisperer voice. "Do not take a nosedive down the doom spiral."

I grunted and gave him a quick scowl. That's exactly what I'd been doing. Was Christy dead in a ditch? Run off with Knox Freeman? Murdered by Amber? My brain was in all those places at once. The last one wasn't that far of a stretch. Jedd thought there was enough evidence to press charges against Amber but sadly, every number he traced back to the burner phones led to Alyssa of all people.

Me: You coming?

Immediately Christy's text bubbles moved.

> Christy: Yeah. Sorry! My truck wouldn't
> start. Pulling in now.

I finished sticking a *Congratulations!* sign against the painted cinder-block wall and forced myself to exhale, releasing some of the tension. When she pushed through the door, with Mrs. Ross in tow, adrenaline rushed my system. And not from the relief of seeing her, though there was that too. Wearing those ridiculously sexy leggings and her Stallions polo, she may as well have been in an evening gown. She looked that good. Hair in voluminous waves, she'd done her makeup differently. Her eyeshadow, maybe. Her warm brown eyes glinted with ambers and golds. I could see that from twenty feet away.

Man, she was beautiful.

I gave her a stupid awkward wave and said, in my most suave voice, "Hi."

Hi?

C'mon moron. Get it together.

My family was even less smooth, all nervously silent, gawking at us. Mrs. Ross too. But then she squeezed Christy's arm. "I'll see you at the game. I'm going to grade some papers in my classroom until it starts."

"Yeah." Christy glanced over and they shared a look. What was that about? "Thanks for the ride." My heart dropped to my knees. She'd needed a ride and she hadn't asked me. Not a good sign.

But then, when Christy looked away, Mrs. Ross gave me a wink and a grin before ducking out the door. What was that about? I didn't know. But it felt hopeful.

I walked to Christy, even though I wanted to run. "What's up with your truck?"

Her brows puckered. "I'm not sure. Not the battery though. We tried jumping it and it didn't work."

I folded my arms, cooly. "If you want, I can give you a ride home after the game and we can take a look at it. Together." I gulped the last word, praying she'd take me up on it.

She tucked her hair behind her ear and I swear she blushed. Either that or it was her expertly placed makeup and I'd just noticed. But then her doe eyes peeked up at me, lassoed my heart, and yanked me toward her. Metaphorically. Literally? It took all my willpower not to close the distance between us.

She hugged herself. "Yeah. That would be great."

Yes!

Her hand ran across her forehead. "Could I possibly borrow your car for a few minutes?" She squirmed like she hated to ask. "I was in such a tizzy about my truck that I forgot to grab the balloons out of the seat when Beth arrived." Must be Mrs. Ross's first name. "I can run to the store real quick and get some more. I'll be super careful with Tessie. I promise."

I could've sent my parents. I didn't want her to leave now that she'd just arrived. Not for a second. But I also didn't want her to think I didn't want her driving Tessie. And clearly she felt like it was something she needed to take care of.

I grinned. "Yeah, of course." I reached into my pocket and slid the keys out.

When I laid them in her hand, her fingers curled around my palm and slid down to my fingertips so quickly that if my nerve endings weren't on high alert, I wouldn't have noticed. But they were, and I did. She didn't have to say a word because her eyes were saying it all. Loudly. Hooded and piercing into me, tugging me toward her again. Her mouth was closed, but curved up at the corners. A "come hither" smile.

Oh man, I hoped I was reading that right. I didn't know

why, but the air between us had changed. Or should I say charged? Yeah. Red hot, crackling. So hot that one spark might blow the entire school up.

She turned and started back through the door. And like a lovesick puppy, I was right there. Too impatient to wait for later.

"I have to grab something from my car," I said half-heartedly over my shoulder to my family, not caring if they heard or not. I was going with Christy, regardless.

She smiled, eyes ahead, biting her bottom lip. I squeezed her elbow as we walked into the breezeway dividing the cafeteria from the gym. That one touch was heaven. Her smile went wider and her gaze flashed over, smoldering. So I took a chance and slid my palm down her arm until our hands were hanging side by side. It totally paid off. She hooked her pinky around mine and my hand attacked hers, engulfing it like a rabid raccoon.

She stifled a laugh as our fingers twined together. Man, how could holding someone's hand be so hot? But with Christy, it was all hot. Like set-the-entire-world-on-fire-and-not-even-care hot. She reached out to pull the gym door open but I placed my hand over hers, stopping it. I was not going to make it through this game on a five-second handhold. I needed more.

So I slid my arm around her waist and turned her to face me. Her gaze burned into mine. She slid her hands up around my neck, and then she bit her bottom lip again, waiting. I wanted to kiss her so badly. But what if someone saw? The last thing I wanted was to cause her any more trouble. So I simply squared her hips and rested our foreheads together.

I had to say it. Was going to explode if I didn't. "I love you." It came out in a rush. "*Please*, you have to know that. I was a stupid idiot and I thought I needed to protect you. I'm so sorry. For everything. Can you ever forgive me?" My hands trembled at her waist.

I didn't know what I was going to do if she was toying with me. I wanted everything with this woman. Her future and mine—I wanted them so interconnected and tangled, that we couldn't unwind them if we tried. I wanted it all with her. And if she didn't want that now, because I'd messed up, because I'd hurt her...I squeezed my eyes shut and swallowed, trying to push past the fear.

She removed her left hand from my neck and rested it over my right, calming me. "Hey," she said softly. "Everything's okay." Her nose nuzzled mine. "I forgive you. Of course, I do." She sighed. "And I love you too. Obviously. Shirtless-kissing, almost-lose-your-job kind of love. We'll talk later?"

I sunk in relief, practically collapsing against her. "Yes. Definitely."

Her nose brushed mine again. "You're all mine, Holden. Your whole heart. I'm taking it."

"You already did," I said in a hush. "A long time ago. I didn't even have a choice. It was gone before I even knew what was happening. Just lassoed it like you lassoed that calf."

She giggled, shaking gently in my arms. Then she shrugged. "Gotta put my roping skills to use one way or another. I don't want them to get rusty."

I tucked a loose strand of hair behind her ear and just took her in for a moment. I hadn't said I love you to anyone other than family since high school. The relief of having it out there— and of having things fixed with her—took all the weight and heaviness of the last decade and bulldozed it straight off a cliff. I pressed a kiss to her forehead. Just a promise of later.

"Let's get you to the car," I finally said.

We had to cut through the gym to get to the parking lot. When we opened the door, volleyballs were already bouncing as the varsity girls warmed up. Our hands came apart just as heads started turning.

"Coach!" Ming yelled, running headlong toward us. But it was Christy she tackled in a hug, which I appreciated. Because a high-five was all they got from me.

"Hey, Ming." Christy laughed, squeezing her back.

Jasmine bustled up next. But her expression was sad. "Coach?" she said to Christy. We followed her gaze to Alyssa, sitting in the bleachers, crying. Her mom and dad were on either side, arms around her. What in the world?

I followed Christy over. At the bottom of the bleachers, I noticed two large boxes. Full of our missing volleyballs. Alyssa was gasping out sobs.

Her mom's expression was pained. My chest clenched as I realized. She was Amber's older sister. I didn't know her. Only knew *of* her. She was much older. Maybe ten years. But the resemblance was clear. But they seemed different too. She seemed less like a viper and more like an actual human with a heart.

She smoothed Alyssa's hair. "She's so worried you're not going to let her play."

"I told her that was ridiculous." Her dad's tone was a touch threatening. And that mustache made me think he wasn't bluffing. "It's not her fault her aunt is a piece of..." He clamped his lips together to refrain from the word he so badly wanted to say. It was evident in every line of his face.

Christy sat on the bleacher directly beneath Alyssa. Then she reached out and took her hand. "Hey."

Alyssa sniffed, face bright red. "I'm so sorry, Coach Christy. I didn't know."

Christy patted her hand. "I know you didn't. It's okay. Sometimes people are just..."

"Jackasses," I said for her.

Alyssa's dad laughed. But her mom looked incredibly sad.

I wanted to have empathy for her. But I also didn't want to touch that family with a ten-foot pole. Except for Alyssa. I'd care about her.

Christy looked up at me, pleading in her worried face. She wanted me to take this.

"Lys," I started. "Of course we're letting you play. You're the best setter in the district. We would lose without you."

"That's what I told her," her dad said proudly.

"Facts."

I turned. Ming had said it. She and Jasmine were at the bottom of the bleachers, arms around each other, silently supporting their friend.

"And," I began again. "You didn't have anything to do with it. We know that." It was a statement, not a question. She needed to know we believed her.

"I didn't. I promise." Her face crumpled and she started crying again. And I hoped they really did nail Amber. If not for Savannah or Christy who both deserved it, then for her niece whom she'd used as a pawn in her twisted game. Alyssa looked at Christy. "I'm so sorry for everything she did to you." Then to me. "And you, Coach Dupree."

I was about to tell her she didn't need to apologize. It wasn't her fault.

But then Christy said, "You know the best thing you could do right now?" There was a twinkle in her eye. "Take it out on the ball. Leave it all on the court. Be there for your team today. Okay?"

Alyssa smiled through the tears. "Let's do it." Then she hopped up and ditched her parents for Ming, Jasmine, and a love of the game.

"Can you girls put the balls away?" I said before they went. The gym was beginning to buzz with incoming fans.

Alyssa's mom stood with a heavy sigh. "We found the balls in my parents' basement. Honestly, it was pretty genius.

There's so much stuff down there, if Alyssa hadn't gone on a rampage looking for them, we might never have known." She glanced at me nervously. "I'm so sorry."

I lifted my hands. "No need to apologize. Let's just be excited for the girls today."

But Alyssa's dad wasn't ready to let it go. "Any idea what will happen to Amber? I heard you were about to be Interim D.A. Thought you might know."

Christy glanced over at me, curiosity in her expression. I hadn't told her about the interim job. But yeah, Jedd's wife, Denise, wanted to start snowbirding. Now.

"I'm not sure yet. With everything though, possibly some jail time. It'll all depend on the evidence." I couldn't tell him more than that.

He seemed placated and gave me a nod.

Alyssa's mom had questions. Questions about Savannah. I could see it in her eyes. But I didn't want to go there today. I was not drudging it up. Not when I'd just let my love for Christy shove it all off that proverbial cliff.

So I put a hand on Christy's shoulder and tipped my head toward the exit. "I'll show you where I parked." I needed out. And maybe a kiss before we had to face the mass of people and intensity of a tournament game.

She hopped up. "Thanks for finding the balls. Can't wait to watch Alyssa play tonight." Then she followed me down the bleachers. As soon as we were outside, her hand was in mine.

"I'll walk you to the car," I said. She, unfortunately, still needed to get those balloons.

I led her as we wove through traffic. This lot was starting to fill.

Thankfully, even though I was parked on the first row, I was down by the tennis courts, as far from the school as possible. Once we were around the back of Tessie, I leaned against the trunk and scrubbed a hand over my face and into my hair.

"Hey." Christy stepped closer, clinging to my waist. "You okay?"

I squeezed my eyes shut for a second. "Can I just kiss you? Is that all right?" I hated the agony in my voice. Vulnerability was not my friend. "I mean, I know we're in public but..."

She pushed up, tilted her head, and pressed a soft kiss to my mouth. And another. And another. My knees rattled and I let out a ragged breath. I'd missed this so much. She didn't stop, gratefully. My hands slid down her back, resting on her hips as I traced her pouty bottom lip with my tongue. Her fingers swirled at the base of my neck. She pulled back, hovering, teasing me. I smashed my mouth onto hers, letting out an embarrassing moan. And she let me kiss her for a few more seconds.

"Hey." She giggled against my lips. "Not the place."

I grunted. And, even though I didn't want to, I made myself stop.

She stretched and smiled so wide. "This is going down on my calendar as one of the greatest days of all time. Today is the day Holden Dupree ate his words. 'We're not a thing, okay?'" She made her voice super deep on that last line, mimicking me from the day we rode horseback together.

I laughed and shook my head. I'd eat a lot more than my words if that's what it took for her to be mine. "Yeah. Well. It's going on my calendar too," I said. "I told Christy Thornbury I love her and she didn't shut me down. It's a day of freaking miracles."

Now she laughed. But then she tipped her head back, thrust her fists to the sky, and let out a "wahoo!"

I grinned.

It was a dream. The best kind. I'd made a lot of mistakes in my life. But this woman right here? She was the one thing I was going to get right. No matter how many times I stumbled, I would get back up and follow wherever she led me. Happily.

But as sometimes happens, the dream quickly shifted to a nightmare.

Because standing there, hunkered down against Tessie's trunk, arms around the love of my life, an engine revved, loud and menacing. Like a bull scuffing the ground with his hoof, threatening to attack, it revved even louder. Our eyes shot to the left, just in time to see Amber's SUV coming straight for us.

A woman screamed like a crazed banshee. I wasn't sure if it was Amber, Christy, or a bystander. And I didn't take the time to figure it out. Without thinking, I shoved Christy out of the way.

And then I dove for it.

The next thing I knew, I bounced off the chain link fence of the tennis courts and fell onto the concrete sidewalk with a thunk. Staring up at the sky, the clouds spun for a second just as the cacophony of screeching metal sliced through the air, ending with a deafening crash.

It took a few seconds to realize it was over.

Christy! I pushed myself up. Amber's horn blared, her airbag was deployed, and her head hung over it like she was sleeping face down into a pillow. Shouts came from every direction.

"Call 911!" someone yelled.

"Oh my gosh, did you see that?"

"She drove straight for them!"

"Christy!" I screamed, but I couldn't find her. My stomach was a ball of dread. I ducked, checking under both cars. Thankfully she wasn't there. I dashed around the back of Amber's car, not giving one crap if she was dead or alive.

And then I saw her, laid out on the blacktop, ten feet away, a woman kneeling by her head.

"Christy!" I yelled again, a sob choking in my throat. But as soon as I knelt, relief flooded me. Her hand was in the woman's and she was trying to sit up.

"I'm okay, I'm okay." She waved us both back like we were making a big deal out of nothing.

I completely ignored that and pulled her against my chest, sobbing. Didn't even care who saw. "Oh my gosh, I'm so glad you're all right."

Then she had the gall to laugh. "You threw me out of the way full-on Superman style. Of course I'm all right. I'm just glad *you're* okay." She inspected me. "Oh, babe. Your leg."

I looked down, barely able to see it through my tears. My pants were ripped from knee to hem. Gnarly road rash covered the entire outside of my right calf. The second I acknowledged it, it burned like fire. Gah!

"She's alive!" Someone shouted over by Amber. I felt no relief at that knowledge. With what she'd just tried to do, I'd kind of hoped she was already in hell, getting comfy with her eternal stay. No worries. I'd make sure she paid. There was no lack of evidence now. Witnesses were everywhere.

I looked over at Tessie who...well...she wasn't Tessie anymore. More like a big pile of scrap metal.

"Uh, ma'am?" The woman kneeling on the other side of Christy said. "I don't think you are okay." She pointed to Christy's right arm. And she was right. The bone was protruding like it was about to pop out of her skin.

I swore. "You've got a compound fracture." I looked at the woman. "Can you get help?" I was not leaving Christy. She nodded, hopped up, and hurried away. "Does it hurt?" I choked on another sob.

"No. I don't feel anything." Christy looked down at her arm and giggled. Yes. Giggled. "I guess that's one way to get out of a Spartan Race." Then she snorted. What in the world? She studied the break for a few seconds, then nodded like she was pleased. "This is kind of cool. I've never had a broken bone. Will you be the first to sign my cast?" She had to be going into shock. Or she had a concussion. There was no other explanation after what had just happened. She grabbed my arm with her good hand, trying to stand.

"Oh, no you don't," I ordered. "You're staying put until the ambulance gets here. There's no telling if anything else is broken."

"But my butt hurts," she whined and laughed again.

So I pulled her carefully onto my lap and cradled her against my chest, still crying like a little boy.

She gave me a sad smile and wiped my tears away. "Don't cry, Epstein." She was trying to make me laugh. "We can get you another Tessie. She'll be even better than that one. Tessie 2.0."

"I'm not crying over a stupid car. What is wrong with you?" I chortled. "I love you. Don't you know that? I can't *live* without you and that nutjob just tried to run you over."

"Us," she corrected and then clicked her tongue matter of factly. "She tried to run *us* over. Get your facts straight, Counselor Dupree. You're going to need them in court." She wasn't taking any of this seriously.

"I don't care about myself. Don't you understand that? *You're the only thing that matters,*" I hissed vehemently. I wasn't even trying to hide my tears. Dripping down my jaw, nose running, body shaking beneath her. I couldn't make myself stop.

Her head tilted and her good hand cradled my face. "Holden, hey, it's over. She won't be able to touch us ever again. And I'm okay. I'm fine. Listen to me. I'm. Not. Going. Anywhere."

I sobbed. "You promise?" I had to ask even though it wasn't hers to give.

Her smile was gentle and soft, and she gave it anyway. "I

promise. I'm yours. All my days, all my nights, they all belong to you. For the rest of your life. If that's what you want."

I nodded, sniffing. "Yeah. That's what I want. And I want it forever. I will never get enough of you."

She curled her hand around the back of my neck and guided my mouth to hers. "Then that's what you'll get. Every little piece of me. Forever."

And then she kissed me.

epilogue 1

HOLDEN

Six months later

"What is wrong with you?" I barked, kicking my boot into the dirt. "I've been wanting to do this for a month. I put it off until you could be here and you show up like this?" I waved a hand over my youngest brother, Ford. Drunk as a freaking skunk, with some tramp he'd probably met at the gas station on his way down here. But hey, he had his guitar, which he'd pointed out first thing after arriving. He was supposed to sing a love song he'd written just for this. But there was no way I was letting him do that now. He smelled like cheap beer and body odor. His hair was a greasy mess, his clothes were rumpled, and he had a weeks worth of stubble. It wasn't a good look on him. At least he'd taken the bus from New York and not endangered everyone on the freeway in his current state.

Unfortunately, we didn't have time for him to clean up. According to the tracking app, Silas, Anna, Blue, and Christy would all be here in the next ten minutes.

Ashton reached out and steadied Ford when he almost tipped over.

"I'm fiiiine." Ford waved a lazy hand, at a fence post two feet to my left. He couldn't even tell where I was. His dark hair, which sorely needed cutting, fell into his eyes. "Stawwp making a biiiig deal outta it."

"Fine my butt," I growled. "Mom's sobbing back at the house. Dad's spitting nails in the barn. You don't show up, after months away from home, completely sloshed, idiot. And you are not messing this up for me." I amended, "For Christy. Her parents came all the way out here to surprise her. And now it's trashed."

Maisy neighed behind me, itching to get going. I tugged on her lead and scratched her nose.

To my right, Ashton shook his head, hands on his hips. "What do you want to do, man?"

My fists curled. "There's nothing *to* do. Scrap it. I'm going to wing it."

He cocked a brow. "You sure?"

I threw my hands out. "Are *you* going to sing and play the guitar?"

"Definitely not." He clapped me on the shoulder. "Just tell me what you need me to do."

I exhaled. "Can you just get everybody set up and make sure the roses haven't blown all over the place? I'll deal with this." I gestured at Ford and his...girlfriend? Man, I hoped not. He'd definitely had his beer goggles on when he picked her up. She was not pretty. Or intelligent.

"You got it." Ash took off for his truck.

Ford cuffed me on the shoulder. "I gotchu man." He held out his guitar with a wobbly arm. "I can plaaaay this wiff my eyes closed." Then he squeezed them shut and demonstrated. It wasn't terrible actually. Maybe this could still work.

The brunette, sporting a black miniskirt like she was

headed to an emo concert, giggled. "Those magic fingers are going to make him millions at age twenty."

Ford clicked his inebriated tongue and pointed a finger pistol at her. "Napshvul, hur we come."

I cocked a brow. "Nashville?"

Then he swung his finger gun on me and winked. "Yup." The p popped sloppily. "Riiiight affer this is oveeeer."

I crossed my arms. "You're going to Nashville?"

"Thaz right." His chin jutted.

I scrubbed a hand over my face. "Ford, you're starting a summer internship tomorrow. Here. In Seddledowne." Dad had wrangled it himself, assuring Marley Butterfield, the accountant for Dupree Ranch, that he wouldn't regret it.

"Nope." Ford's P popped again. "I'm done wiff accountant-ing. I'm going to Naaasshvul. Gonna make it biiig."

My mouth parted and I spoke to the girl. "What is he talking about?"

She clapped her hands together. "Two of his NYU friends got an apartment down there and talked him into dropping out. He's got an audition, the day after tomorrow for a new talent show, like American Idol."

"He dropped out of school?" Mom balked from behind us. I spun. She released a loud sob. Oh, good grief.

"Yeah." Bimbo squealed, bouncing on her toes. "He's really going for it. Just wait, Mrs. Dupree. He's going to build you a big, fat mansion."

At that, Mom wailed. Dad, who had ambled out from the barn, put an arm around her shoulder. "She doesn't want a mansion," he said to Bimbo. "She just wants her son to get his head on straight." Then he said, "Come on, Ford. Let's get you to the hill."

"Ford, no singing," I said. "Just play something simple. But no words, man." I was chancing it by letting him do this at all. He clicked that dumb finger again and stumbled straight into Dad's back. Then he righted himself before disappearing around the edge of the barn.

I shoved my foot in Maisy's stirrup and stroked her jaw. "You up for a double ride, Maisy girl?" Then I clucked my tongue and took off for Mom and Dad's house.

When we arrived, Christy was standing there looking confused. Man, she was a sight. She always was. Whether she was in a dress, pajamas, or jeans and a T-shirt, it didn't matter. My heart was stupid-happy to see her, regardless. But today, she could not have worn anything more fitting. Her pale yellow dress had puffy sleeves. She looked like pure sunshine.

At the sight of me, she smiled, surprised. "Oh, hey." She threw her hands out. "What's going on? Silas said we were having an end-of-school-year dinner, but no one's here." She gave me the once over, and her brows wiggled. "You look very schmexy." Her brow cocked. "And way too dressed up to be on a horse. Is something happening that I don't know about?" I had gotten a new shirt and new boots and was wearing my nicest slacks. I wanted to look at least halfway worthy of her.

I chuckled and reached down for her hand. "Wanna ride?"

Her eyes narrowed and I could see the wheels turning. "Sure?"

With one good tug, she was up, riding side saddle in front of me. She snuggled into my chest and I pressed a kiss to the top of her head.

"So you don't think I'm normally schmexy?" I asked right against her earlobe, eliciting a tiny shiver.

"I mean, you're always sexy." Her voice was husky. "But something's going on, isn't it? Anna and Silas were acting weird."

"Just going for a ride." I clucked my tongue, spurring Maisy forward, my heart racing.

As we loped toward the hill where it was all going down, I

took the opportunity to love on my future wife. A kiss to her cheek, a tickle up her arm, my nose against her neck.

"How was your last day as assistant principal?" Somehow, Alvarez had suckered some big-city school in Richmond into hiring him. The Seddledowne School Board had happily hired Christy as his replacement. So as of tomorrow my girl was the new Athletic Director. I couldn't have been prouder.

"Good. But I have a feeling it's about to get better?"

I laughed. "Nice try." I steered Maisy to the left, across the pasture. Every gate was open, waiting for us. So far, so good.

Christy rested her arms on top of mine and it was heaven letting the late spring sun warm us. There was a four-inch scar where the doctors had repaired her arm. But the break had long since healed and the bruises were nothing but a memory. The scar was a constant reminder that she was here, she was breathing, and she was mine to love. And Amber would be behind bars until she was an old lady.

I'd spent so many years under the stress of not knowing when Amber would pop up, that I hadn't realized just how anxiety-ridden things had been. But in the last seven months with Christy, the peace that had teased me for so long had found a permanent home in my heart. There were still times when the voices in my head tried to take me down, but they were getting fewer and farther between as I continually worked at it.

"Mmm," Christy murmured, eyes closed, face to the sky. "I could get used to this, Clark."

I chuckled at the nickname. Clark, as in Clark Kent. She'd been calling me that ever since the day Amber tried to run us over. Said I was her own personal Superman.

But really, she was mine. A real life Super*woman*. Because her love had saved me when no one else's ever could. And today, I was going to make sure she knew I'd spend the rest of my life repaying that love tenfold. Christy was not going to regret taking a chance on me. I'd make sure of that.

"You better," I whispered. A kiss to her temple. "'Cause this is your life now."

I slid a hand across her waist and pressed kisses up her neck. She swiveled her head and kissed me hard and long and raw. And I wished, for a split second, that we weren't headed for the hill.

Then someone cleared their throat from behind a bush and I remembered real quick what we were doing. Christy's head snapped up and she glanced around. But then she must've thought her mind was playing tricks on her because she leaned back in for another kiss. And dang if I didn't have to deny her.

"We're already here." I smiled.

Her eyes lifted to mine one last time, full of questions. "Where?"

"Our hill," I said simply. This is where we were building a house. The contractor had it staked. Excavation for the basement started in a week.

She looked around and let out a little gasp. It was kind of obvious, what with the large leather chair set neatly on the grass inside a heart-shaped bed of lavender rose petals. I'd never tell her how much those had cost. And the massive light-up letters "H & C" set up as a backdrop. Mom had insisted on renting them. And the twinkle lights that a very pregnant Lemon had insisted on adding. Yeah, it was pretty clear what was happening.

I slung my leg back over Maisy and hopped down. Then I turned and, hands around her waist, lowered Christy in front of me. Once on her feet, she smiled, eyes already damp. I pulled her to a stop.

"Don't you cry already," I whispered. "How am I supposed to get through it if you're crying?"

She rolled her shoulders back. "Okay. Yeah. No tears."

"Good. Now eyes straight ahead." I put my hands on her hips, guiding her toward the chair. As we walked across the grass, Ford, perched on a stool off to the right, began to strum. My nerves ticked up with every chord, wondering if Christy, or worse, her parents, would be able to tell he was smashed. But we made it without him messing up.

I peeked over my shoulder to make sure everyone was in place. Ashton must've drilled them well. Because they'd tiptoed up so slowly, I hadn't even heard them.

I helped Christy to the chair and turned her toward me. As she sat, her eyes lifted. The look on her face was going to be one of my favorite memories from today. I already knew it. It was full of joy and surprise. Then she started blinking.

"No crying," I reminded her.

She beamed and blushed at everyone. "Hey, Mom. Hi, Dad." She gave them a little wave.

They waved back. "Hey, sugar," her dad said.

It looked like maybe her mom had been crying too. She wasn't thrilled at the idea of Christy living out here. But we'd talked about moving to Laramie. I'd miss Seddledowne, my family, and the ranch, but I just wanted to be wherever she was. She'd shot it down immediately. Seddledowne, and on my family's ranch, is right where she wanted to be. It's where our jobs were, sure. But this was her home now.

I'd spent a week with the Thornburys at Christmas. Her sisters had backed way off since I'd entered the picture. Rowan was downright terrified of me. He'd learned real quick never to call Christy Tink. I'd overheard Ari telling her husband I was a textbook Alpha-hole. Fine by me. I'd keep the fangs out as long as necessary to protect Christy.

Her dad was nice enough. But her mom might take some time to get used to. Even now, as her oldest daughter was being proposed to, she was wiping tears for herself. I'd spent the last six months needling it into Christy in every way possible that she deserved all the good things in life. That she deserved my love. And it was okay to put herself first. She'd done the same for me. We planned to keep doing just that.

Everyone important was there. Mom and Dad. Silas, Lemon, and her watermelon-sized belly that looked like it was going to pop any second. Anna and Blue. Ashton, Ford, and Bimbo—who was now snuggling up to Ashton since Ford was off to the side, serenading us all. Yep, against my wishes, he'd added lyrics.

It was all going well. Until it wasn't.

Ashton shook Bimbo off and held his fingers out in a cross. "Stay back. Seriously. Get."

Christy's cute "psycho-cackle" as she called it threatened to burst out of her adorable nose and she slapped a hand over it.

I gave everyone a silencing glare. And then I dropped to one knee.

"Awww," Lemon whispered.

"Christy," I started. "You unexpectedly came into my life—"

Anna burst into a wailing sob.

"Oh my gosh," I said with a groan. "I barely even started."

"It's not you," Blue said as a dark blue car with fully tinted windows rolled to a stop fifty yards back. "I'm sorry y'all, I have to go."

"Seriously?" Silas grumbled. "I thought you told him to come at five."

"I did." Blue's gaze volleyed between the car and Anna. He was moving. To California. Right now apparently. His dad wanted him to go to a school with a stronger football program. He was determined for Blue to go pro. And Seddle-downe wasn't cutting it.

"Blue!" A dark-haired man yelled out of a half-opened window. "We're leaving! Now!"

Anna threw herself into Blue's arms, weeping into his chest. He stood there, biceps locked around her, looking sick. He'd thrown his hands up at Fate and she'd laughed in his face. Poor kid. I wished I could take it for him.

After the man I was assuming was his dad yelled again, Blue tried to step away from Anna, but she yelled, "No! I don't want you to go!" And then sobbed even louder than before.

And I was trying to compete with that?

"Oh my gosh," I said, my heart breaking for my niece but also wanting to get this dang ring on Christy's left hand.

Lemon held up a finger, pleading in her expression.

"Go on. We'll wait," I told them. Then I shifted. My knees were starting to ache.

"I got it, babe," Silas said to Lemon, but she waved him off.

Blue headed for the car. But in an unprecedented turn of events, Silas stepped in front of him, pulled him into a tight hug and squeezed.

Blue pounded him on the back. "See ya, Mr. D," he said as he stepped away.

Silas nodded and it looked like he was blinking back tears.

Anna was right back in Blue's arms, sobbing. Lemon took Anna from Blue and the three of them walked—actually Lemon waddled—toward the car.

"Bye, Blue!" Christy yelled. Everyone followed suit.

Ford strummed a dramatic chord to get our attention. "While we waaiiit." Spit shot out on the T. "I'll suuurunade y'aaall," Ford slurred. Another loud strum, "Beeaauuuuuutiful guuuurrrllll," he bellowed. Anna's Bassett hound, Huckleberry, who I hadn't even realized was there until this moment, took that as an invitation to join in. "Aaaaroooooooooooo," he howled.

"Fo-shiz, get your woman off me!" Ash bellowed, running circles around Mom and Dad to get away from Bimbo.

I glanced back at Christy about to apologize but she was doubled over, arms around her middle, laughing so hard tears were rolling down her beautiful cheeks. Her gaze flitted to her parents and she laughed even harder. They looked utterly mortified. Christy was going to dump me. She might be laughing now, but as soon as they got her alone, they were going to make her see sense.

"Oh my gosh, I can't breathe." She exhaled. "I love you people so much. I can't wait to be a Dupree."

"Thank goodness for that," I muttered with a chuckle.

Blue hung out of the window, waving goodbye. Anna grabbed his hand, trying to keep the entire car from leaving with that one grasp. Of course, it didn't work. Blue's jerkwad dad took off so fast the tires spit gravel and Fate ripped their hands apart. Once they disappeared, Anna hiccuped her way back to us, Lemon's arm around her.

Mom's hands were to her heart. Lemon, Silas, Mom, and Dad surrounded Anna, petting her like a dog about to be put to sleep. Even Christy looked like she was fighting the urge to run over and pull poor Anna into her arms. Now I felt like a jerk. Like somehow I should've planned this on a day when Anna's heart wasn't cracking open. Like I could've known.

But here we were, everyone watching expectantly.

"Are we ready?" I asked.

"Oh my word, yes. Please hurry," Ashton said, slapping Bimbo's hands away. I didn't know if she was high. I hadn't thought so before, but she clearly thought he was throwing down a challenge. The more he fought her off, the more aggressive she got. Just then she grabbed Ash's head, stuck her tongue out, and licked him from chin to forehead.

"Gah!" he yelled. "Mom, help!" He shoved her face away, palming it like a basketball.

"Hey!" Ford thundered, tripped over his guitar, righted himself, and then took off for them. "Get yer haaaands off her!" He full-body tackled Ashton to the ground.

Christy slapped her thigh, the laughs coming so hard she couldn't even make a noise.

"Get off me, you freaking nutter!" Ashton yelled at Ford.

"You have got to be kidding me," I said.

Silas was already on it.

But before he could get there, Mom stepped over, grabbed Ford by the ear, and twisted it until he was her paralyzed puppet. "What is wrong with both of you?" she exploded. "Holden is trying to *propose* and you two are rolling around like you were raised in a barn!"

"Mom!" Ford yelled. "My ear!" His words were suddenly clear as day. Then he let out the loudest belch I'd ever heard— didn't even know a noise like that could come out of a human being—and puked all over the ground.

Lemon covered her nose with a gasp.

Ford heaved again, and it spattered on Silas's shoes. Silas swore, which made Christy's mom let out an appalled squeal.

All this time, Mom had never let go of Ford's ear. Pretty sure from her fury that she took vomiting as a personal affront. She twisted harder, forcing Ford to a bent-over stand. "You take this..." She glowered at Bimbo. "*Person*, back to the house. And drink at least three cups of coffee. You better be in your right mind by the time I get back, do you understand me, Ford Sutton Dupree?"

"But Holden wanted me here," Ford whined. The puking seemed to have sobered him up. Or maybe it was the ear twisting.

Mom looked at me, eyes blazing as if to say, *do you still want him here?*

I shook my head. "Just go, Ford. You're not going to remember it anyway."

Anna's continual background sobs gutted me. This whole thing was a disaster.

I looked back at Christy. *My* beautiful Christy. She deserved so much better than this. "Maybe we should do this another day."

She leaned down and booped me on the nose. "No way. Don't even think about it. This is amazing. We're going to have the best story to tell our kids." I smiled at her, so stupid in love. Because that right there was precisely why she was going to be the mother of my children.

Ford stomped over to his guitar, swiped it off the ground, and stormed back to Bimbo. Grabbed her by the hand and yanked her toward the side-by-side.

"And don't you go anywhere near the bedrooms!" Mom yelled just before they rode away.

Anna hiccuped another sob.

Ashton was finally on his feet, smoothing out his shirt, looking disgusted. He caught my eye and mouthed, *sorry, dude.*

I wasn't even going to ask everyone if they were ready again. The universe was obviously taking it as a dare.

"Christy." I exhaled. "Last summer you came into my life unexpectedly." I paused making sure Fate was truly done having her laugh. No one so much as twitched. Deep breath. "I had no idea making out with my brother's ex would be so rewarding."

Her mom squealed again. But Christy snorted. I'd added that line just for that snort right there. Success! At least one thing had gone right.

I took another deep breath and plowed on. "But now—"

"Uh, hold up, Holden," Silas bellowed, his voice verging on hysterical. We looked over to see Lemon, knock-kneed, trying—and failing—to stop what looked to be a gallon of liquid from exiting between her legs. "I think we're having a baby today!" Silas hooted.

We lost our entire audience at that. Even Christy's parents swarmed Lemon who was laughing giddily as she gasped out short breaths. At least Anna's sobs were sidetracked. A grin split her face.

"Hey."

I turned back around to see Christy, elbows on her knees, chin on her fists, beaming at me. "Looks like this was meant to be a you and me moment. So have at it, big guy."

I looked back at the group and then back at her. It was an easy choice.

"Yeah, okay." Enough with the monologue. I didn't want to tempt Fate again. I slipped my hand into my pocket and fished out the ring box. Then I popped it open for her to see.

Big, bright swoony eyes, her mouth went into a stunned O. It was exactly what I'd hoped for. "Christianna Juliet Thornbury, you are the love of my life. Will you marry me?" I chuckled. "Even if I do have the most ridiculous family on earth?"

She nodded, eyes sparkling. "Yes. Absolutely. I cannot wait. One hundred percent. Let's do it."

I blew out my breath as I slid the round diamond, surrounded by a rim of sapphires, over her petite finger. A perfect fit. "The blue stones are for—"

"Stallions blue. So we never forget coaching volleyball together, the shirtless kiss, the car accident in the parking lot? All of it?"

I grinned. "Yeah. I hope that's okay. 'Cause if you hate it, we can take it back." Total lie. I'd had it custom-made. But I wouldn't tell her that. She could have any ring she wanted so long as she was mine.

She cupped my face in her hands, pulling me into a full

kneel. And then, the ring finally on her finger, she kissed me. "I love it. I love you. It's absolutely perfect." She waved her hands at the decorations and the crazy group of people we called family. Her eyes teared up then. "If I had to do it all again, date all the jerks, cry all the tears, knowing you were my prize at the end, I would." She pressed another kiss to my mouth. "Because you were so worth waiting for, Holden."

There I was, on my knees, in front of this stunner of a woman who made me laugh, cry, and feel things I never thought I'd feel again. I didn't know what I'd done to deserve her. But I wasn't going to spend a single second questioning it. I was hers. She was mine.

That was all that mattered.

"Clark," she whispered as she checked out the ring. "Remember that time you told me we weren't a thing and we never would be?"

I groaned. "Really? We're doing this now?" She liked to throw those words back in my face every few weeks, always with a delighted laugh. Like she'd slayed the town's monster, slung it over her shoulder, and brought it home for everyone to celebrate.

"Mhmm. Right now." She giggled. "And remember when I told you I would always win?" She put her ring right in my face. "Looks like somebody is eating a big fat slice of humble pie right about now."

My jaw jutted. "Just wow."

She beamed. "Say it."

I glared and bit back a grin. "No. And you can't make me."

"Do it, Epstein." She cocked her head to one side. "Tell me what I want to hear."

"Never."

She raised a brow. "Is that right?"

It was basically a memorized script at this point. The exact same words every time, followed by her doing something to make me yield. A steamy kiss, a tickle across the abs. The woman always found the chink in my armor. But not today. Today *I* was in charge.

I crossed my arms. "That's right. I know all your tricks now."

Her brows puckered, not the least bit intimidated. "Well, that's a shame." She slipped the ring off and held it out for me. "It really is a pretty—"

"No!" I yelped, jamming it back on. "Fine. We are totally a thing."

She laughed and rewarded me with a quick kiss. "Yeah, we are." But then she wrapped her arms around my shoulders and looked deep into my eyes. All the teasing was gone, replaced by an intense, burning gaze. "Holden and Christy are one hundred percent *a thing*," she murmured. "And?"

My hands slipped down around her waist, pulling her closer. "And we will be. Forever and ever."

She pressed one last kiss to my lips. "Without end."

epiloque 2

CHRISTY

Three Years Later

It was the first spring day warm enough to be outside, and I'd stayed there on our wraparound porch as long as I possibly could. The air smelled like honeysuckle and the red tulips Holden and I had planted two years ago were in bloom. The breeze was just warm enough to tease at a hot summer.

My big toe was the only thing touching the boards on the porch as I sat on our padded swing, reading an article on my phone. Holden pulled up in his black truck. I stood, carrying our newest little bundle in my arms. He hopped out, cowboy boots hitting the concrete driveway, wearing my favorite suit. The charcoal gray one that hugged him just right.

He tipped his head, lips in a straight line, exasperated. "Don't get up. You need to rest, babe."

"Holden." I laughed. "I need to move. My muscles are atrophying from all the sitting."

He pursed his lips and shook his head but he didn't protest again. Then he opened the back door of the truck and

266

quickly loosened the car seat buckle. "C'mon here, little man." He held his hands out, and our adorable blond-haired, blue-eyed two-year-old, Liam, jumped into his arms with a "whee!"

Holden set him down and he ran over and up the porch stairs, "Momma, momma! Up!" He held his arms out for me.

"Hey, cute boy," I said while bouncing the baby in my arms. "I missed you."

"Hold up, bud," Holden said as he hurried over. He pressed a kiss to my lips like he did every single time he saw me. Didn't matter if it was first thing in the morning, or the fourth time he'd come in the house from doing ranch work. Hot Lips was still going strong. But now I was the only girl on his list.

Well, me and Maddie.

Holden took the baby, gingerly settling her in the crook of his arm. He peeled back the pink swaddling blanket. "How's Daddy's girl?" He bounced her. "How's my Maddie Ro?" I wrapped my fingers around his bicep and rested my chin on his arm, peering down at her. Her big blue eyes, which I was pretty confident were turning brown just like her daddy's and mine, looked up at him, wide and aware.

"She already has a crush on Dad. Don't you, cute girl." I kissed Holden's stubbled cheek. "Get in line, Miss Mads. He was mine first."

"Don't talk dirty," Holden said. "We still have two more days till you're cleared for...you know." He winked.

I slapped him on the rear end. "Eh, if you're keeping count."

"Don't tempt me, woman."

I wiggled my brows. "Who's talking dirty now?"

"Momma!" Liam was still reaching up. I squatted and put my arms around him. He squeezed my neck so tight I thought my head might pop off. I blew a raspberry into his chubby cheek and he giggled. It was my favorite thing. Well, one of them. I had many when it came to being his mom.

"Careful and slow," Holden said.

"I got it." I rolled my eyes with a smile. "Always so concerned." Then I slowly lifted, using my legs, not my middle. "See, piece of cake," I said, once Liam and I were fully upright.

Holden held the front door open with one arm, baby girl in the other. We went inside.

"Oh, that's a big yawn for such a little girl," he said. "Did she eat?"

"Mhmm."

He glanced at Liam and then grinned at me, eyes greedy. "I think he needs a nap. What do you think?"

I laughed. "I thought we still had two days."

He shrugged. "He's pretty tired. That's all I'm saying."

I snorted. "Yeah. Sure."

Fifteen minutes later, both babies down for the count, Holden flopped back onto the bed next to me. I climbed on top of him, loosened his tie, pulled it through his collar, and threw it on the floor. He'd left his suit coat in the living room.

As I unbuttoned his dress shirt, I asked, "Liam had a good time with James and Griffin?" Lemon and Silas's boys. They'd delivered a third baby two weeks before us. Another boy, named Bowen after Holden and Silas's dad. So, three in four years for them. I was so not trying to keep up with that.

"Yeah. Though he and James were fighting over a toy truck when I got there."

I peeled back his shirt and ran my fingers down that swole chest. He still ran those obstacle course races and I was ever so grateful for what it did for his body. But now, we ran them together.

"Good grief, man." I groaned. "Are you trying to make my ovaries explode?" It was a cheesy line I'd read in a romance novel while I was on minor bedrest with Madeleine. We threw it into conversation daily, always with a laugh.

With a jerk, he flipped me over so fast, I got dizzy. Then he was on top of me. "I think we better give those ovaries a rest." But then he leaned down and pressed a long, smutty, throb-inducing kiss to my lips and slipped his hand under the hem of my shirt.

"You need to quit." I laughed. "Unless you want me to ignore the doctor's orders." But his lips were on my neck now, then down to my décolleté. "If you pass the point of no return, I will not let you stop," I said in a threatening voice. "We will be going all the way. Do not mess with me."

"Fine." He huffed and slid off. Once his head was on the pillow next to mine he unbuttoned my jeans. But I knew where this was going. He peeled back the waist just enough to trace his fingers over the nickel-sized Superman tattoo I'd gotten as a surprise for our first anniversary. Right above my right hip bone. Practically microscopic because I didn't love tattoos but I also wanted him to know that I loved him more than my dislike of tattoos. And also because...

I slipped his dress shirt down enough to see my name there on his bicep where the suicide prevention tattoo had been. He'd wanted to have it removed but I wouldn't let him. It was part of his past. And his past was part of him. But he wanted it to represent something happier. Our future. So he'd had a design drawn up—a swirling flower with my name in cursive in the middle. The semicolon was still there, but it was part of the bigger picture, and if you didn't know, you would never see it. I thought it was a beautiful metaphor for life after tragedy.

He pressed a kiss to my forehead, still tracing circles over Superman.

I leaned up on my elbow so I could see him. "How was the awards assembly? Was Tally surprised?"

"Yeah. She started crying. I don't think she believed she deserved it." He was still tracing Superman.

Jilly, Holden, some of Savannah's other friends, and Dahlia and Randall had started a scholarship in memory of Savannah. Surprisingly, but also impressively, Alyssa's family had been some of the first donors. It was an award that gave one full college scholarship—within reason—every year to a girl who had struggled in some way. Mental health, teenage pregnancy, abuse of any kind.

"Hmmm," I murmured. Mostly because Holden's swirling was getting me a little revved, and I had to focus to put a coherent thought together. "We'll have to tell her to sign up for Ashton's class." Ashton had accepted a job at James River College, a private liberal arts school forty miles away, starting in the fall. And that just so happened to be where Tally had chosen to attend.

Holden chuckled. "For sure. He'll die when she walks in. They'll get the gloves out immediately and start duking it out in front of the whole class. I'll get Anna to convince her." Still tracing Superman.

My fingertips trailed along his jaw. "Hey, did you see about Ford?"

He pressed his eyes shut, his expression pained. "Yeah. Idiot is going to screw up his music career." Ford had made it big, just like his hussy friend predicted. We'd never seen her again after that day, but we still included her every time we told our engagement story. Ford indeed went to Nashville and won one of those TV talent competitions. But now it was all loose women, drinking, and gambling. "Next time I see him, I'm going to pound him for the number it's doing on Mom."

It broke my heart too. I hadn't known her as long as Lemon or been around when they were kids, but Jenny was an amazing grandmother and mother-in-law. She'd never been anything but welcoming to me. But she was crushed for her youngest.

I pushed up when I remembered something. "Did you see about Blue Bishop though?"

He scowled. "The kid Anna was all heartbroken about after her freshman year?"

"Yeah."

"What about him? I thought he was in California. Do they even talk anymore?"

"I don't think so. But he's not in California for long. He was recruited by The University of Knoxville."

"Wow. That's one of the best football programs in the country." He nodded, impressed. "Knoxville's not that far from here. Maybe he and Anna will pick things back up."

I shook my head. "Last time Ashton mentioned Blue's name, Anna tried to kill him with her laser beam eyes and told us never to mention him again because he was dead to her, remember?"

He chuckled. "You never know. Sometimes us stupid men just need a second chance."

My lips quirked, and I looked deep into his eyes. "Is that right?"

"Mhmm," he murmured, and dang if his fingers weren't still tracing Superman.

If I'd known Holden would use the tattoo as an electric push-start button, I might've gotten it placed somewhere else...

Pfft. Who was I kidding? I lived for this.

Taking a play out of his book, in a flash, I growled, shoved him onto his back, and pinned his arms down, straddling him. I lowered myself right over his face, my hair making a curtain around us. His eyes were ravenous just like I felt.

"You know," I said. "For somebody so set on doing exactly as the doctor ordered, you are pushing me very close to the edge, Holden Dupree. Do it one more time," I dared him.

"And all bets are off. Clothes will be flying. Intense love-making will be happening. You *will not* stop me."

He smirked. And preened. And then he pried an arm loose. He tugged the neckline of my shirt over my shoulder and crunched up to press a kiss to it. "I love you, Christy Dupree."

I stared into his autumn eyes. "I love you too, Clark. So much."

But then his lips pulled into a smile. And his hand dropped. His fingers trailed across my stomach, and very slowly, and very intentionally curlicued Superman...

One more time.

Ready for more Seddledowne? Book 3, All to Pieces is out now!

Millions watch him play. Except the one who matters most.

Read All to Pieces (Book 3 of the Seddledowne Series) today! Available in KU, ebook, and paperback.

Rate and review on Amazon.

Rate and review on Goodreads.

Rate and review on Bookbub.

To read Anna and Blue's First Kiss, go to my website and click on the extras tab at www.susanhenshawauthor.com or click this link.

. . .

Is Facebook your thing? Come join Susan's Southern Charm Readers Group, and discuss all things Dupree, as well as future projects.

Let's be friends!

To sign up for my newsletter and get writing updates, snippets from future books, and cover reveals go to www.susanhenshawauthor.com. Scroll to the bottom of the page and plug in your info.

Follow me on Instagram.

thank you

Thank you for reading Book 2 in the Seddledowne Series. I hope you loved reading it as much as I loved creating it.

When I sit down to start a book, my biggest fear is that the words won't come. For me, the story tells itself. And if I'm heading down the wrong path, I hit a wall. This happened a couple of times as I tried to get Holden and Christy's story out. It's a signal that I need to back up, rethink, and try again. And one person was always there to help me brainstorm and get back on track. Etta, thank you for being the world's best plotter. For loving my characters and Seddledowne as much as I do. Thank you for taking a nose dive with me into our dark sides, as we schemed up ways Amber could mess with Holden's life. If I didn't know we were both good, Christian girls, I might be worried at how much fun we had. I couldn't have written this without your endless ideas, constant encouragement and epic beta reading skills.

To my phenomenal beta readers, Kenzie, Crystal, Natalie and Emma. Thank you for telling me when it wasn't working and squealing with me when it was.

For my amazing cover artist, Angelica Hagman, who has the patience of a saint and a serious talent for capturing the emotion of a book she hadn't yet read.

To my stellar editor, Emily Faircutler, who once again made sure I didn't make an idiot of myself. Ever so grateful.

For my oldest brother, Glen, who came in clutch when I needed a repulsive yet hilarious joke about Senator Bromhorst to get Holden fired. I truly could not have come up with that on my own. Haha.

And once again, I have to give credit to a kind and loving Heavenly Father who shares the gift of storytelling with me and continues to fuel my words daily. I'm grateful for the walls I hit in this story that were His way of telling me I was taking a wrong turn. And Who set me on the right path again.

All my best,

Susan

also by susan henshaw

Seddledowne Series Book 1: One Last Thing

**One shattered farm girl. The cowboy who has always loved her.
Ninety days under one roof.**

Silas Dupree spent the last decade two thousand miles from
Seddledowne, Virginia for one reason and one reason only: to get
away from Clementine Shepherd, his sister's best friend.

But when his twin sister, Sophie, dies tragically, Silas is forced to
return home.

In an unexpected twist, Sophie leaves her teenage daughter, to Silas
and Clementine, jointly, with a stipulation: the three must reside
together for ninety days or a judge will decide Anna's fate.

Can Clementine endure an entire summer with the quiet, closed-off
man who ghosted her the minute they graduated high school?

And can Silas keep his word to his new fiancé back in Wyoming while
sleeping across the hall from the only woman he's ever truly loved?

**Perfect for readers who enjoy a sweet, slow burn. There will be
hilarity and heartbreak, tears and tire-slashing. But always a
hard-earned happily ever after.**

Made in United States
Orlando, FL
22 March 2025

59712013R20173